ON THE BRICKS

by

Penni Jones

© 2016 by Penni Jones

This book is a work of creative fiction that uses actual publicly known events, situations, and locations as background for the storyline with fictional embellishments as creative license allows. Although the publisher has made every effort to ensure the grammatical integrity of this book was correct at press time, the publisher does not assume and hereby disclaims any liability to any party for any loss, damage, or disruption caused by errors or omissions, whether such errors or omissions result from negligence, accident, or any other cause. At Pandamoon, we take great pride in producing quality works that accurately reflect the voice of the author. All the words are the author's alone.

All rights reserved. Published in the United States by Pandamoon Publishing. No part of this publication may be reproduced, stored in a retrieval system, or transmitted in any form or by any means—for example, electronic, photocopy, recording—without the prior written permission of the publisher. The only exception is brief quotations in printed reviews.

www.pandamoonpublishing.com

Jacket design and illustrations © Pandamoon Publishing
Art Direction by Don Kramer: Pandamoon Publishing
Editing by Zara Kramer, Rachel Schoenbauer, Kathy Davidson, and Heather Stewart: Pandamoon Publishing

Pandamoon Publishing and the portrayal of a panda and a moon are registered trademarks of Pandamoon Publishing.

Library of Congress Cataloging-in-Publication Data is on file at the Library of Congress, Washington, DC

Edition: 1, version 1.0

ISBN-10: 1-945502-30-4
ISBN-13: 978-1-945502-30-9

Dedication

Sorry, Mom. You tried.

ON THE BRICKS

Chapter 1

Every foolish decision I've ever made had a man at its juicy center. If men weren't in my life, I would be a successful lawyer or actress, living in some big city high-rise and driving a fancy car. Instead, I'm in the pen on my way to my third parole hearing. Maybe this one's the winner. It's just so damn hard to convincingly say I've learned my lesson when I'm innocent. Maybe I wouldn't be a successful actress after all.

My name is Cass. It's not Cassandra, not Cassidy, just Cass. Like my mom forgot she was in the middle of something and just stopped naming me. I don't even have a middle name. The worst part is that my sister is named Evangeline Ann. I used to think my parents gave her all the names and ran out before they got to me. We all call her Vangie Ann. Evangeline isn't a fitting name for a meth-head. Excuse me, *former* meth-head.

Sometimes I forget Wayne Talbot's the one who put me here, and I catch myself daydreaming about him. Mostly about his body. Dicks are scarce in the women's prison, and Wayne had a nice one. I assume he still does. Long and perhaps a little too thin, but always as eager and obedient as a Golden Retriever. When the memories start, I can't help but touch myself. Then I feel as foolish as if I had slept with that loser again.

My cellmate will take care of things for me when I let her. I can't let her if Wayne is on my mind, though. That wouldn't be fair. Tabitha, with her cornrows and thick waist, is just not the same as a man for me. She tries, though, and I can't say that she's not one of the best friends I've ever had. Tabitha strokes my mousy brown hair when I cry, tells me that she loves me when nobody sends me letters. She's told me about her mama's yard, complete with a massive weeping willow tree, so many times it's started showing up in my own childhood memories.

It's hard to believe sometimes that Tabitha stabbed her husband with a stainless steel grilling fork. He used to beat her up pretty bad. The public defender said he could have gotten her off if she had stopped after two or three stabs. The jury found forty-one to be a bit excessive and perhaps a sign of a violent personality. I suppose none of them had ever been hospitalized by someone who had vowed to love and cherish them forever.

"Cass Blankenship." The guard sounds bored and she has her thick thumbs stuck through her belt loops. She lets out a giant sigh when I stand up from the bench. Maybe she expected me to do something more entertaining.

She opens the door and I nod instead of saying "thank you." I walk into the large room with the wooden walls and floor and sit down on the folding metal chair. All the wood makes me feel like I'm sitting in a giant coffin, facing a table of five people in fancy suits.

I rub my moist palms on my murky gray scrubs. I try to channel the Cass that existed ten years ago, when I was an elementary school teacher and not a convict.

"Thank you for joining us, Ms. Blankenship," the warden says. As if I would decline a chance, no matter how remote, to get out of this shithole.

"Thank you," I say, because "you're welcome" seems smug.

The fluorescent overhead lights reflect off his bald head as he opens my file. "You've served ten years of a twenty-year sentence for second-degree murder. Your actions led to the death of"—he stops to flip a page. I could tell him the name and date but that would be inappropriate—"Ms. Judith Talbot on January 10, 2001. Can you tell me how things have changed for you since then?"

I sigh and gather my thoughts one last time. I've given a speech in response to this question two other times, but I didn't say the right thing and the parole board sent me back to my cell. I'm trying another route this time. If it doesn't work, my words will be different next year. All five of them are staring at me, judging me even though no words have spilled out of my mouth. Old white people, all of them. I'm white, too, don't get me wrong. I'm just a different brand of white. The kind of white who's done time and messed around with her black cellmate. I'm not the same race to these people.

"If I could go back in time, that day would be different. I wish I could change things. I wish I was still teaching second grade, still living in my little apartment, and had never even met Judith Talbot. What I did to her was terrible, and I can't take it back. But I sure wish I could. I wish I could erase the pain I caused her children and her parents, and I wish more than anything that Judith Talbot was still alive." I had to cross my fingers in my lap the entire time to say all the lies. I told the truth the previous two years, declared my innocence, and they sent me back for my lack of remorse. Truthfully, I don't even wish Judith Talbot was alive. She was a miserable bitch. Of course, if she was alive, I wouldn't be here.

"Ms. Blankenship, if you are released, where will you go?" a woman with gray hair and giant glasses asks me. She looks at me like she thinks I'll answer "a crack house."

"My sister Evangeline runs a transitional home for abused and displaced women. She always needs help there. She can't pay me much, but she'll provide me with room and board." I don't mention that Vangie Ann is in recovery for drug abuse. If they want the details, they'll find them out.

My friend Jessie just got paroled a month ago. She promised me a job at her aunt's boutique in Southern California, in a town called Camarillo. I've only ever lived in Arkansas, but in California I'll get to help people get dressed for a living. It's my shot to start over. But I don't mention that, either. I figure I'm more likely to get released to my sister's halfway house than to another ex-con in a different state. Plus, I have an inheritance waiting for me at home. If I can get it out of the hands of my stingy stepmother. I'll apply for a probation transfer once I get settled.

"Where is the home located?" a man in a bowtie asks. It's red with blue dots. Why is he wearing a bowtie? Does he want to look like a present?

"In West Plains."

"How far is that from Pleasant Fields?" Mr. Bowtie asks. I hope this is a good sign. He's really interested in my plans.

"About a half hour. I won't have any reason to go there whatsoever." That's true. I don't want to go there. Don't want to run into Wayne and his Wrangler snake. At this point, I'd be tempted to screw him until he's unconscious and then cover his face with a pillow.

"If we grant you parole, you would be required to stay away from Pleasant Fields for at least two more years," Big-Glasses lady says. Those frames are huge. They take up half her face. How does she not know that the amount of glass far exceeds the size of her eyeballs? Then I realize this might actually be happening. She said "if."

"Your behavior the past ten years has been exemplary. And it sounds like you've learned from your mistake," another man says. This one has on a brown suit and has thinning blond hair. I'm afraid to respond so I don't.

They ask me to leave the room for a few minutes. I walk back out to my bench. The guard has her arms crossed, and she's staring at me like I'm about to make a run for it. Even if I wanted to, I couldn't, because my legs are almost numb from excitement. I might be getting out.

I look down at my fingernails which haven't been manicured in a decade. I used to get French manicures. My nails were always chipped and ugly by the time I made it back to the salon for maintenance. I should have taken better care of them, but I had no idea how luxurious it was to have pretty fingernails.

My hair was beautiful back then, before I got arrested. One of my best features. Now it's limp and mousy. I'm in need of a dye job and conditioning treatment. Not sure how I'll pay for that. I didn't make much as a teacher, but I didn't have any debt.

All I had to pay for was my apartment. My old car was long since paid off, and so were my student loans. All my money went toward what I wanted. Clothes, hair, nails, skin care, shoes, and of course, having fun. Narcissism is extremely satisfying. Anyone who says it's not doesn't know how to do it right. But I'm older and wiser now, with coffee as my only vice. I'm certain I'll make smarter choices now.

I don't know how long I sit on that green metal bench. Long enough for my ass to get sore and to count one hundred ceiling tiles, but I'm not sure how long that is in minutes.

"Ms. Blankenship, they're ready for you," the guard says and opens the door again.

I take a deep breath and stand up. I feel woozy. I wish someone could get the answer for me and come and tell me. If I throw up, will they change their minds one way or the other?

My feet shuffle into the room and my body follows. I feel like I might lose bowel control, but fortunately I don't. The warden motions for me to sit down.

"Ms. Blankenship, you've been granted parole." He rattles off a lot more words—the rules and restrictions I'll have to follow to stay out of jail—but I can't hear him over the loud humming in my brain. It's like the noise that remains in your ears the day after a rock concert. I'm sure I'll get this information in writing because it's certainly important.

I realize they're all silent, waiting for me to speak. "Thank you," I say. I'd like to say more, but I don't want to say anything that will sabotage my release.

"You're welcome," Big-Glasses says.

I stand up and the guard leads me back to my cell, back to Tabitha. She's waiting for me, looking both hopeful and sad. Either way there will be tears. That's the thing about prison. She wants me to stay, wants me to leave.

"Well?" she asks.

I nod at her and tears stream down my face. She envelops me in her arms and smothers me a little with those boobs, heavy and pendulous. Maybe I would have been more into her if she didn't have those. I was never quite sure what I should do with them and they are impossible to ignore.

"I promise I'll write and visit." I mean it, I really do. Letters are the only things that make life bearable in this place sometimes. Little reminders that people still remember that you exist, that you ever existed outside of these cinder block walls.

Tabitha presses her lips to mine and says, "I love you, Cass."

"I love you too, Tabitha. Thanks for being my friend." I rub her cornrows with my open palm and inhale her scent, trying to commit it to my memory forever. She won't be out of here before we're old, and we both know it.

Chapter 2

One week later, I walk outside of prison into a hot-as-hellfire day. I'm wearing what I wore ten years ago when I walked in: faded Levis, green Pumas, and a white t-shirt. Feels fabulous after those prison scrubs. Might as well be a silk dress and tiara. And since my old clothes are long gone, this is what I have for a while.

Vangie Ann pulls up in her beat-up Nissan. She jumps out, dressed like an off-duty stripper. Her curly hair is long and unruly and a cigarette dangles from her lips.

"Cass!" she shrieks as she jumps from the car. She wraps her arms around me and I can smell her cheap perfume.

"Thanks for coming to get me." I return her warm hug, grateful for it even if her stink is making me nauseous. Family is family, no matter how smelly.

"What do you want to do first?" She has already let me go, returning to the driver's side of the car.

"Well, I'm only supposed to go straight home. I can stop for food, anything work-related. That's pretty much it." I open the car door and a wall of smoke assaults my nose. I'm in no position to complain, so I don't. Sitting in the seat feels good and comfortable, like relaxing on an old couch. Worn velour and cigarette burns, much better than cold metal and a lumpy mattress.

"How about some waffles?" she asks with a smile. Her cleavage is poking out at the top of her tight white dress, and I wonder if she brought a jacket that she'll put on before we go anywhere to eat.

"Sure, Vangie Ann. That sounds great." And it does, really. The only waffles I've had the past ten years were the frozen variety that kids eat. I can live the rest of my life without seeing another toaster waffle.

She pulls into a diner thirty miles from the prison. I would have liked some more distance before we stopped, but I don't complain. I'm hungry anyway.

"This place should work. I need some coffee." She turns to me and asks, "Do you drink coffee these days?"

"Yeah." I didn't drink coffee before prison. I only drank sodas or tea back then.

Vangie Ann grabs my hand and pulls me toward the door. She doesn't put on a jacket. We sit in a tiny blue booth and read laminated menus. The menu is the shiniest thing I've seen in ages. It's also very smooth; my fingertips are in love.

The waitress approaches and her proximity makes me nervous. Her nametag reads "Heather." My sister orders us a round of coffee while I stroke the menu and try to focus on the words. It's been so long since I've read a menu I've forgotten how they work. Too many choices overwhelm me. A waffle, I just want a waffle. So many choices of batters and toppings. Why is it so difficult? Is everything going to be this difficult?

"You look spooked, Cass." Vangie Ann smiles at me, looks like she might start laughing. I'd like to punch her smug little face.

"I just got out of prison, idiot. I haven't ordered food in a decade."

"Oh." She puts her menu down and clasps her hands together. "Don't overthink it. You've always done this, you know. Remember that time you got highlights in your hair? You looked at the color chart for an hour."

"Yeah. And my hair turned orange. I looked like Bozo's whore sister."

"Exactly. You should have gone with your gut. Just order a waffle. Just say 'plain waffle' when Heather comes back with our coffee." Vangie Ann picks up her menu and her eyes dart over the offerings. I wonder for just a second if she's back on the crank, but I realize she's a little too chunky for that. Can't say anything, though, or she'll be on the express train back to Methville.

Heather returns with our coffee and sits it down in front of us. The mugs are heavy enough to knock someone out if you hit them hard enough with it. Not that I would. But it's always good to know where the weapons are located. I saw an inmate bite another woman right on the cheek once. She took a hunk of flesh out of her face. A mug would have come in handy to fight off that attack.

"Have you ladies decided what you want?"

"I'd like a plain waffle, please." I say the words quickly, in case they slip my mind. Heather nods at my declaration, and I realize how unimportant it really is.

"I'd like two eggs over easy, wheat toast, two sausage patties, and a waffle," Vangie Ann says in one long breath.

"Alrighty," Heather says with a nod and walks away. Her shoes squeak on the linoleum, even though it doesn't look clean enough to squeak.

"I've got some bad news, sis." Vangie Ann grabs my hands in hers and smiles like she's about to tell me that I have cancer but at least it's not AIDS. "Wayne got married a few years back."

My stomach churns a bit and I can feel the blood creeping up my skin from my chest to my neck. "Why should I give a shit?"

"Well, it's kind of a slap in the face." She crinkles her nose and pulls her hands back.

"Why? Who did he marry?" I know how these things go. There aren't a whole lot of single folks to choose from after a certain age, and the certain age around here is only about twenty-five.

"He married cousin Melody." Vangie Ann frowns, her face a sympathetic mask.

A slap in the face is an accurate description. It doesn't seem possible. "When did this happen?"

"Five years ago." She grabs one of my hands again. "I'm sorry. I tried to talk her out of it. I promise I did."

"Well, maybe he'll kill *her* this time." My first thought is of the kids. TJ and Danielle are grown by now. I was supposed to help raise them, not Melody.

Her eyes widen and she jerks her hand away. "You don't mean that."

"Of course I don't. But I really don't understand how she could marry him. After what he did to me. To Judith. Really?" I cross my arms over my chest. "What's wrong with her?"

Vangie Ann shrugs and our food arrives. I've lost my appetite after her announcement, but I grab my fork anyway. I'm so accustomed to eating on a schedule, I don't know how not to anymore. The waffle is delicious. It tastes like childhood and my appetite returns with the first bite. I guess I'll never have to worry about starving myself over Wayne and Melody's union.

* * *

Blankenship House for Displaced Women and Children sits on a heavily populated residential street in West Plains. West Plains neighbors the town where I grew up. We spent plenty of time here, since Pleasant Fields doesn't have its own Walmart or hospital. Pleasant Fields' population of 2,301 makes West Plains look like a big city with its whopping 5,328 folks.

There are over 60,000 people in Camarillo, California. My face will be one in the crowd there. No one will know about my teen years, riding up and down the main drag with my girlfriends in my Chrysler convertible with french fries and homework littering the floorboard. No one will know that I threw up at my senior prom after too much Strawberry Hill, leaving my white sequined tea-length dress stained pink, forever ruined. And no one will know that I served time for the murder of another member of our tiny community.

But for now, I'm here in West Plains, obligated to live in an old house, large and rickety like a diabetic pensioner. The pale blue paint is chipped, revealing gray wood beneath, and the entire house looks like it might be just a little off-kilter. It's a three hour drive from the prison.

"Needs some work," says me, queen of the obvious.

"It's better than prison, though." Vangie winks and grabs her fake leather purse.

"True." I feel like an asshole. She's spent the last several years getting clean from meth and helping others, while I was reading books, doing everybody's laundry, feeling sorry for myself, and playing house prison-style with Tabitha. I turn around and get my vinyl duffel bag from the backseat. I'm a few years short of forty and my worldly possessions fit in a bag not much bigger than a lunchbox.

We get out of the car and stretch our road-tightened limbs. "I depend on donations, so things get done as they can. I have a few folks who do jobs for me for free, but it's mostly emergency stuff. Plumbing and stuff like that. Hopefully it will get better someday. I'm trying to organize a fundraiser. Maybe you can help me."

"Sure, V." The last thing I planned was a Christmas party for second graders. I can't imagine what she thinks I'm capable of at this point. Maybe a prison-themed bash where the attendees all dress alike and dance with same-sex partners.

The creaky steps and front porch remind me of a haunted house we used to go to every year when we were little. We would pile into our parents' Cadillac and make the half-hour drive, trembling in our princess outfits, except the years when we were dressed like hobos. Then I realize this *is* the haunted house.

"Is this the haunted house?" I ask.

"Sure is! Isn't that cute?" she asks as if the word "delightful" is right on her tongue but just didn't make it out. Vangie Ann opens her big tatty purse, and a brown leather-bound notebook falls out. She pulls a giant key ring from the bag as I pick up the notebook.

"What's this?" I ask.

"It's my journal."

"You keep a journal?" I'm tempted to look inside, but instead I hand it back to Vangie Ann.

"It's part of my recovery." She stuffs the notebook back in her bag and unlocks three locks. "Can't be too safe." She pushes the metal door open and we walk through the threshold. She turns to me. "To tell you the truth, the place is kind of on its last legs. I'm not sure how much longer I can keep it going."

A response gets stuck in my gut. I'm not in a position to help much anyway.

"Evangeline!" A woman with wiry red hair rushes to the door. She's skinny like someone who can't afford both food and cigarettes, so she chooses cigarettes. "The upstairs toilet is backing up again and Paul won't answer his phone."

"Sonya, this is my sister Cass. Cass, Sonya."

"Nice to meet you," she says and holds out a limp-wristed hand but flashes me the stink-eye. I shake her cold, damp hand, immediately wondering where it's been.

"Nice to meet you, too," I say.

"Paul will call back if you left a voicemail. Get a plunger after it in the meantime. You ain't helpless." Vangie Ann closes the door behind us and secures all three locks.

"Okay." Sonya sighs loudly and heads up the stairwell. The stairs are wooden, with lavender carpet running up the middle. The color is something a young girl would have selected. I wonder if she inherited the carpet when she bought the place, but I don't bother to ask.

Vangie Ann turns to me and whispers, "She's a prostitute, but she's trying to turn her life around."

"I'm not sharing a room with her, am I?" I wipe the hand-shaking palm on my jeans, wondering if chlamydia is moist.

"No. You're on your own tonight." She starts up the stairs and motions for me to follow. "There are two twin beds in your room. I think you're getting a roommate tomorrow, but I don't know much about her yet."

"Okay." I'll get one night on my own before some stranger moves in with me. At least in prison my roommate was a friend.

She opens a scarred, naked wooden door to a bedroom with two single beds and two slim dressers. "Pick whichever bed you want." Vangie Ann smiles as I walk past her into the bedroom. I pick the bed closest to the window. An outside view will remind me of my freedom if I forget.

"Thanks for this, sis. You don't know how much this means to me." I sit down on the bed and throw my bag on the floor.

She sits on the bed across from me. "I always thought I'd be the one in jail, you know."

"Yeah, I know. I did, too." We both chuckle even though it's the truth. Life is one hell of a comedian. "There are a lot of women in prison because of meth. I'm glad you got clean."

"Me, too. And I'm glad you're here." She stands and kisses me on the forehead, just like she did when we were children. Just for a second we're little again, still innocent, before drugs and men and prison. She takes a step back. "Look, I don't want to harp on this. But things really aren't going well. We're all going to have to pitch in to keep this place going."

"Alright, V. I'm here to help. I'll do whatever you need me to." I slip my shoes off and cross my legs on the bed.

Vangie Ann draws her lips together in a fake smile. She takes a deep breath and says, "I'm glad you feel that way."

"Oh." I realize what she's after: my inheritance. Dad's attorney sent me a letter after Dad died. He said I was set to receive a portion of the estate, but only under conditions which I would learn upon my release. And I had to go through his wife to find out what. Dad included that part because he wanted us to be close. He refused to accept that familial bonds can't be forced. My dad has to be in charge even when he's dead.

"I put all my money into this place. My inheritance is gone." I know what she's going to say next with that same apologetic tone, and I don't want to hear the words. "It's time to talk to Lucinda." She puts her hand on my arm and squeezes it lightly.

"Can I have a few hours of freedom first?" I want my inheritance, but I'm not ready to deal with that woman. The last time I saw our stepmother was in the visiting room at prison. She came to tell me that the blame for my dad's death lay at my feet. That was one year after she threw out all the clothes I had asked her to store when I went away. She told me she figured I'd be in too long to care, and they took up too much of her attic space.

But I realized in prison that I have to be more proactive in my own life. Standing aside is what landed me there. Well, that and Wayne the Jerkface.

"What if it's not enough?" I ask. I don't mind helping her, but I can't give her everything.

Vangie Ann pulls her hand away and says, "Trust me. It will be. And I'll only need a small percentage to get back on track." Her face goes soft and she says, "The bank is going to take the House."

My stomach rolls and I hang my head. "Fine."

Vangie Ann nods and walks out of my new room. I just got out, and already I'm responsible to someone. I should have at least tried to go straight to California.

Chapter 3

Someone is knocking on the bedroom door—scratch that, banging on the door—during my first nap as a free woman. If it's not a well-hung young man with a bottle of champagne and a box of dark chocolate, I'm going to open a vein.

Instead it's recovering whore Sonya, holding a broom and a toilet brush.

"It's chore time, new girl," she says around a giant wad of gum. She has to have at least three pieces in there, all bright green.

"Oh, all right." I want to argue, to tell Sonya to fuck right off. But who am I but another displaced woman? Anyway, I am here to help.

I turn around to find my flip-flops and Sonya edges her way into my room.

"How long were you in prison?" Smack, smack, smack.

"You're not shy, are you?" I ask.

"Nope." Smack, smack, smack. She hovers six inches from me, close enough for me to feel her breath, full of spearmint and nicotine.

"I was in for ten years." I slide my feet into my flip-flops.

"I heard all women go gay in prison. Is that true?" Sonya leers at me, like she knows a secret.

"Sorry, can't speak for all women." The details of my life aren't for Sonya's entertainment. "Give me that broom." I snatch the broom from her sweaty hand.

"I usually start in the kitchen. But Paul's down there right now."

"Okay." There's a man in the kitchen. Hell yes, there's a man in the kitchen.

I march down the lavender stairs, stopping at the bottom to smooth my hair and wipe the sleep from my eyes. *Dear Lord, I know you're not okay with sex outside of marriage but if you could be so kind as to just this once put a handsome, available man in my path for an immediate sexual experience, I would appreciate it so very much and would work very hard to get my act together quickly thereafter. It's just been so long. You understand, right? Thank you. Amen.*

I put on a movie star smile and drag my broom into the kitchen. Vangie Ann is still in that damn white dress. She stands with a disappointing specimen holding a toolbox. He looks too puny to support the weight of a wrench.

"Cass, this is Paul. He's a plumber and a saint." He holds out his hand, and I fear another moist handshake. I accept anyway, and my fear is confirmed.

"Hi, I'm Evangeline's sister." I surreptitiously wipe my palm on my jeans.

"Well, you are just as pretty as she is," he says and smiles sweetly. He has a few teeth missing, but it's probably because he's at least ninety years old. *Thanks a lot, God. Why did I expect Him to listen, anyway?*

"Thank you." I can't help but smile. Andy Rooney's eyebrows survived and found their way to Paul's face.

Vangie Ann hands me her cell phone, as if I know what to do with it. It looks like a toy, a prop someone would use on a science fiction movie. "There's a voicemail on here from your parole officer."

"How do I get to the voicemail?"

"Oh, right. Sorry about that." She pokes at the screen and hands the phone back to me. I have instructions to call my parole officer, Mack Brown, right away. I haven't been out a full day yet and he's already up my ass.

"How do I dial this phone, Vangie Ann? There aren't any numbers." No keypad. Seriously, I don't get it. She giggles and tosses her hair.

"Even Paul here knows how to use a phone, Cass. We've got to get you used to modern society." She presses the screen, showing me the missed calls and the number where my parole officer called from. She presses the number and hands the phone back to me.

"Mack Brown." All business. Obviously takes himself too seriously for his level of income.

"Hello. This is Cass Blankenship returning your call." The broom is still in my hand. I prop it against the wall and head outside to the porch.

"Ah, right. Ms. Blankenship. We need to set an appointment." His tone is deep, but I can't tell if it's his real voice or his "I'm the boss" voice. A lot of men in the penal system have that tone.

"Sure. My schedule is pretty open at this point." I sit on an unpainted rocking chair and feel the breeze gently lift my hair.

"You're at the Blankenship House in West Plains?" He's flipping through papers. I can imagine my manila folder on his desk. I'm a manila folder to many people.

"Yes. That's right."

"I'll come there tomorrow at 9:00 a.m. Does that work?"

"That's fine. Thank you."

"You're welcome," he says with a question in his voice. Maybe not all of his parolees are as grateful as I am.

The phone line is dead without me hanging anything up. The phone slips into my jeans pocket and I lean back in the rocking chair. A woman about my age walks by pushing a double stroller on the sidewalk. The children are loud, one gleeful and one angry. There's no sign outside of this House but everyone in the neighborhood knows what it is. The woman sees me, doesn't know why I'm here, but knows this isn't the place for people like her. She averts her gaze quickly, just in case I can send her any telepathic badness. The woman keeps her stride steady, walking toward the life I'll never have.

* * *

Bitterness gripped my guts those first few years in prison. It was ugly and harsh and foreign. Nothing in my life had ever made me feel that way. No breakup, no backstabbing friend, not even the drunk old man who ran my mom down with his car. Bitterness had never been a part of me and it was as strange as an extra limb.

Frown lines formed between my eyes, and a hole burned in my stomach. Sleep eluded me as the bitterness grew into a raging hate.

Wayne let me take the rap. And that's what I did. I took it. I could have fought harder. But I didn't, because I knew he wouldn't let me go down for Judith's death. It would be okay. It was best if I kept my mouth shut. My lawyer thought I was insane. My dad and stepmom used words like "lazy" and "naïve." The jurors found me sympathetic enough to take it easy on me, but that's probably only because I was young and pretty.

That's what I'm thinking about this morning, what's keeping in me in bed even though Sonya's been banging on the door, ordering me to help with breakfast. Vangie Ann's been in to tell me that my roommate will be here soon, and of course, my parole office will be here within the hour. I'm finally free and I can't get my bones out of this tiny bed because my brain refuses to leave the prison. I need to see Wayne, to slap him senseless. But I can't go back to prison just because I want to make myself feel better.

I decide to get up and take a shower on the off chance that the parole officer is jumpable. That would take the edge off of the bitterness for sure.

The warm water rolls down my spine and I start to let go a little, at least for now. Big-Glasses gave me a pamphlet before my release that told me all about how this would be a process, almost like grieving or divorce. I threw it away because I thought I wouldn't need any help adjusting.

Back to my room for jeans and a t-shirt. I want money so I can shop. I want to feel a silk dress against my skin. Do people still wear silk?

I'm rubbing my hair with a thick pink towel when the doorbell rings. I can hear Vangie Ann's shoes clacking to the door, and then the deep male voice.

Clack, clack, clack up the stairs. My door swings open and Vangie Ann stands before me looking winded and excited like a child who just won a game of chase.

"Mack Brown is here to see you." Her smile has grown large enough to include her eyebrows.

"What do you need to say, sis?" I stand up and hope she's going to tell me what I want to hear.

"He looks like he probably played football in high school. You know, big shoulders. And he has dimples. Dimples!" She puts her hands on her hips and frowns. "But you look like shit. I'll stall while you put on makeup."

She closes the door and I jump into action. Makeup. I used to love the process but I barely remember how to do it. The only makeup I could buy at the prison canteen was cheap shit that made my eyelids peel, and there was no reason to bother.

I decide to go for a basic, natural look. If I try too hard, I'll screw it up. After a few old moves, I think I'm okay. My hair still needs a lot of attention. But my face looks decent.

I walk down the stairs like I'm revealing myself to a date. Slowly, poised, then I remember that I'm not a teenager and I feel like a dumbshit.

He's standing by the door. Vangie Ann neglected to tell me that he's completely bald, shiny head bald, with a thick neck. But he does have beautiful, bronze skin that makes the shiny head more appealing.

"Hi. I'm Cass Blankenship."

"Hi, Cass. I'm Mack." Then I see the dimples. We shake hands. His hands are large and meaty. It's like shaking a firm slab of ham.

"Does it matter where we do this?" I ask.

He shrugs and looks down at the brown file in his left hand. There's no wedding band. "No. I just have to go over a few things with you this time. It won't take long." He's wearing slacks and a shirt that's neither yellow nor ivory. It's a perpetual nicotine stain of a color.

"How about if we sit on the porch?" I think I'm flirting, but I'm not sure.

"Okay."

Mack opens the door and waits for me to walk through. It takes me a second to realize it, though, so he's just standing there with the door in his hand, looking toward the street.

"Oh, thanks," I say once I finally get what's going on.

There's a stiff-spined police officer standing on the steps. My heart jumps and I almost run back inside. I turn to Mack with my mouth wide open as if to ask "What the fuck?"

Mack smiles softly. "Officer Johnson isn't here for you. He's here for me. They send someone with me on home visits when there're enough officers on staff."

"Looks to me like you can take care of yourself." I didn't mean to say that out loud, and my cheeks turn pink immediately.

"Well, we never can be too safe."

I sit on the rocking chair and he sits next to me on a white wicker chair that doesn't look sturdy enough to support his weight. He opens my file on his lap.

"So, Cass, is this going to be your residence for the foreseeable future?" He doesn't look up.

My probation is two years. A relatively short term considering I went down for murder, but it still feels like a really long time to answer to someone constantly and pee in a cup randomly.

"Yes. But I want to apply for a probation transfer. My friend Jessie has a job lined up for me in California."

Mack looks up at me like he's waiting for me to laugh. "I'll get you the paperwork." He jots something down and says, "I want you to check in with me every week. I'll come here or you can come to my office. Do you have your own transportation?"

"Not yet." I don't even have a car. Another great realization.

"Driver's license?"

"No."

"Well, I'll come here until you get that worked out." He stares at me for a beat, then smiles a little as a spark of recognition hits his face. "I remember you from high school. You graduated a few years before me."

"Oh." Mack's face doesn't connect with anything in my memory. But a few years is a big age gap in high school. Younger kids have a better view of the older kids. They watch those going before them to learn what to wear and how to abuse their peers.

"I didn't think you'd remember. I wasn't one of the cool kids." He smiles in a way that tells me he doesn't mind not being remembered.

"Sorry," I say for lack of something better to say.

"Do you have any questions for me?" He looks up, and I wish he had hair but his eyes are sparkly like a child's.

"How am I supposed to get over being in prison? You know, the anger of the situation, the bitterness? To forgive so I can move on and grow as a person?" I glance to

Officer Johnson, who is still standing perfectly still and staring into the street. He has a round belly, and I don't understand how he can be comfortable standing that way.

I put my elbows on my knees and lean forward. I'm inches from his dimples. It's electrifying to be so close to a man. My skin is tingling and I wonder if he feels it, too.

Mack leans back and the wicker chair makes a sad creaking noise. He draws his lips tight and looks toward the sky. He takes a deep breath and says, "You know I'm not a therapist, right? I'm a parole officer. I'm here to help with a job, school, keeping you out of jail…shit like that."

And just like that, the charge fizzles.

Chapter 4

Sex with a man is an actual option for me now, but how do I get it? The longing is even worse on the outside. Being so close to something I can't have. Smelling a man, but not able to touch. Feeling the heat from his skin radiating close to mine, but having no actual contact. These feelings were easier to deal with when the only men around were the guards. Big-bellied men with jangling keys and shitty attitudes. Nothing attractive about them other than the possibility of what might be lurking in their trousers. Not worth investigating because it would only be bringing attention upon yourself that you couldn't afford. But here on the outside it should be so easy. A touch, a glance, that "come hither" look made famous in the movies and cosmetic commercials. But it's not. Have I become undesirable? I know I have forgotten how to seduce.

But I'm here now. In a chat room with Hairychest68 and I don't even like hairy chests. But I suppose this isn't something I could do in prison. We had computer access, but chat rooms were blocked. I only know about this from a girl named Becky Ann who did a short stint for drug possession. She told me every detail one day when we were bored in the laundry room.

"What RU wearing?"

Really? He's too lazy to spell "are you"?

"Black cotton panties. You?"

"Mmm. Nice. I'm wearing nothing."

I imagine he's fat, hairy, and naked. Gross. I decide to cut to the chase. "Tell me what I'm working with."

"What do U mean?"

Idiot. "How big is your package?"

"Huge & hard. Tell me about your tits."

No reason to tell the truth here. "36D—want to touch them?"

"Oh yes. Push them together so I can slide my big cock between them."

Because everybody knows a woman's G-spot is on her sternum. "Then what? Don't forget that I'm still wearing panties."

"I'm sliding those off right now."

Finally. I unbutton my pants and lean back against the headboard, positioning the laptop beside me. "Tell me more. Where are your hands?"

"One hand is rubbing your big tits and the other is massaging your clit."

There we go. I slide my left hand in my panties and type with my right. This is complicated. "I have my hand wrapped around your shaft…"

"Cass!" Bang, bang, bang on the door. Shit.

I close the lid to the laptop and button my jeans. "Just a second, Vangie Ann."

She opens the door anyway. "What are you doing?"

"Just checking my e-mail." I can feel the heat in my cheeks. She knows I'm lying. Nobody ever e-mails me.

"We need to chat."

Chat? Does she know what I was doing?

"What's up?" I slide the laptop to the bed. Heat is rising to my cheeks, and sweat forms on my upper lip.

"Lucinda's here."

The heat deepens on my face. Shame mixed with anger. "Why?"

"I called her. You weren't going to do it. You have to be nice to her, okay?"

"I'll try." I stand up and stomp down the stairs like a hormonal teenager.

* * *

"Why haven't you called me, Cass? I had to hear through the grapevine that you were out of prison." I found her on the porch, smoking a cigarette. Her voice is even deeper than I remember; it's almost frightening. She puts her bony fingers on her hips and stares at me.

"I've been out less than twenty-four hours, Lucinda. Anyway, I didn't reckon you would want to see me." I turn and sit down in the rocking chair. I can tell this is going to take a while. "I didn't really want to see you." I don't bother mentioning that my sister telling her wouldn't really be considered a grapevine.

"Oh, we're just going to throw it all out there, are we?"

I sigh loudly and wait for her tirade to begin. Lucinda is real good at tirades.

"The last time I saw you it didn't go so well."

"I was upset, you know." Lucinda pulls the long skinny cigarette to her lips, and her giant diamond ring sparkles in the morning sun. "Losing your dad made me say things I shouldn't. But it's not exactly a coincidence that his heart attack came after you got yourself incarcerated."

I try to never think about how much it hurt him when I was convicted. But sometimes late at night, it's the only thing I can think about. Lucinda doesn't need to remind me.

"Don't do this again. I just got out of prison. I'm desperately trying to get my shit together here." I realize I'm balling my fists, so I cross my arms across my chest. "You're the one who fed him that high-fat diet when you knew his blood pressure was through the roof. You killed him as much as I did."

"I fed him what he liked. He was a grown man and made his own choices."

"You smoked in the house and cooked a pound of bacon every two days."

Lucinda takes a drag of her cigarette and her face softens. "Look, sweetie. I'm sorry. I didn't come here to fight. You and Vangie Ann are all the family I have left. I know we ain't never got along. But I'd like to try."

I rock back and forth for a few seconds. The chair squeaks rhythmically on the porch.

When I got the call that Dad was dead, I started crying and didn't stop until he was buried. By then I was dehydrated and my face was chapped. But Lucinda doesn't know that. Only Tabitha does.

"Please, Cass."

"We can try. But I'm not making any promises."

She smiles and the skin of her red stained lips look like they might split from the strain. "That's good enough."

"I didn't kill Judith. It's not my fault I was incarcerated."

"Why didn't you try harder to prove it, Cass? Why?" She sits on the chair across from me and ashes on the porch floor.

Tears pool in my eyes, and I can't stop them. "It's not something I can explain to you. I guess I just thought it was going to be okay."

"It wasn't okay, Cass. For any of us." Her voice is barely above a manly whisper.

The tears fall from my eyes. I lean forward and put my head in my hands so I can hide my face from her. She stands and rubs my back, a strange but welcome sensation. I release the tears freely, hoping for catharsis.

"You're out now. Let's get your life on track, okay? There's nothing you can do to get those years back."

Her words are meant to comfort me, but they only serve to make me feel hollow. Like she always does, Lucinda gets it wrong.

Vangie Ann walks out with an unlit cigarette dangling from her lips. "You ladies all caught up out here?" She lights her cigarette with a pink lighter and gives Lucinda an impotent half-hug.

I wipe my face with my palms. "I think so."

"How are you, Vangie Ann? You're looking healthy." Lucinda flicks her cigarette butt into the yard.

"I know that means fat, Lucinda," she answers.

"I didn't say that." Lucinda sweeps a lock of hair out of Vangie Ann's face. "You got any coffee?"

"Yeah. I just started a pot," she said.

"I need some, too. I'll go with you." I stand up and lead Lucinda inside. Vangie Ann hangs back with her cigarette, even though I want her to follow us. I haven't been alone with Lucinda in a really long time. And I'm not eager to do it now.

We walk in and Lucinda sits down, waiting for me to pour her a cup of coffee. "You still take sugar?"

"Yes, thanks." She twists her diamond and clears her throat. "Your sister told me you two need money."

I sit down at the table with our coffee. "Yeah. Isn't that handy? Me needing your help."

She smirks at me and pulls her mug closer. I catch the familiar scent of Aqua Net and cigarettes, mixed with coffee. For a moment, I feel like a teenager again. "Your dad left you a lot of money in his will."

My stomach flutters, and I feel like I might pee my pants. "He did?"

"Yep. A half a million dollars."

"Well, hot damn." A slow smile spreads across my face. It's plenty enough to help Vangie Ann and move to Camarillo. I can get my life started.

"Wait. You have to do something to earn it." She points at me with a long, red, fake fingernail.

"I know." My dad always made us work for his money. It came from a place of love, I suppose. To make us responsible and all that. But couldn't he give all that up once he was dead? "What do I have to do?"

"You have to prove your innocence. Your daddy wanted you to clear your name." Lucinda takes a drink of coffee and peers at me from over her cup.

"How the hell am I supposed to do that?"

"I don't know, sweetie. But I'm sure you can figure it out."

I sit back in my chair and sip my coffee. If I could prove my innocence, I would have done it over a decade ago. But I have a chance to do something my dad wanted me to do. I'll never have a chance like that again.

A thought pops in my head that distracts me from the quandary.

"Do you have any of my old yearbooks?" I ask.

"I think so. There's a box of school crap in the attic." She taps her nails on her coffee mug.

"So you kept the school stuff, but not my clothes?" I told myself I was over the loss of my wardrobe, but I guess I'm not.

"Clothes rot over time. Everyone knows that."

"Whatever. If you can find the yearbook from my senior year, I will really appreciate it."

"I'll take a look." She takes a sip of coffee. "But I don't think that will help you get the money."

"You don't say?" I roll my eyes and immediately regret it.

"Brat," she says under her breath. It's reassuring to know that some people never change.

Chapter 5

We're facing each other, staring one another down like we're both ready to pounce. I can tell she's been to jail, too. Maybe not hard time like me, but she's at least been in county. I can't tell her that I've only been here one day. That I haven't found my legs yet, so she can't kick them out from under me.

"Who are you?" I ask.

"Name's Tilly. Who are you?"

"I'm Cass Blankenship. My sister owns the place." That's right. Ownership. Don't cross me.

She grins out of the side of her mouth. Her over processed blonde hair is pulled into a tight ponytail, and she tugs at it without taking her eyes off of me. Tilly's been in the House fifteen minutes, and the pissing contest has already started.

"You an ex-con?"

"Yeah." I nod my head once in her direction. "You?"

"Just been to county. But you're the real deal, ain't ya?" Tilly puts a cigarette between her lips and presses down. She puts it between two fingers and pulls it out.

"Yeah." I put my hands on the bed and lean my shoulders forward. "Why were you in county?"

"Drugs." She narrows her eyes and puts her cigarette back between her lips. "Murder?" Her eyebrows are raised to punctuate the word.

"How do you know?"

"I'm going outside." Tilly flashes her lighter at me, and walks out of the bedroom. I try to follow, but Vangie Ann walks in before I can get out.

"What did Lucinda say?" She leans against the doorframe. She's wearing an electric blue tube dress. I'm not sure how it's staying up.

"Dad left me a half million."

"Fantastic. What do you have to do to get it?" Vangie Ann stands up straight and brings her hands together.

"What did you have to do?" I ask.

"Use your head, Cass. Why do you think I got off drugs?" She walks to Tilly's bed and sits on the edge. "I had to attend an intensive three-month inpatient program. But that's how I got this place off the ground and paid for rehab. That place was pricey."

"Oh. That makes a lot of sense."

"What do you have to do? Go back to school or something?" she asks.

"I wish. All I have to do is clear my name."

A chuckle escapes Vangie Ann's throat and her right hand moves to her mouth. "Sorry about that," she says. "I didn't mean to laugh. But if you could clear your name, would you have done a dime in prison?"

"Exactly." I sigh and my shoulders slump instinctively. "I don't want to do this. I've given up so much of my life for Judith already."

"If you don't do it, it won't get done." Vangie Ann leans toward me, and I'm getting a much better view of her cleavage than I need. "The cops think the case has already been solved."

"I know." Where can I even start? "I wish I could talk to Wayne. He's the one who knows what happened."

"Are you kidding me right now?" she asks. "Wayne testified against you. Why do you think he'd help? Stay the fuck away from him. Don't be an idiot."

"I don't know that he would help. But if I could get information out of him, it would be a start." I pause and look around the room, as if inspiration is going to spring from the taupe walls. "If he saw me face-to-face, he'd have to tell me why he said I did it. Maybe the guilt would cause him to confess."

Her eyebrows pop up. "You have to stay away from him."

"You're right." I grab a sheet of paper from the bedside table. "I'm going to make a list of 'persons of interest.' It will be suspects and people who might have information."

"Who's going on the list?"

"Just Wayne for now. I need to keep thinking." I write his name in black ink. Seeing his name fills me with something akin to grief, even though I thought I was over all that by now.

Vangie Ann stands up abruptly. I guess she's done talking about this. "Can you go to the grocery store for me?"

"Is it part of my job?" Can't leave the House unless it's for work. It's prison light.

"Yes, it is. And you can take my car." Her smile becomes broad and welcoming, and I feel guilty for judging her tacky clothes.

"Oh, wait. I don't have a driver's license. Can you take me to the DMV?"

"Let's go," she says and motions for me to follow her.

Ten minutes later, I walk into the DMV. It's just as I remember: beige tiles, tired-looking folks behind the counter, a bright red number dispenser in the middle of the room. Vangie Ann sent me in alone so she could make some calls in the car. Or so she said. I think she just didn't want to come in to this drab place.

God must be favoring me today because I only have to wait twenty minutes. The woman behind the counter has black dyed hair. It looks like she was trying to cover her grays and got a little too optimistic.

"I need a driver's license, please." I slide my state issue ID and social security card to her. "I've been incarcerated." I add a smile, as if incarceration happens to every girl.

"Hm," she grunts and taps on the computer. "Go to the end of the row and I'll take your picture."

My first driver's license picture in about eleven years should be great, so of course I smile like a serial killer. At least I brushed my hair before I left the House.

Me and my shiny new license go to the car.

"Look, V! I have a driver's license, just like a grown-up!"

She's smoking a cigarette and looking at her phone. "You don't have to be a grown-up to get a license."

"Well, do you have to a bitch to be my sister?" I smile and wink at her as she looks up to let her know that I am mostly kidding.

Vangie Ann puts the car in gear and pulls away without a response.

* * *

Vangie Ann gives me a list for the grocery store. I demanded that she be as specific as possible.

I pull into the parking lot just as my stomach drops. This is tougher than I thought it would be. *You're middle-aged, girl. Get over yourself and go to the grocery store like a normal adult. Sure, you haven't been to the grocery store in over a decade. But people go to the grocery store all the time. You can't let normal, everyday tasks terrify you if you're going to survive in the real world.*

Bright aisles. Fluorescent lights like I haven't seen in so many years seem foreign and strange like something left by aliens. Labels with primary colors and photographs of fake food. The cart rolls off to the side, a wonky front wheel leading the way. I should go get a different cart, but that seems like too big of a task. I just drove a car for the first time in a decade; my senses feel a little too scrambled.

Four giant cans roll back and forth, banging against the sides of the cart. The wheels squeak. *Squeak, bang, squeak, bang.* My eyes squint, and for a second I wonder if this is real. What if I'm in prison? What if I'm in the cafeteria, passed out at a bench? I'll wake up with my head pressed against Tabitha's giant breasts and she'll stroke my hair until my tears dry and I forget what upset me to the point of passing out in my mashed potatoes.

I have to snap out of this. A grocery store trip can't intimidate me to the point of fantasizing about prison.

Two giant boxes of Cheerios from the shelf to the cart. The boxes are bright yellow and smooth. They remind me of my mom, her White Shoulders scent first thing in the morning. "Come get your breakfast, girls. The bus will be here soon." And just like that, I'm lost again.

I look down at the list to find myself. Got the Cheerios, got the canned foods. I still need milk, eggs, cheese slices, shredded cheese, cheddar cheese. These bitches love their cheese. I can do this. My hands grip the cart and I walk toward the dairy section, determined not to think about my mom, or Tabitha, or anything other than dairy products for the next two minutes.

That's when I see Melody Talbot nee Blankenship standing with her ass turned away from the yogurt. Fuckety, fuck, fuck. What am I supposed to do with this?

I turn around, away from the milk, eggs, and various cheeses. I walk toward the bread. We need bread.

"Cass?"

Shit. I turn back toward the dairy case slowly. Melody's jaw is hanging low, but she's still prettier than I remember. Prettier than I want her to be.

"Hi, Melody." I move toward her like I'm going to hug her, then stop. We don't get to hug now.

"You're out of prison." It's a statement. Flat. Not a question.

"I just got out." My gaze shifts to the contents of her cart. She's buying steaks for Wayne. Rib eye, his favorite.

"Wayne told me you were getting out, but I didn't know it would happen so soon." She looks me up and down, looking for signs of something different. I'm sure I look older, but so does she.

"I wouldn't call ten years 'soon.'"

Melody smirks and rolls her eyes. "Are you staying with your sister? Is that why you're in West Plains?"

I nod slowly. "Why are you here?"

"My mom's in the hospital here." Melody looks down at the floor and then looks back to me. "She has pneumonia. Don't try to go see her." Just like she always used to, she thinks she can boss me around.

"I suggest you don't tell me what to do. Okay?" I put my hands on the cart rail and grip it until my knuckles turn white. My breath is suddenly hard to find.

Melody takes a step back and her eyes grow wide.

"Sorry. I hope your mom's all right." I turn away from her, away from my responsibilities, and walk toward the checkout. I don't know if Melody follows me, and I don't turn around to look.

Chapter 6

The tiny bed is my refuge. Just me and the bed, so I can think about my choices: going to California with no money in my pocket and leaving Vangie Ann and the other women here homeless, or stirring the dead-Judith pot. Vangie Ann will never forgive me if I don't try to help her.

There's a knock at the door. Soft this time.

"Come in."

Vangie Ann pushes the door open but doesn't walk in. "Your parole officer is here again."

"Fuck. Again?"

"I'll tell him you'll be right down."

She closes the door, and I drag my bones from the mattress and down the lavender stairs.

"Hey, Cass. How's it going?" Mack asks. He glances at my sheet-creased face and looks away.

"Fine. Weren't you just here yesterday?"

"Yeah. I have some information for you. Want to go to the porch?" He opens the door for me before I can answer.

I follow him out and we take our places. There's sunshine and a light breeze, a beautiful day to be a parolee. I should be spending more time outside.

"Where's your bodyguard?"

"We're short-staffed today so I'm on my own." He grins and I feel a little woozy. He says, "So don't try any funny stuff."

I'm not sure if that's a joke or if he knows I've considered diving into his pants, so my response is a blank stare.

"Here's the phone number for a therapist who specializes in transitional cases like yours." He hands me a business card. His fingers brush against mine, and my breath catches in my throat. I put the card in my back pocket without looking at it. "I know about your opiate problem. She can help you with that, too."

It's not like I've forgotten that I used to pop pills like candy, but I choose not to think about it anymore. That was a lifetime ago. His mention of it feels like someone coming up behind me and pushing me down for no reason.

"I haven't had an opiate problem in a very long time." The first time I took hydrocodone was when my wisdom teeth started pushing through, angry and ripe. The dentist gave them to me as an act of mercy. I was twenty. The pills allowed me to float above the pain, above my body, the shell that holds me down. Two years after the wisdom teeth came out, I was in a car accident with a boy in his Ford pickup. His truck plowed into a drainage ditch and my body slammed against the dashboard. Hello, Percocet. The injuries healed quickly, and my dependence grew rapidly. For the next five years, I needed opiates to feel normal, to not have a hungry pain in the base of my skull. I only took a few a day, never enough to lose my ability to function. But a functioning addict is still an addict.

"Transitions can bring up old issues." He hands me a small stack of papers. "And here's your transfer application."

"Thanks."

He pulls out another sheet of paper. My transcript. One piece of paper in the brown folder that defines my life now. "I understand you earned credits toward your graduate degree while you were incarcerated."

"Yeah. I'm about three quarters finished with my master's degree in education." I had been working slowly toward my master's before I was arrested. Then I had ten years to finish it with nothing but time on my hands. Having endless time laid out before me make it impossible to do anything in a hurry. And it was hard to see the point. "But I'm pretty sure I can't get a job using that kind of degree, and I already have something lined up."

"Don't be so sure. What about a community college? I can put you in contact with a job placement office to see what your options are." He smiles for a second and shows those damn dimples again. I almost think he cares. "You need to have a plan B in case your transfer isn't granted."

"Oh." I hadn't even considered that I might not be allowed to go to California, to the place where winter never arrives.

"Look, even if you don't plan to stick around, you need to get focused. You don't need to have too much time on your hands." Mack leans toward me with my file in his lap. His hands are clasped together.

"Makes sense. I'm staying busy, though. I got my driver's license and Vangie Ann sent me to the grocery store this morning."

"Oh, really. How did that go?" He leans back and the chair sighs.

"Terrible. But it was a first effort. I'll give it another shot." I look up at the green of the trees against the blue sky. "I guess I can't stay holed up here all the time."

"No, not really." He hands me another sheet of paper. "Here's a list of places you can finish your education. A couple are brick-and-mortar schools, the others are online universities."

"Thank you."

Mack looks at my face and forces a half smile. "You'll be fine. But you have to put some effort into it." He stands up and tucks my brown file under his left arm.

"All right." I nod at him, but don't get up. I watch him get into his official-looking black sedan. He's not the type of guy who would be interested in an ex-con.

* * *

Tilly and I are staring at each other again. We're both sitting on our own twin beds and glaring at each other like predators. If I hadn't been to prison, this woman would scare the shit out of me. She's tiny but looks like she could tear me apart.

"So what do you know about me?" I ask.

She grins slowly. "I'll tell you for a hundred dollars."

"I don't have any money, numb-nuts." I know better than to give cash to anybody who looks like her anyway. She'd smoke it or snort it, and I'd never get what I wanted from her.

"Fine," she sighs and says, "The woman you murdered"—she uses air quotes when she says *murdered*—"used to buy meth from my boyfriend."

"What else do you know?" I'm careful to keep my face stoic.

"Judith and me used to hang out and do drugs. She wasn't so bad, you know? Just fucked up. Anyway, she was real messed up that night, right?" Her eyes grow wide like she's excited by her memories. "She had been over at Matt Morgan's place snorting meth with us. Matt was my boyfriend. She would come over to buy meth and stay sometimes. I don't think she had many places to go."

Matt. A man named Matt paid a visit to Wayne once when I was at his house. I never saw his face.

"And?" I want to slap her in the back of the head to see if relevant information will come out faster.

"Matt told me you didn't do it. He followed Judith that night." She turns to pull a cigarette from her back pocket and starts twirling it between her fingers.

"What did he see?" I scoot to the edge of the bed. My predatory focus is gone, and so is hers. We've found our bond with gossip. And this little skank might just turn out to be my savior.

"I don't know, Cass. He wouldn't tell me. He just said it wasn't you. He couldn't go to the cops. He followed Judith because he wanted to sell her some heroin."

"Where does he live? What's his phone number?" My heart races. Is it going to be this easy?

Tilly shrugs and sticks out her bottom lip. She looks childlike, and I wonder how old she is. She looks like she could be anywhere from twenty-five to forty.

"He's in the state pen. I don't know how to reach him. We broke up before he got busted."

"Do you know any of his family or anything?"

She grins and stands up, reaching her arms over her head in a stretch. "No. I was just a tweaker he was screwin' for a while. He never introduced me to his family." She walks toward the door. "Matt does have a cousin who was around him all the time. Johnny Morgan. He's the only family I ever met. I'm going to go smoke." Tilly closes the door softly behind her.

No. It's not going to be that easy. I pull out the persons-of-interest list and add Matt's and Johnny Morgan's names. I put Tilly on there for good measure. I put it in my back pocket for safe keeping. No leaving it in the room now that my roommate is on there.

I wonder if anyone else saw Judith die that night. Sure, I didn't care for her. She was a meth-head, hateful and crazy. But she was the mother who made two kids I loved so much.

It's so peculiar to me that someone can watch someone else die and make no move to intervene. This man knew I was innocent and let me go to jail. Of course, the same could be said for Wayne and he was supposed to love me. Why would I expect more out of a drug-slinging stranger?

Chapter 7

For my probation transfer application, I need Jessie's address, phone number, the name and address of the store, my starting salary, title, and supervisor's name. As I write the e-mail, I'm consumed with a fear that it won't work out. That Jessie has changed her mind, wants to distance herself from everybody she knew in prison. Or maybe her aunt doesn't want me there because I'm associated with a part of her niece's life she doesn't want to think about. I try to make the e-mail sound as upbeat and positive as possible, to let her know that working at the boutique in California will make my life real. I reread it three times and press "send." I close the lid to Vangie Ann's laptop and pull out a pen and paper.

Tabitha needs to hear from me. Of all the people in my life, she's the only one who's ever saved me. I can't let her think I've forgotten her.

During my first week in prison I scored Vicodin from a guard. It took me five minutes on my knees in a custodial closet to earn ten pills. Tabitha found me on my bed after I took the first four. If ten had been enough to kill me, I would have taken them all. But instead, I just took enough to get really high.

Wayne didn't know about my pill problem until I was arrested. The cops knew I was high, and the prosecution used it against me. For two years, Wayne didn't know I used pills. But Tabitha knew right away. She said it was because my eyes didn't look right. Tabitha took the remaining pills out of my grip and returned an hour later with face cream and a novel.

"It wasn't for nothing," she said when she dropped the goods on my cot. "But never again, girl. You can't die in here." Tabitha pulled my head into her lap and massaged the cream into my face. She did that every day until the cream was gone, nothing left even in the seams of the tiny jar.

I should be writing her every single day. But my pen has nothing to tell the paper. The only development is the possible inheritance, and I can't let the prison officials read that I need to clear my name. Does she need to know that she's still the only sex I've had in the last decade? Knowing Tabitha, she probably would like to know that.

Before I can erase the emptiness from the page, Tilly runs into the room and slams the door behind her.

"There's a kid here."

"What do you mean?"

"A new girl just got here and she has a kid with her." She sighs and hops onto her bed with her tennis shoes on. "I fucking hate kids. They're always dirty and they talk too much."

"The word 'children' is in the name of the place. You knew it could happen."

"Not here by choice, smartass," Tilly says.

"I'm going to go see what's going on." I jump up and head down the lavender-carpeted stairs.

There's a large woman at the bottom of the stairs. She has stringy brown hair and a black eye the size of a bagel. A boy stands clutching her leg. He's so skinny that I wonder if she's eaten all of his food before he had the chance.

"Hi. I'm Cass," I say to him as I reach the bottom of the stairs. "What's your name?"

His mother puts her hand on his back and pulls him closer. "This is Troy. I'm Dana."

"They just got here, Cass," Vangie Ann says. She's wearing one of those stripper dresses again. This one is purple. "They'll be across the hall from you and Tilly for now." Vangie Ann smiles broadly and Dana relaxes her grip on Troy.

"I can take you upstairs," I say.

"That's okay. We can go up on our own. Evangeline already pointed the way," Dana says. She brushes past me and pulls Troy up the stairs. She cuts her eyes at me as she passes. She and Troy go into their room and close the door.

"Did you see the way she looked at me?" I follow Vangie Ann into the kitchen.

"Yeah. Sorry about that. She doesn't like you." She turns to me and gives me a half grin and shrugs.

"She doesn't know me."

"I know. But she did know Judith. She worked with her at the bank or something."

"What the fuck? Can I not go anywhere without running into somebody who knows me or Judith?" I grab a coffee mug from the cabinet and slam it on the countertop.

"No. Not around here."

Reassurance that I shouldn't be here. I should be far away in a boutique where I belong.

"I saw Melody at the grocery store. Did you know that Aunt Rita's in the hospital with pneumonia?"

"Yeah." She grabs a newspaper from the countertop and sits at the table. "I didn't know if I should tell you because you shouldn't go to the hospital."

"Thanks a lot, V." I look down to my coffee mug. My sister wants me to give her a bunch of money, but she doesn't trust me with simple information.

* * *

I know I shouldn't be doing this. Melody will flip right out if she sees me. But I can't help it. It's not illegal for me to see Aunt Rita, and I want to see her. I should have asked Vangie Ann to come with me, but I want to see Aunt Rita alone if possible. I'm only supposed to be out on my own if it's work-related, but I'll think of some excuse if I have to.

I told Vangie Ann I was going to the dentist when I asked to borrow her car. She's right not to trust me.

The parking lot spreads out before me, and seeing Rita suddenly feels daunting. I park the car and get out. I force my feet to move one before the other, and the automatic doors open to greet me.

The gift shop catches my attention as I walk in. It's nestled to the left of the front door, and it holds brightly colored stuffed animals, glossy magazines, and every kind of candy bar I haven't had access to in a decade.

Before I can buy a bag of candy corn that I planned to eat between the shop and Aunt Rita's room, I see Wayne shuffling down the hall. The familiarity of the way he walks catches my attention just before I realize it's him. And I get the tickle in my stomach just like the first time I saw him. I hate how attractive he still is to me. The tickle borders on nausea, but I'll be damned if I'm not excited. He's older, a little thicker through the middle, but still terribly handsome. He sees me and stops moving. He looks at me for a second, and starts walking toward me. It takes him about fifteen seconds to reach me, but it feels like days.

"Hi, Wayne." I can tell he's sizing me up, probably thinking I should dye my hair. I remind myself that he's probably a murderer, that he definitely made me lose my freedom. I can't be attracted to him. I'm not twenty-five anymore.

"Cass." His voice hasn't changed from the way I remember it. I don't know if I want to kiss him or stab him. I replay the way he said my name, trying to judge the tone.

"We need to talk." I put the candy corn back on the shelf next to the red licorice. He's the only one who can help me.

"I suspect we do." He looks around the gift shop. "Come with me."

I follow him outside to his truck, and climb into the cab. It's a different truck from a decade ago, but the smell is the same. That grungy truck-part smell, dirty and oily but not unpleasant. I realize when I climb in that I could be making a mistake, but I don't think I have a choice.

"So, you're out?" He turns the key in the ignition.

"How did you come to that conclusion, genius?" I cross my arms and push my body into the seat.

"You don't have to be an asshole." Wayne pulls the truck onto the street.

"Get to the side streets. I can't be seen with you." I put my hand over my face like I'm shading my eyes from the sun.

"You ain't supposed to be coming to the hospital." He turns onto a residential street.

"It's not against the law." I take my hand from my face. "I can visit my aunt if I want." I'm not sure if that's true or not.

The street turns to dirt. Wayne picks up his speed. I turn around and watch the dust billow behind the truck.

I turn to Wayne. "I don't understand why you did this to me."

"What do you mean?" He pulls onto a one-lane dirt road and puts the truck in park. He stretches his right arm over the back of the seat and raises one eyebrow. He's wearing a cap with a gas station logo. I wonder if he's hiding a bald spot.

"I thought you loved me. You said you did."

"I did love you. And you killed my ex-wife. How is that my fault?" His jaw is set and his lips push forward.

"You know that's not true. I need to clear my name. You have to confess."

"I didn't kill Judith," he whispers.

"Then who the hell did? You had more of a motive than anybody." I keep my voice steady.

Wayne told the cops that he had been there right before she died. That TJ wanted to see his mama but changed his mind. Wayne said neither one of them went into the apartment until she was already dead.

Wayne glares at me. Redness is creeping up his neck and face.

"She was the mother of my kids. You know I didn't kill her. I wouldn't do that to them." Wayne stares out at the cotton field in front of us. "But I didn't want to believe it was you, either."

I shake my head. "But you let me go down for it."

"I'm sorry, Cass. What was I supposed to think?"

I stop shaking my head.

"You thought I was capable of killing her." I look at his face. "It wasn't me, Wayne. I didn't kill Judith. I thought it was you."

"You thought I was capable of killing her," he says quietly.

"So we're both assholes?"

"I guess so." Wayne reaches toward me and I flinch.

"Cass, don't be afraid of me." He face registers a flash of pain. And I know I have to get the fuck out of here before I do something really, really stupid.

My breath catches in my throat, and I reach for the door handle even though I have no idea where I'm going. I pop the door open as he grabs my arm.

"No." He pulls me close. "You want to be here. I think you know that, or you wouldn't have got in the truck with me."

"This is a mistake." I can barely get the words out because my breath is still missing.

His proximity has an unexpected effect. There's anger, sure. But the heat of anger is morphing into desire. I hate myself, but more than that I want in his pants immediately. Fear and anger have made my body all mixed up. The endorphins and adrenaline are making me confused and unbearably horny.

"I'm sorry." Wayne's eyes search my face. "You're so beautiful, Cass." Those eyes hold a question, and I answer with a nod. Wayne lets go of me, opens his door, and comes around to my side of the truck. I wrap my legs around his waist. It doesn't make sense; but he's a man, a familiar man.

"I missed you," he says. He wraps his arms around me. "You look like the same girl."

"I missed you, too." I did. I missed him even when I thought he let me take the rap for murdering Judith.

My lips meet his before the moment passes and he can start to feel guilty. He pulls me closer, and I unbutton his jeans.

"So I guess this is okay with you. It's not going to be weird?" he asks.

"I haven't been with a man in a really long time. I don't want to talk about my feelings," I whisper in his ear as I wrap my hand around his hard dick. I need to feel him inside of me.

Wayne unzips my jeans and steps back. He pulls my jeans and panties off and throws them on the floorboard. He smells like a man, not quite sweaty but sort of. He feels strong and his muscles are hard with soft edges. I've missed him so much it hurts to have him close. He rocks against me, thrusting in and out until we both come. I wanted it to take longer, but it feels good for it to end quickly, before thinking has time to start.

"My parole will be revoked if anybody sees us together." I grab my jeans and slide them on as fast as possible. There's no time for tenderness.

Wayne's face drops as he watches me, but pulls up his pants, too. "Yeah. And if my wife sees us together, she'll kill me."

I kiss him on the cheek. It's a foreign gesture, and I'm not sure why I do it. His face flashes a resigned smile, and he closes my door. I lean against the back of the seat and breathe deeply.

Neither one of us speaks as he drives me back to the hospital. It's like the walk of shame but in a pickup.

"Will I see you again?" He parks beside Vangie Ann's car.

"I don't think that's a good idea." I open the door and turn to look at him. "It was good to see you."

"Yeah," he says. "Goodbye."

"Wait. Do you have any idea of who killed Judith? I have to find out."

He shakes his head slowly.

"Bye." I get out of his truck and close the door behind me. I'm not going to visit Aunt Rita now. My head's not in the right place. I should ask Wayne more questions, figure out if he's leaving something out. But I'm not in a good place for that, either.

After I take a few hours to clear my head, I'll go see Johnny Morgan. Nothing will be better for me than staying on task.

Wayne watches me get in Vangie Ann's car, and he takes off. I feel good, satiated. But also empty and sad. Was it always like this?

Chapter 8

Vangie Ann is waiting for me when I get back. "Mack Brown is looking for you, Cass," she says. She's sitting on the porch, smoking a cigarette. "How was the dentist?"

I sit next to her and let the breeze caress my face. "Didn't go to the dentist. I went to see Aunt Rita."

"Oh. How is she today?"

"I don't know." I sigh, building the strength to continue. "I saw Wayne leaving, and we went for a drive."

"You did what?" Her eyes are wide but she's almost smiling. "You screwed him, didn't you?"

My face turns red and it's too late to deny it. "Yeah."

Vangie Ann bursts into mad laughter, like she's never heard anything so funny. "You idiot," she says once she finally catches her breath.

"I know." I suddenly wish I smoked. It looks so damn satisfying. "He didn't kill Judith."

"You mean he *says* he didn't do it."

"I believe him. You didn't see his face." The words sound ridiculous as they come out of my mouth.

"You mean I didn't see his dick." She's laughing again, ignoring the cigarette and its ash growing too long.

"Stop telling me what I mean, Vangie Ann."

"You can't see him again. You'll go back to prison," she says and the laughter stops. Her face is suddenly solemn. "And I'm responsible for you now. We have enough trouble without you violating your parole."

"I know. I won't see him again. It's not worth it. Plus I don't want to ruin his marriage." I place my elbows on my knees and lean forward. I'm not sure if I'm telling the truth.

"If he didn't do it, who did?" She takes a deep pull from her cigarette. The ash drops all over the front of her dress and she brushes it onto the porch with her hand, leaving a gray smudge on the fabric concealing her right breast.

"No idea, V. No idea." I stand up and go toward the door. "I guess I better go call Mack. Where did you say I was?"

"I told him you went to the dentist. I thought I was telling the truth." She doesn't look at me, so I'm not sure if she's annoyed. Instead, she just keeps smoking and staring into the street.

"Mack Brown." He answers on the first ring.

"Hi, Mack. It's Cass Blankenship." I lean against the kitchen wall.

"Hi, Cass. Thanks for calling me back. How was the dentist?"

"Fine, thanks." How the hell is the dentist supposed to be?

"Great. Have you looked over any of that school information I gave you yet?"

"No. I'll do that today." Geez. He is really up my ass.

"I'd like for you to go ahead and schedule an appointment with the therapist as well. I think transitional help would be extremely beneficial for you."

"Sure." I roll my eyes, and I'm thankful that he can't see me.

"I'll come by tomorrow to check in."

"Tomorrow?" This guy is really starting to annoy me.

"Yep. See you in the morning." He hangs up before I can argue.

I sigh loudly and walk back out to the porch. "Mack's coming back again tomorrow. He won't stay off my ass about school and therapy and shit." I plop down into the chair next to Vangie Ann.

"Well, he's looking out for you. It's his job. Could be worse." She pats me on the knee. "Come on. It's time to clean this place. We can't stay out here all day, you dirty little slut." She winks at me, and I know that if she was annoyed with me, she's over it now.

I follow Vangie Ann into the House and we each grab a broom. I start sweeping the hardwood floors in the living room.

I start to lose myself in the soft rhythm of sweeping when I hear someone bounding down the stairs like there's a fire. I look around the corner and see Dana and Troy.

"Hello," I say.

"Hi," Dana grunts.

"Mama, I thought we ain't supposed to talk to that lady." Troy points at me, and I cross my eyes at him.

"Come on, Troy." Dana says and pats his back.

"Your eye is looking better, Dana," I say. "More yellow than purple now." I resume my sweeping and she goes in the kitchen to find Vangie Ann. She doesn't notice that Troy stays behind to stare at me.

"What are you looking at?" I ask, smiling at him.

"My mama said that you shot a lady in her own house."

"How old are you?" I stop sweeping again and make eye contact with the kid.

"I'm almost seven."

"Well, Troy, I did not shoot anyone. But a lot of people believe I did. Sometimes what people believe about you becomes true." I start sweeping again, dismissing him before his mom returns.

"That don't make no sense."

"No, I guess it doesn't." I turn away from his little face. "Go find your mama, Troy."

He turns around, and I resume my rhythm again. *Scratch, scratch, scratch.*

* * *

Johnny Morgan's address is in the phone book that I dug out of a drawer next to the refrigerator. It's from 2005, but hopefully he hasn't moved. Not many people around here do.

The listing even reads "Johnny," not John or Johnathan. Maybe he got gypped in the name department, too.

He lives about ten miles north of West Plains. Vangie Ann let me borrow her car again, even though I lied to her earlier today. She offered to come with me in case Johnny Morgan is as unsavory as he's likely to be, but I figure I can handle him on my own. Just in case, I told her to call the cops if I'm not back in two hours.

The directions I printed out lead me down a one-lane county road. After about five minutes, I have to pull to the side and wait because a truck is barreling toward me. The truck slows down, and the man in the driver's seat rolls down the window.

"Lookin' for somethin'?" He has a thick wad of tobacco stuck in his cheek.

"I have directions, but thank you." I throw on a sweet smile, then realize that this might be the man I'm looking for. My lazy side tells me to let him go, then I won't have to deal with him today. "Actually, maybe you can help me. I'm looking for Johnny Morgan."

He spits into a Styrofoam cup and says, "You're gonna go about another mile, then take the road on the right."

"All right. Thanks."

The man nods and starts to roll away before I can get the window all the way up.

I'm still wiping the grit from my face with a paper napkin when I get out of the car in front of Johnny Morgan's modest farmhouse.

The house used to be painted white, but now it's brown with uneven white streaks. It's a small place with a grand porch. It looks like an old farmhouse that used to stand proud, but now it's probably a cheap rental. The fields are bare and there are no tractors in sight.

The screen door is closed, but the main door is wide open. A TV blares a sermon from inside.

I knock on the screen door's edge, and the door bangs against the doorframe. The TV goes silent. I wait a minute, but there's no noise from the house.

"Hello?" I say loudly.

"Yeah. Just a sec." The voice comes from the back of the house.

Sweat beads on my forehead as I wait. My armpits feel sticky, and I hope I didn't forget to put on deodorant. A tall man appears in front of me as I'm lowering my arm from the sniff test.

"Can I help you, ma'am?" He pushes the screen door open.

"Are you Johnny Morgan?" I step back a couple of paces.

"Yes, ma'am." Johnny runs his hand down his stomach, smoothing out the wrinkles in his short-sleeved button-down shirt. He has small eyes and a pointed nose that make him resemble a horse.

"I'm Cass Blankenship." I realize now how half-baked my plan is. "I'd like to ask you a couple of questions about your cousin Matt."

Johnny looks down to his bare feet and looks back up. "Sure. Come on in."

I follow him down the hallway, dark from wood floors and wood paneling on the walls. It opens into a living room. He points at a plaid couch.

"Have a seat. Would you like some iced tea?" He smiles, revealing a mouth full of teeth. They're stained a little, but not tweaker-yellow.

"Yes, please." I sit down and lace my fingers in my lap.

The room is heavy with religious artwork. A small Ten Commandments scroll hangs over the TV, and a pastel Jesus with his arms outstretched hangs on the wall above the plum-colored velour recliner opposite from where I'm sitting. A brass cross hangs over the doorway leading to the back porch.

"Here ya go." Johnny appears with two glasses of tea. He places the glasses on the squat coffee table, and sits in the recliner.

"Thanks." I take a sip, not expecting it to be so sweet, almost syrupy. I fight the urge to make a face, and put the glass back on the table.

"I know who you are," he says. "How long you been out?"

The thick swallow of iced tea rolls down my throat, threatening to choke me. "About a week. I'm wondering if you know where Matt is these days."

"Last I heard, he's doing time in the state pen."

"You haven't stayed in contact with him?" I reach for the glass, then remember what the tea tastes like and change my mind.

"No, ma'am. Me and him used to be best friends. But he went to jail, and I found the Lord and got clean." Johnny looks to the ceiling like that's where God lives and looks back at me. "He didn't want anything to do with me after that."

"Do you talk to his folks?"

Johnny shakes his head slowly from side to side and says, "His dad and my dad were brothers, but my dad passed away a couple of years back. I haven't seen Matt's dad since the funeral."

"Oh." I wasn't expecting a dead end so quickly.

"I was with him that night." Johnny leans back in the recliner and starts rocking slowly.

"You were?" I try not to appear too eager, but it's difficult. I wonder what other details Tilly left out.

"We were selling heroin. I can't believe my life got so bad."

"What happened?" I hope he doesn't think I want the story of his rock-bottom. "That night, I mean."

"We were really high. So my memory isn't what it should be. So happy to be free of drugs now. I am truly blessed to have made it out of those days alive."

"Yeah. I've had some struggles myself." I sit on the edge of the couch and angle my body toward Johnny.

"I guess you have. Prison and all that." Tears well up in his eyes. "You didn't do it, did you? You didn't kill that woman."

"No. I didn't." I hope this man I don't even know doesn't start full-on crying in front of me.

"I stayed in the car. But Matt, he told me that Judith was dead and no one else was in the apartment." He takes a sip of iced tea. "When word came out that you had been arrested, he said he knew you didn't do it. I tried to get him to go to the cops, but he was scared."

I take a deep breath, gathering my courage. "No offense or anything, but do you think it could have been Matt who killed her?"

He starts to speak, but he stops when his bottom lip trembles. He takes a breath and starts again. "I've thought about that quite a bit. He was really messed up. We both were. He may have been capable of something like that, but I didn't hear any gunshots."

The tea is the only liquid nearby, so I take a syrupy gulp. "Did you see anything that might help? Anyone in the parking lot? Anything like that?"

Johnny stops rocking and leans forward with one elbow on the recliner's armrest. "When we pulled in, there was this girl tearing out of the parking lot in a Ford Explorer. I remember because I thought it was a real pretty shade of red."

"Did the girl have blonde hair?" The sweat is back on my forehead. I'm glad I remembered deodorant.

"I think so, but I didn't get a good look at her."

Of course she had blonde hair. She promised that she would kill Judith if she didn't back off. Judith had become a real pain in the ass before she died.

Panic rises in my chest, and I have to get out of here. "Thank you for your time, Johnny." I stand up.

"Oh. My pleasure." Disappointment registers on his face like he doesn't get many visitors. But the disappointment quickly turns to resolve.

Johnny walks me to the door, and I take a deep breath of hot summer air. "Please don't come back here."

"Excuse me?" His statement feels abrupt, and I'm not sure I heard him right.

"I don't like being reminded of who I used to be." There's sadness in his voice.

"Thanks. I understand."

I get in the car. It's become an oven from sitting in the sun for twenty minutes. I turn the ignition and start back toward the girl in the red Ford Explorer: my sister.

Chapter 9

"Did you know that Sonya was a hooker?" Tilly's eyes are wide and she looks young again. I want to ask her how old she is, but then I can't keep playing this game with myself.

"Yeah." It's early. But I need to get up and get dressed. Mack will be here soon, and I'd like to get showered before he arrives.

"I've done a lot of shit, but I ain't never sold my body for money." She sits against her headboard and looks out the window. "I guess technically I probably gave it out in trade for drugs. Does that make me a hooker, too?"

"It might, Tilly. But I think maybe we've all been a hooker a time or two for some reason or another." I get up and stretch. It's great to have a twin bed instead of a prison cot, but a full-size bed would be luxurious. "I'm going to hit the shower."

I walk into the hallway, forgetting to close the bedroom door behind me. It's simple things like that—doors don't close automatically behind me—that remind me that I'm free. I turn around to close it when I see Sonya leering at me in the hallway.

"What's your problem?" I ask.

"You're not pulling your weight around here, that's my problem." Her roots are out of control, at least four inches of dark hair. I can't help but stare. The rest of her hair is red, but the type of red that was meant to be blonde.

"Yeah? Go file a fucking complaint." I go into the bathroom and lock the door. I don't know why Sonya thinks she can intimidate me. I dealt with worse than her on a daily basis in prison, and she should know that. Maybe she's only been to county lockup. That would explain a lot.

I finally have a little bit of cash from working around here. I'm going to get some new clothes and dye my hair. I need to feel more like the old Cass, the pretty Cass, the young Cass. It's not that I want to be young again and lose the things that have made me strong, though. The things that protect me from people like Sonya. My life will never be free of folks like her now.

I get in the shower and turn on the hot water. My muscles relax, and I wash Sonya away. I try not to think about being with Wayne, but it's all I can think about. It was perfect. He fucks with the body of a man and the emotion of a woman. Just like he always has. I want him again. But I can't have him. No man is worth going to prison over even once, let alone twice. Plus Melody would divorce him if she found out, and I don't want that on my conscience.

Right now, I have to figure out who killed Judith Talbot, get the money, and move to California. I can do this. I have to come up with a plan. But first I'll wash my hair.

* * *

I'm sitting on the porch when Mack Brown pulls up in his blue pickup with its rattling muffler. He gets out of the truck, and I watch his large manly frame approach.

"Where's your fancy sedan?" I ask.

"My boss wanted it today. So I get the privilege of writing off my mileage." He smirks and nods toward the truck. "And I'm alone again today. I think Officer Johnson doesn't like it here."

"You gonna get that muffler fixed?" I ask.

Mack grins slightly and steps up on the porch. "I already did two days ago. I think it's trying to commit suicide." He sits down with the brown file that is me. "Speaking of suicide, you call that therapist?"

Mack's junky truck has presented me with an idea. I pause and try to choose my words carefully so I don't send myself back to jail. "Not yet. I've been a little busy with another project. But the thing is, I think I need some help."

He cuts his eyes at me. "What do you mean?"

"My dad left me a lot of money in his will. But I have to clear my name to get it. And I can't do that on my own."

"Don't know what to tell you. There's not much you can do without violating your parole."

"What if my parole officer offered me some guidance?"

He rubs his head with one those giant hands and sighs. "The guidance I'm here to offer has nothing to do you clearing your name. It's about protecting your future."

"This would protect my future. If I don't do this, I'll be homeless."

Mack looks to the street and turns back to me. "Is clearing your name even a real possibility?"

I cross my arms over my chest. "I'm not a murderer." But my sister might be. Maybe this is a bad idea.

"No one's guilty, Cass. None of y'all did anything wrong."

"You really think I did it?" For some reason, I thought he knew I was innocent.

"It doesn't matter. You are a parolee either way."

"I'm not the only one who'll be homeless. There are other women in trouble who count on this place. There's a lady in there now with a black eye that takes up half her face. She showed up with her son in tow to get away from her husband."

Mack pulls a chair and sits down across from me. "You have thirty seconds of off the record time to tell me what you are suggesting. Anything over thirty seconds will be included in your file."

I take a deep breath and get started. "You have access to people and information that I don't. You can help me and I'll compensate you for your time once the insurance money comes in." I point to his pickup. "You can't tell me you don't need it." I don't know why I keep pushing this. If it was Vangie Ann, it's better if no one is involved. No point in both of us serving time for it. But I don't think I can do this on my own in a timely manner.

"Where do I even start with everything that's wrong with this, Cass? Bribery? Is that a good place? What do you think?" He leans forward. "You don't even enjoy being free, do you?"

"I'm just asking you for help, and I'll pay you for your time. It's a simple exchange." I stop talking in case my thirty seconds is up.

"You want me to risk my job to gain access to information for you, correct?" He crosses his arms over his chest.

"How you assist me is up to you." I'm looking at my jeans and picking at a thread to avoid looking at Mack.

He swats at my picking hand with his massive paw. "Knock that shit off."

My attention is fully on Mack, but I remain silent. It's like getting in trouble in grade school, but the consequences are much worse than my name on the board.

"Call the therapist. Think about getting some direction in your life." Mack turns away and stomps off the porch.

I'm fairly certain I just fucked up.

* * *

I want to blame Vangie Ann for my worries. If Mack sends me back to prison, it will be hard not to hate her. She's the one who insisted that I get the money, even though it was my bright idea to ask for his help.

But no matter who I blame, it won't change my fate.

A knock on my bedroom door interrupts my self-pity before it boils over into tears or an internet chat room.

Vangie Ann sticks her head in. "TJ is here to see you." Her face is solemn.

"TJ?" I stand from my tiny bed.

"Yeah. He looks high. He's on the porch, twitching and shit."

"Are you sure?" I stand up stretch my arms overhead.

She nods. "Hey. You never told me how it went with Johnny Morgan."

"He didn't have much to say, unfortunately."

Vangie Ann steps aside. I walk down the stairs slowly. I'm not prepared to see him if he's tweaking. I know plenty of damaged folks. Hell, most people I know are damaged. But the last time I saw him he was a child, full of potential and hope.

TJ is standing on the porch, smoking a cigarette and fidgeting. He sees me and smiles halfway. He reminds me of one of those boys from the wrong side of the tracks. The ones that would feed a dog gunpowder to make it tougher, then shoot it in the head when it got that crazy look in its eyes. And shrug it off like it's no big deal, just something that happens.

"Hi, Cass." He hugs me with one arm, holding his cigarette far away with his other hand. Chemical sweat radiates from his skin.

"TJ, you're grown." I force a smile, trying to pretend that the sight of his skeletal frame doesn't torture me. He knows what he looks like. He's seen his own scars left from hours spent in front of the mirror digging out whiteheads.

"Yeah. That happens, I guess."

I sit down in my favorite chair and wait for a breeze, but nothing comes. The air is still, stale, hot as hell. There is no relief. TJ stares at me and fidgets.

"What brings you by?" I ask.

"Heard you were out. Wanted to check on you."

"Did you hear about me from Melody?" I look around for something, anything to fan myself with.

"No. It was dad." He takes a deep drag from his cigarette and flicks it in the driveway.

A flash of what happened when I visited with Wayne pops in my head. My face is already red from the heat so I don't bother blushing.

"What are you going to do next? I mean, with your life and all?" He grinds his teeth. He doesn't even know he's doing it.

"I'm trying to work that out. I haven't been out long. Just taking it day by day right now."

TJ lights another cigarette and bites down on the filter as he takes a deep drag. He stares at me without really looking at me. I don't know if there's something he is not saying or if he's just high.

"Dad didn't date anyone for a real long time after you went away. He and Melody were just friends for a few years before they become a couple."

A punch in the gut, and I'm not sure why. It shouldn't bother me. I shouldn't give a shit. This boy, this young man with big ears and a meth problem, shouldn't affect me this way.

"I didn't 'go away.' I was sent to prison for killing your mother when I didn't kill your mother." I don't look at him.

"It was hard on us, you know. We lost her and then lost you." There's venom in his voice, blame.

I turn to him. "I know, TJ, and I'm sorry for you. But it wasn't my choice or my fault. Don't forget that you and your dad nailed my coffin shut with your testimonies."

"I know what I saw."

"Are you sure about what you saw?" I force myself to face him.

"I've had years to think it over, Cass. Years." He looks away and looks back to me. "You were there. In the apartment."

I wipe a single tear from my eye and squeeze my lips together. I close my eyes and soak the heat into my skin. The discomfort from the heat is preferable to the pain TJ is inflicting on me.

He sticks the cigarette between his nicotine- and drug-stained teeth and stares into the distance as he takes a drag. "I ain't had a life, Cass. Everything's been taken from me."

His words turn my guilt to anger. "For fuck's sake, TJ. Stop feeling sorry for yourself. Get over yourself and go to rehab." I cross my arms over my chest and stare at him. My anger refreshes me, renews my interest in the conversation. "I lost my mama young, too. So did Vangie Ann. She went to rehab and she's doing fine. I would have been fine, and I'm working on being fine again."

TJ smiles and says, "Maybe you're right. But I feel like I lost two mamas, you know."

"Are you talking about me?" I ask.

"Of course. That's another reason I'm here. Dad told me you're looking to clear your name." He flicks his cigarette and takes two steps toward me. "I'd hate for something bad to happen to you now that you're finally free."

"What do you mean?" My stomach flutters but I don't move.

"A lot of folks care about you, Cass." He sighs and tilts his head, grits his teeth and begins to speak again. "But some folks don't mind if you just disappear. And ex-cons disappear all the time."

"Anyone in particular?" I stand up.

"Just leave well enough alone, all right?" He looks at his watch, or pretends to. "Oh no, I need to get going. Dad's expecting me at the shop."

"TJ, I need to know what you're talking about." I stand up and grab his arm. His skin is oily and cold, reptilian.

He pulls away and turns toward the street. "We'll talk soon, Cass. Good to see you." He's on the street before I can respond.

I go back inside, and add TJ's name to the list. That boy obviously knows something.

I check my e-mail. More than anything I want to get the hell out of Arkansas. The response I have been waiting for is in my e-mail inbox. Jessie is waiting for me, my job is waiting for me, my life is waiting for me in sunny California.

* * *

I am scrubbing the bathtub with all my might, hoping for inspiration. What am I supposed to do? What if Mack rats me out? Mexico. I could make a break for Mexico. Unless it's already too late. He said I had thirty seconds off the record. I shouldn't have trusted him. Trusting men doesn't turn out well for me. And I really, really just want to go to California.

Chewing my nails would feel great right now. Stupid gloves and cleaning products.

"Well, I'll be damned. You're cleaning." It's Sonya. She plops her ass down on the toilet and proceeds to pee inches from where I'm squatting down to scrub.

I stand up and peel the gloves off. "What's your problem with me, bitch?"

"You think you're better than me, don't you?" She stands from the toilet and flushes, then moves to the sink to wash her hands. For some reason I'm surprised that she's washing her hands.

"What if I do?" I wonder how she could tell.

"I'm used to shit like this, you know. Ever since I can remember, bitches like you have looked down on me." She turns so we're face-to-face.

"Why the fuck do you care what I think?" There were countless women like her in prison. Women that would come out swinging if you looked at them wrong.

"You and me ain't so different, you know." She points at me just in case I'm not sure who she's talking to. "Like it or not, you're just as trashy as me."

I smile at her. "I don't recall claiming to be better than you." But I really hope I am.

Her face softens, as much as a face like hers is able. "I have seniority around here." She turns and walks away. She looks over her shoulder and says with a smile, "Don't think that just because Evangeline's your sister, you'll get special treatment."

I shake my head and get back to scrubbing. I'll have to make friends with Sonya if I want to live here in peace. But for now my mind wanders to Wayne. It's easier to think of him than to worry about Mack Brown, Vangie Ann, or Sonya the Hooker. I know I have to stay away, but I miss him. His touch is warm, and my body feels cold and lonely. There is a cold that no number of blankets can fix. I can't imagine that Melody appreciates a man like him. But then, I can't really claim to know much about her any more. When we were young, she was more girlie than Vangie Ann or me. She was also more proper. Also a better cook, which I'm sure Wayne appreciates. But I can't imagine that she can let go and enjoy the way he touches a woman. There's no way I can know that for sure. It could just be my hopeful thinking.

Chapter 10

"Let me in. It's hot out here." Mack's standing in the doorway. The sight of him makes my stomach lurch.

"Good morning, Mr. Brown. Please come in." I stand aside as he walks in. "I have something for you."

I grab the probation transfer application from the kitchen table and hand it to him. "Everything's here."

He nods and follows me to the sitting room, to the left of the front door. His bald head is shiny from sweat.

"Did you call the therapist?" he asks as he shoves my application into his briefcase. One of the pages gets creased. I want to say something about it, but I keep quiet.

"I left a message." *Liar.*

"Really, Cass?"

"I'll do it today." I put my hands in my lap and look down.

He sighs. "I've been giving your offer some thought. I need to know that you are truly innocent, and you're not trying to get me to help you frame someone else for your crime."

I'm not sure how to convince him. No officials have believed me this entire time. "I promise, Mack. I did not kill Judith."

Resignation sweeps his face. "Look. I get it that this place is in trouble. To tell you the truth, I need some help, too. I'm already broke, and I'll be putting my job in jeopardy."

I nod slowly, afraid to say anything that can change the course of the conversation.

"If I'm going to do this, I expect a real payment. Fifty grand." He stands up straight; his face tells me he thinks I'll try to talk him down.

"That seems fair." I smile too broadly and feel like a dork.

He leans toward me, and for the first time, he seems interested in what I have to say.

"But I still want you to call the therapist. And if I learn anything at all that makes me believe you're guilty, the deal is off." He stares at me until I nod in agreement. "Where do we start?"

"Right. Well, my roommate Tilly said her ex-boyfriend Matt Morgan was there. He knows who killed Judith. But he's in the state pen. Can you arrange a meeting with him for you or me, or both?"

He sits back in the blue velour recliner and taps his finger against his temple. "Yeah, probably. You'll have to say you're my secretary or something. If anyone catches us, I'll lose my job." He shrugs and looks at me. "But, I'm not great at this job anyway."

I smile at him again. "Do you think he'll tell us anything?"

"No way. Why would he?"

My smile drops. "Well, that sucks."

"Sorry, Cass. Consider who you're dealing with. Maybe ask Tilly if there's anything you can use to bargain with. I doubt he's going to do anything for you out of the goodness of his heart." He looks toward the window and back to me. "Why is he in?"

"Dealing meth? Maybe cooking, too. I'm not sure." I realize I sound like a first-rate idiot now.

"Okay. This guy has no reason to help you. You have to give him one." He leans back in his chair. "Tilly is the only link you have. Need me to grill her for you?"

I consider his offer. "Not just yet. I don't think she'll talk to you. Let me give it a shot first."

"Watch what you're doing. You're likely to be messing with some unsavory characters."

"Okay." Maybe he's a little concerned. That makes me happy.

He stands and extends his substantial paw. "I look forward to working with you, Ms. Blankenship. I trust that everything from five minutes ago forward will be held in the strictest confidence." He grins and I see the damn dimples.

"Yes, indeed, Mr. Brown. I look forward to working with you, too. And don't worry. My lips are sealed tighter than Mother Teresa's crotch." I put in extra effort with my smile. I'm going for sparkly like a pageant contestant.

Mack blushes but maintains his grin. "Well, okay. Talk to Tilly. We'll discuss nothing over the phone or text."

"Text?"

"You don't know what that is, do you?" He chuckles and continues, "I'll come by in a couple of days. One more thing," he sighs and says, "You have to stop it with the eyelash batting and leaning toward me and shit."

"The what?" My mouth hangs open at the hinges. I'm mortified, but also shocked that he noticed.

"You know what I'm talking about. Just because you've been locked up doesn't make me a piece of meat."

"Okay." It's the only word I can form.

He walks outside to his black sedan, and I go upstairs to speak with Tilly.

* * *

"Tilly, tell me about Matt." I lie back on my bed and put my hands under my head with my elbows out.

Tilly's on her side, facing me. "Well, what do you want to know?" Her over-processed hair is in a messy bun. It looks better than usual.

"I just wonder what he saw. You know? I'm wondering if there's anything about him that you can tell me that will give me any clues." I turn to my side and face her.

"I don't know, Cass. We were so fucked up back then. So many drugs." She leans back. "Ya know, I miss him a little bit. I think it's just because I miss men, though. Know what I mean?"

"Unfortunately, yes."

"He fucked like a maniac." Tilly smiles and angles toward me again. "Maybe that was the drugs, too. So much passion. I wonder if normal men know how to screw."

"I don't know if I ever fucked any normal men. No druggies, but I like the wounded types. You know, emotional fuck-ups," I say. I try to keep my mind from wandering to sex. I can get lost there for hours. "Did he cook or just deal?"

"Cooked, dealt, both." She rolls over to her back. "Your sister used to hang around him some. Not much, though."

"She's never mentioned him."

Tilly sits up on her bed. She swings her tennis-shoed feet back and forth. "Look, you've already done the time, right? Maybe you should just let the Judith thing go. Move on. Isn't that the healthy thing to do? I learned that in one of my rehab classes. I mean, it was something like that, not exactly because the circumstances were different." She stares at the ceiling a minute and then brings her focus back to my face.

"It would be great to just let this go. But that's not really an option for me."

"Why not?"

"The thing is, I need to clear my name to get the money my dad left me. We need that money to keep this place going."

She folds her hands in her lap. "You need to be careful, okay?"

"What do you mean?" I sit on up on my bed.

"What if you start messing around with the wrong folks? Judith was caught up with a lot of dangerous people. Crystal dealers aren't usually reasonable folks, you know." Her lip trembles slightly.

"Is there something you're not saying?"

She takes a deep breath and says, "I saw you talking to TJ Talbot. He's real bad news."

"I'm not afraid of him. He's just a messed-up kid. He was almost my stepson, for fuck's sake."

"Don't underestimate him. Everybody on the scene knows he's dangerous." She smiles, but flinches at the same time. "I wouldn't cross him if I were you."

"TJ wouldn't hurt me." I shake my head and do my best job of nonchalant.

"It's a shame that boy turned out like he did. His mama would be so sad," she says.

"Well, it's partially her fault. Don't you think?" I ask.

Tilly shrugs. "There is one little bit of information I have that might help."

The renewed hope shoots my back up straight. "What?"

"Nuh uh. It'll cost you, sweetie." Tilly looks up to face me again. She smiles and says, "I need a bag of weed."

"You can't smoke weed. And I can't find weed."

"Don't worry about my end of it. I have enough goldenseal to pass every drug test for the next year."

"Where am I supposed to find weed?" My shoulders drop. I'm officially deflated.

She gasps and sits up suddenly, and I know she's thought of something important. My heart lurches. Maybe this will be easy.

"What is it?" I jump to my feet.

"Do you think there are any corndogs downstairs? I'm freaking starving!"

"Let's go look," I sigh. Not the most disappointing thing that's ever happened.

Chapter 11

Tilly and I are sitting at the table, dipping corndogs in mustard when we hear someone knocking on the front door.

"I'll get it." I get up and wipe my mouth on a paper napkin.

A man with a large beer gut and moles on his face stands on the other side of the door. "I'm looking for my wife."

"Oh yeah? Good for you," I say. I don't know why I unlocked all three locks and opened the door without looking through the peephole. That's how the bad guy in the movies always gets in. "Who's your wife?" No time to kick myself.

"Dana Hendricks." He's wearing a shirt with sweat and tobacco stains. I can smell whiskey from his breath. He's truly disgusting, and I wonder how Dana got close enough to him to procreate.

"Never heard of her." I move to close the door, but he stops the door with his palm. I wonder if it's the same hand that gave her the black eye.

"Bullshit," Pit-stains says. "I know she's staying here. She's here with my boy."

"Look. Unless you want me to call the cops, I suggest you get your fat ass off of my porch." I raise my voice and Tilly runs to stand behind me. She crosses her arms and sticks her chin out like she's ready to rumble. She's only about five-foot-two, so she comes off more cute than tough. I appreciate the gesture, though.

Pit-stains points a finger in my face, and I try not to think about where that finger has been. I don't breathe too deeply. "You tell that bitch Dana that I'll be back. She ain't got rid of me."

He backs up enough for me to slam and lock the door.

"He's so gross," Tilly says. "Makes me feel better about some of the jerks I've done it with."

"Yeah, no shit."

We go back to the table. Vangie Ann walks into the kitchen. "Was somebody at the door?"

"It was Dana's nasty-ass husband," Tilly says. "He was so gross. Pit stains, tobacco stains"—she takes a bite of corndog and continues—"smelly."

"I think he's going to be a problem," I say.

Vangie Ann sighs. "Well, he won't be the first problem husband we've had around here. I'll let the cops know he's been around. Do me a favor and don't answer the door for him next time, okay?"

"You got it," I say, and I feel incredibly foolish. It's so simple: just don't answer the door.

Chapter 12

"Okay, ladies. We need cash." Vangie Ann is sitting at the head of the table. She's wearing glasses. I don't know if she actually needs them, but they make her look official. She wore fake glasses for six months in junior high once, so she could get the attention of a boy in the honor society.

"I know how to make money real fast," Sonya says.

"No, Sonya." Vangie Ann shakes her head and smiles. "We're going to throw a fundraiser. We need a theme. Auction items. Stuff like that. There aren't a lot of us staying here right now, so I need everybody involved."

I like how she includes herself. She's a displaced woman, too. Maybe the queen of displaced women. Surely she didn't kill Judith. Sure, she was strung out and angry. But she can't be a murderer. I feel bad for even considering it.

"People like raffles," Dana says quietly, without looking up from her coffee mug. Troy sits to her right, coloring vigorously in a coloring book that looks like it's been passed through a few hands.

"Sure." Vangie Ann writes the word "raffle" on her legal pad and underlines it. "Anyone else?"

"What are the restrictions?" I ask.

"What do you mean?" Vangie Ann asks with her eyebrows at full attention, far above the rim of her glasses.

"Can we have alcohol at the party? That will determine the theme, I think."

"I don't think so. This is pretty much a glorified halfway house." She taps her pen on the side of her glasses. "That would be really inappropriate. I might lose the little bit of state funding I have."

"You can't have a party without alcohol. What will everybody do?" Tilly asks.

"We'll have lots of snacks and games. And, of course, the raffle. A silent auction." Vangie Ann takes notes as she talks. "And guess what? I found some of the old haunted house decorations in the attic. So there's our theme!"

"That sounds fun. Can I dress like a slutty zombie?" Tilly asks.

"You thought of that awful fast," Sonya says.

"How about a few bottles of wine?" I ask. "No keg or anything. Nothing crazy. Just a few bottles of wine. No liquor. Snacks, a raffle, and a silent auction. How about a speakeasy theme? People love that shit. It could be a haunted speakeasy."

"Ooh yeah," Sonya says.

"Shit," Troy says and giggles.

"Sorry," I say to Dana. "I forgot he was sitting there." She glares at me and then shrugs, as if the glare zapped all her energy.

"No alcohol." Vangie Ann is looking at the legal pad as if it's going to give her an answer. "Do you want me to get shut down? Can you even have alcohol when you're on parole?"

"No. You're right," I say. "Just seems boring to have a party without alcohol."

"When do you want to do this?" Tilly asks. "I'm so excited. I haven't thrown a party since right after my first stint in rehab. It was such a great party I had to go back to rehab!" She laughs, and I'm not sure if that means it's a joke or not. I don't bother asking.

Vangie Ann stands and grabs the calendar from the refrigerator. "How about August 11? That's a Saturday."

"That's only a month away, V," I say.

"We can do it!" Tilly says. "Where should we start? I guess we should make a list of places to hit up for auction items, right?"

"Yeah, that's right," Vangie Ann says and smiles. "I know it's not much time, but we need money now. We can do this."

"All right. Let's get to work." I grab a sheet of paper from Vangie Ann's notebook and get started on my own list, wondering how the hell I'm supposed to ask strangers for donations when I can't even grocery shop without fighting off a panic attack.

***

I knock on Dana's door. I'm not sure why, but I feel like I have to talk to her. After spending all those years with Tabitha, my heart goes out to women who take a beating from a man, I guess. And since she knew Judith, maybe she has some insight on her death.

"Yeah, come in," she says.

"Hey." I walk in and close the door behind me. "Where's Troy?"

"He's playin' in the backyard." She looks me up and down, like I might be carrying a weapon.

"Mind if I sit?" She's sitting on one twin bed, and I gesture toward the other one.

"Guess not."

"Thanks." I sit down and brush my palms down my faded jeans. "Did V tell you that your husband came by looking for you?"

"Yeah." She looks up. There is no fear in her eyes. There's nothing.

"I don't know what you're going through, Dana, but if you need to talk to anybody, I'm here. Okay?"

Dana looks at me blankly. I'm the last person in the world she'd want to talk to.

"Are you here because you want to know what happened, Cass?" She leans forward on her elbows.

"Not really, no." I do want to know, but I won't say so.

"Well, I'll tell you. I had sex with someone else. Sleeping with my husband is like being smothered. He puts his face over mine and breathes while he's screwing me, and I feel like I can't breathe, and when he's done I still feel like I'm smothering, so I had sex with somebody else because I wanted something for me. He found out and backhanded me right in the face."

I sit there on the bed staring at her. I don't know what to say, mostly because I'm wondering how she's getting so much action and I've only managed to get laid once since I've been out of prison.

"I had to get out of there because I was afraid he was going to do worse." She puts her face in her hands. "You can think I'm a whore or a slut and I don't care." Her hair is parted down the middle, dirty and stringy.

"I don't think that, Dana. You didn't deserve to be hit, no matter what you did." Seriously, it's not fair. How did she find somebody else to have sex with? "What are you going to do?"

"I don't know. I'll stay here for a while. Elijah will cool off eventually. Me and Troy will probably just go home, pretend all this never happened."

"Is that what you want?"

"I don't know." She wipes her nose with the back of her hand and then wipes her hand on her pants leg.

"You can't go back to an abusive environment. It's not good for Troy."

"Who are you to tell me what to do?"

"I'm sorry. You're right." I don't want to make her angry. I need to backtrack before it's too late. "I know I'm not your favorite person. But I'm just wondering if maybe you know who might have killed Judith. It's really important that I clear my name."

"How dare you? Yeah. I know who did it. You did." Small drops of spit fly from her lips as makes her accusation.

"No, I didn't." I'm losing my ability to be nice.

"Yes, you did."

"No, I didn't."

"Yes, you did." She stands up and goes to the middle of the room.

"Oh. You were there, were you?" I meet her in the middle of the room. I stand at least three inches taller than her. I can see the top of her greasy head clearly. "Do you know that we have shampoo in the bathroom?"

"You're such a bitch." She tries to push me backward, but my feet remain planted. "Do you want to take this outside?"

"Yeah, why don't we?" I don't notice, but my voice has grown loud.

Vangie Ann appears in the doorway. "Cass, get out of here, right now!"

I relax my stance, immediately feeling guilty. My sister shouldn't have to reprimand me for my behavior. "Sorry," I say to Vangie Ann and slink across the hall to my room. She follows on my heels.

"You can't make everybody like you, Cass." Vangie Ann stands in front of me with her arms crossed.

"No shit." I'm sitting on my twin bed on top of the blue and white quilt with my knees to my chest. "I was just trying to be nice."

"No. You were trying to win her over to make yourself feel better. Just like you always do. Give it up. You can't be everybody's best friend. Just stay out of Dana's way. She was friends with Judith, for fuck's sake. She will never like you." She pauses and says, "To you, Judith was a pain-in-the-ass ex-wife and a druggie. But that's not always who she was."

"Sorry. I thought she might be able to help." It feels like I'm being reamed by my mom. Humiliating and soothing at the same time. "Have I really always been this way?"

Vangie Ann smiles and relaxes. She sits on the bed with me. "Yes. You hate it when people don't like you. How on earth did you survive prison?"

"I don't know. It was different there. When you're in for murder, the other women tend to stay out your way. All I had to do was walk around all tough." I cross my legs on the bed in front of me. "I'm more insecure on the outside."

"Dana's pretty messed up if you haven't noticed. She's not your problem." Vangie Ann moves a lock of hair out of my face and then grabs my hand. She laces her fingers with mine. Her hand is smaller than mine, daintier, but with longer nails.

"I'm worried about Troy, though. That kid can't be raised in a home where his dad hits his mom." I stretch my legs out. My knees ache from keeping them bent just a couple of minutes too long.

"It's not your problem, Cass. When you do this type of work you learn that you do what you can and that's it. You can't change people. Hopefully Dana will make the right decision and not go back, but we can't make her do anything." Vangie Ann stands up and stretches, and I fear her boobs will pop out of the stripper dress du jour. "And she definitely won't help you. She made it clear to me when she arrived that she thinks you killed Judith."

Of course she does. "Tilly said you used to hang around Matt Morgan some. Do you know anything about him?"

"Not really. I bought drugs from him sometimes, but I didn't really know him. I haven't heard his name in years." She puts her hand on the doorknob. "Want to go to the hardware store with me? I think you could probably use some fresh air."

"Yeah. That would be great."

"Do yourself a favor and put some makeup on first. Maybe brush your hair, too. Okay?" She leaves my room and closes the door gently behind her.

I stand up and grab my makeup bag and mirror and get started. Every time I apply, I have to remember how. I wonder if it will ever become second nature again like it used to be.

Chapter 13

Thanks to a couple of extra stops on the way back from the hardware store, I have hair dye and three new dresses. It will take years to restore my wardrobe to its former glory, but this is a good start. And I bought enough dye to fix Sonya's hair, too, in attempt to make her my friend.

"You sayin' I need my hair done?" Sonya has her hands on her hips and her eyes narrowed.

"Well, yeah." I'm standing in front of her with three different boxes of hair dye. One is red, one is brown, and one is auburn. "I got three choices for you. I'll even dye it for you."

Once again I'm trying to make someone like me, but at least I'm going about the right way this time.

Sonya grabs the box of auburn and stares at it. "You'll really do it for me? Why?"

"Because I'm making an effort." No reason to pretend it's something it's not.

"Okay." She looks at me and smiles, revealing her nicotine-stained teeth. I almost suggest bleaching them, but that might be going too far.

"Sit here." I point to a kitchen chair.

Sonya nods and sits down. "You've done this before, right?"

"Yep. I used to do my own all the time. I'm going to do mine next, in fact."

"You're doing mine first?" she asks.

"Yeah. It's easier to do someone else's." I open the box of dye and pull out the instructions.

Vangie Ann walks in as I'm mixing the color at the sink. Her eyes take a second to assess the situation.

"Really, Cass? Playing beauty parlor now?"

"I'm trying to make a friend." I put my finger over the top and shake the plastic bottle.

"Didn't we just talk about this?" She puts her hands on her hips.

"Talk about what?" Sonya asks.

"Cass wants everybody to like her."

"Who doesn't?" Sonya asks. She pulls a magazine from the table and opens it, already bored with our sister drama.

"See, V. Who doesn't?" I smile and shuffle over to Sonya.

Vangie Ann smirks at me, and I'm pretty sure she's trying not to smile. "Just don't ruin her hair."

She's taunting me, daring me to say what I want to say. Something like "how the hell could I make it worse?" But I don't.

"It's going to look great," I say and start squeezing the dye on Sonya's head.

Sonya sniffs the air and says, "It stinks."

"Watch out for her, Sonya. She likes the ladies." Vangie Ann winks at me and walks out.

Sonya slaps the magazine on the table and says, "Is that really what this is about? I knew it was weird that you were being so nice."

"No, Sonya. It's not. I'm just making an effort." I'm rubbing the dye around her scalp, making sure to get all the roots.

"Okay. I hope so. 'Cause I don't swing that way." She picks up the magazine, then puts it in her lap. "I did swing that way once, but it was for a lot of money. You know what I'm saying?"

"Yeah. Pretty sure I do."

But Sonya still feels like she needs to explain it. "The John was named Bill. Or was it Bob? Anyway, he liked to watch two girls together."

"Gotcha." I should be used to hearing stories like this. Prison was lousy with hookers, and they loved to tell their stories. But it's different when I have my hands in one's hair.

"The girl I was with that time was named Madison. I don't think that was her real name. I think she was just trying to sound fancy."

"Certainly sounds like a name someone would use to be fancy," I say. "Have you ever had auburn hair before?" *Let's move on.*

"Yeah. My natural color is brownish-red. I could show you my pubes so you'd get the idea."

"No. That's okay."

She turns to face me, as much as she can with my hands on her head. "See. I knew you wasn't coming on to me. You don't even want to see my pubes."

"I'm done with this part. Just have to wait thirty minutes and rinse it." I pull off the thin plastic gloves and toss them in the trash.

"Thanks." She smiles and says, "And just so you know, if I was gay, I'd give you a go."

I nod and smile. "Thanks."

"Cass, friends do favors for each other, right?"

"Um, yeah." I fidget on my feet, waiting for what will come next.

"And we're friends now."

"Yeah." I cross my arms. "What are you after?"

"I need some clean pee." Sonya holds her hands out in a way that makes me expect jazz hands.

"Why?"

"I smoked weed the other day and I'm pretty sure my PO will test me tomorrow. All you have to do is pee in cup. I'll put it in a balloon and tape it under my armpit. He never follows me to the bathroom." She spouts off the words like she's explaining how to turn on a lamp.

"Do you have weed?" It would be so great if I could find it here in the House.

"Not anymore. I might have some in a couple of weeks. My source isn't very reliable."

I sit down at the table. "I'll give you the pee, but can you let me know when you can get weed?"

"Sure." Sonya holds out her hand. We meet palms for a shake, and hers is moist again. "Sounds like we have a deal, friend."

* * *

"It's so fucking hot out here." I fan myself with the stack of flyers.

"Don't wrinkle those," Vangie Ann says. "They were expensive." She takes them from my hand and throws them to the backseat.

"Where are we going first?" We are out soliciting donations for the fundraiser. Thankfully, I'm not on my own. Vangie Ann used to guide me through the neighborhood when I sold Girl Scout cookies. She's adopted the same attitude for this.

"We're going to hit the strip mall on Main Street. There are a half dozen shops there. We'll see if we can get any gift certificates or anything." She flicks a cigarette out of the window.

"Oh, yeah. I think there's a spa there."

"Don't get your hopes up. This isn't for you, princess."

"I can't help it if I miss the finer things. I really need a facial." I bring my hand to my cheeks. My skin feels papery.

"Get you a rich boyfriend. I'm sure there's some old fool who'd love to get a piece of you." She pulls into a parking spot in front of an embroidery shop.

"Sounds great. Just what I've always wanted. An elderly lover."

"Well, you went gay. Might as well cover all the bases." She grins and grabs her fake leather purse and the stack of flyers.

"You know, V, sometimes I think you're really smart. And then I realize you really don't get it at all." I get out of the car and stretch.

I follow her into the embroidery shop and stand beside her at the counter. She hands the flyer to the clerk and asks to speak to the manager. She gives her pitch and we leave with a fifty-dollar gift certificate. I wonder if I will be able to do the same thing.

"Can I shadow you here, too, V?" I ask as we walk into a clothing store.

"Sure. But I want you to take the next one."

She works her magic again. This time she scores a coat that retails for a hundred dollars. Sure it's July, but it will be winter again sometime. It always is.

"Okay, Cass. This one is yours."

We walk into a tanning salon. I breathe deeply and give myself silent positive affirmations. *I can do this. I can do this.* I approach the counter. The clerk looks like a teenager. She has dyed black hair and goth makeup. Her skin is too pale for her to actually be using the tanning beds. I hand her a flyer and introduce myself.

"We're collecting donations for a fundraiser. Items we can use for a silent auction. Gift certificates, things like that."

She rolls her eyes at me and looks down at her cell phone. "You'll have to speak to the owner and she won't be here until four." She's pressing buttons on her phone the entire time.

There's a pop sound behind my eyes. I reach for her phone and wrap both hands around it. The girl looks at me. Her eyes are full of panic and rage. She doesn't let go of the phone. She has one hand on the phone and the other hand on my left wrist.

"Hey, Elvira. Why don't you let go of the fucking phone and listen?" I say each word slowly, as if she's special and doesn't understand.

Vangie Ann grabs my arm and yanks me backward. "Cass!"

My hands relax their grip, and I let go of the phone. Vangie Ann picks the flyer up from the counter, removing the evidence we were there. She pulls me outside. The little teenaged bitch stands behind the counter with her mouth wide open.

"What is wrong with you?" Vangie Ann asks once we're on the sidewalk.

"I wanted to throw the phone through the window. What a rude little bitch!"

"You can't just do shit like that." She walks ahead of me and gets in the car. She slams the door shut.

I get in the car and see the tears streaming down her face. "What is it, V?"

"I can't babysit you, Cass. I have enough to deal with without taking care of you all the time. Can't you act like a fucking grown-up?" She lights a cigarette and puts her other hand to her forehead. "That girl could be a minor, for fuck's sake."

"I'm sorry, Vangie Ann. It's weird to get used to stuff, you know. But I'll try harder. I didn't know I was making things rough for you." My stomach turns, and I have to roll down the window to keep from throwing up. I don't remember the last time I felt so awful.

She sighs and starts the car. "It's okay, Cass. Just try to use your head. All right? Get your temper in check. You're not in prison anymore. But you are on parole, dumbass."

"True," I say. I put my hand out the window and let my palm ride the waves of wind.

Chapter 14

Mom died when Vangie Ann was ten and I was six. She went for a walk alone because she and Dad had a fight about something. I don't know what. I asked him once, but he didn't want to talk about it.

He married Lucinda at the worst possible time, when I was a shape-shifting preteen and Vangie Ann had just started driving. Lucinda was a police dispatcher who didn't know the first thing about girls. The poor woman never stood a chance.

But here she sits in front of me, twisting her gaudy diamond and sipping coffee with her wrinkly lips. My senior yearbook is on the table in front of her.

"Thanks, Lucinda," I say as a pull it toward myself. I flip it open to the freshman section. Mack Brown was scrawny and had a full head of hair. Almost a mullet. He was cute and baby-faced, not even close to the broad-shouldered man he is now. I flip the page to see if he has any activities or clubs listed, but Lucinda won't leave me be.

"I heard you need to work on your temper." The reprimand sounds ridiculous coming from her croaky voice. Like a wide-mouth frog is trying to give me life lessons.

"I heard you need to mind your own business." I sip my coffee and stare at her.

She stares back, unblinking for an unnatural amount of time. Vangie Ann walks in.

"Why did you tattle, V?" I ask.

"I was hoping someone could talk some sense into you." She pours herself some coffee and sits down with us.

Lucinda finally blinks, and I release a sigh of relief.

I lean back in the chair and look at Vangie Ann and Lucinda. They're both staring at me. "When you're in prison, your defenses are always up. I was in for a decade. I can't just relax automatically. I am trying."

"Are you going to see the therapist that Mack wants you to see?" Vangie Ann asks.

"I don't know. I don't like dumping my problems on people."

"Well, if you haven't noticed, you're kind of dumping your problems on me whether you want to or not." Vangie Ann takes a drink and then sits her mug down.

"What you do affects other people, Cass. There are trained professionals who can help you."

"Your sister is right," Lucinda croaks in.

"Fine." I cross my arms over my chest.

"We're trying to help you. Don't act like a little brat," Lucinda says.

"I can't help but feel like you two are ganging up on me a little bit here. What about the things I'm doing right?"

"Just what are you doing right?" Vangie Ann asks.

My anger rises and I resist the urge to hit her. "I get out of bed every day. I help clean around here. I haven't punched anybody in the face. Most of my decisions haven't been awful. I'm trying to clear my name like I'm supposed to so we can save this place and I can concentrate on living my life."

"Why did you go to jail, Cass? You don't understand how hard it's been on the rest of us," Lucinda says.

I sigh and rub my hands on my face. "Ten years. I lost ten years. For what? Fucking nothing. That's what. I thought it was to keep two kids from being orphans and it turns out that's not true. Sorry if I have some anger issues. But guess what? I haven't burned any houses to the ground yet. Have some patience with me, please. How do you think either of you would behave if it was you? I know I fucked up. Believe me. I had ten long years to think about everything I did wrong."

"You rolled over and took it, Cass. You just took it. You went to jail. You didn't say you did it, but you didn't fight like you should have. You say it was to protect Wayne's kids. But was it, really? Or was it to make Wayne keep loving you?"

"Excuse me? Didn't you start doing meth to keep a man?" I feel guilty as soon as the words come out, but I don't apologize.

Vangie Ann stares at me for a moment through narrowed eyes. "You've always been so afraid of what it would be like if nobody loved you. There are worse things than being rejected by a man. I fucking hope you hit your rock bottom. Because we can't take it if you drag us down any further." She wipes a tear from her cheek.

"I'm sorry my decade in prison was so rough for you two. It wasn't a holiday for me. I had motive and opportunity. Plus, all of the people who heard me say I wished she was dead. Didn't matter that I didn't mean it. I was facing the death penalty. I had to make a deal." I suck in a breath, determined to get the truth out of my body. "I called you that night. As soon as I saw her. You weren't at work." The words are pushing out of me after being held for way too long.

"What are you trying to say?" She narrows her eyes.

"You were fucked up and angry. I was afraid that if it wasn't Wayne, then maybe it was you." I want to stop talking, but it feels out of my control. "You told me you'd kill her if she kept messing with me."

Her mouth drops open like I've slapped her. No words come out.

"Johnny Morgan told me he saw you leaving the parking lot at Judith's that night." My voice is barely above a whisper.

"You really think it was me?" Her face turns red as tears pool in her eyes.

"Can you tell me why you were there?"

"How dare you?" Her voice is low and quiet. It would be creepy if she were a stranger. She takes a slow sip of coffee and says, "Gabe lived in the same apartment building as Judith. We had a date that night. We got in a fight about something, don't remember what, and I left."

"Oh." I feel like a jerk, but I'm glad it's over. I don't have to wonder if she sent me to prison anymore.

"Sometimes it's hard to love you," she says.

I stare at Vangie Ann for a second and then push away from the table. I go outside to the porch and sit down on the steps. It's hot, but there's a decent breeze. The breeze sends my hair brushing against the skin on my face, neck, and shoulders. I close my eyes and pretend I'm on a beach in California, far away from here. For the first time, I miss the comfort of my cell, the insular feeling. I miss Tabitha.

I'll have to see Wayne.

Chapter 15

We're crossing a line that can never be uncrossed. I'm afraid she'll walk in. My childhood friend, my family. She'll see me on top of her husband. We didn't bother to get naked this time, either. I'm still wearing a flimsy sundress.

I drove here of my own free will, even though it could cost me my freedom. I told myself I was only coming here to ask for help in finding Judith's killer. But when he declined with a vague excuse, we started kissing. This is pre-meditated adultery. I'm a moron.

Melody swore to love him forever even though his dick's definitely a bit too thin. She took his motherless kids on as her own. I don't want him for more than this. He believed I killed the mother of his babies, and I believed he did. We were doomed a decade ago. Why am I doing this?

Part of me is tempted to destroy his life for the years I spent in prison, but only the darkest part that doesn't have anything to do with who I really am. Anyway, things have already been pretty fucked up for Wayne.

I try not to think about it, but I realize what Vangie Ann meant. I am afraid of not being loved. I need someone to love me at all times. That's why I carried on with Tabitha. That's why I'm here right now, on top of Wayne, on top of his desk.

"We can't do this anymore." I stop moving and look at him.

Wayne opens his eyes and looks at my face. "Can we at least finish this time?" he asks.

"Sure," I say, and find my rhythm again, careful to commit every detail to memory in case it's a while before I get laid again.

He hands are around my waist. He sits up and kisses me. I know this probably means more to him than it does to me.

When it's over, I curl next to him on the desk. He wraps his arms around me.

"I'm sorry for everything," he says.

"Thank you," I say, because nothing else seems appropriate. "I thought about you a lot when I was in prison. Sometimes I missed you. Sometimes I was mad at you. Sometimes I wanted to sleep with you. Sometimes I wanted to kill you."

He looks at me and smiles. "I missed you. I never stopped." He kisses me on the forehead. "I want to keep seeing you."

"We can't." I shake my head.

"I know."

"I need to go. Vangie Ann thinks I went to the store. She's going to get suspicious." I stand up and look for my panties.

"Will I see you around or anything?" he asks.

"Probably not. I'm supposed to stay away from you. You know, parole and all." I find my panties under the desk and shimmy them on.

I see his boxers on the floor and pick them up. The memory of men's cotton boxers against my bare skin floods my mind and takes place of the misery I'm feeling. Sleeping in boxers and a cotton t-shirt in the summer time, comfortable and at peace. "I'm taking these."

"Okay." He grabs me, puts both hands on my face and kisses me. "I'm really sorry for everything that happened. I wish it had been different."

"Yeah. Me, too." I grab my shoes and walk out barefoot. I don't want to take the time to put my shoes on in case I change my mind.

My feet hit the driveway and it starts raining. Maybe the rain will wash away what I just did, make everything clean again.

* * *

It only takes two days for Wayne to confess. I don't know why it took us having sex twice for him to tell her, but it only takes two minutes for Melody to get in the car to make the thirty minute drive to come after me.

Melody Talbot nee Blankenship is on the porch and in my face, her arms are crossed over her big boobs, and her jaw is set. "Who do you think you are? You can't just go around having sex with people's husbands!"

"Calm down. It was only twice." I sit down, resisting the urge to knock her off the porch. She has every right to be angry with me, and she deserves the rant. "Why on earth did he tell you?"

"Because he's not a sociopath and he feels guilty." Melody narrows her eyes at me. "You really think this is no big deal, don't you, Cass?"

"I feel bad. Okay?" My voice comes out more shrill than I intended. "Sorry. It was kind of like visiting an old friend, you know? Hanging out. Doing things we used to do. I confronted him about Judith. He said he didn't kill her. So we had sex because that's what we'd always done. To my credit, it'd been a really long time since I'd been with a man. That gets rough." I shrug, trying to get her to understand that it was out of my control.

"What about the second time?" Melody stares at me through slits of eyes. "You're selfish."

"So I hear."

"I can get you sent back to jail, you know. You aren't supposed to contact Wayne, or even go to Pleasant Fields." She drops her hands to her sides and pulls a piece of paper from her back pocket. A copy of my parole agreement.

"Where did you get that?" I ask. My stomach drops, and I feel like I need to evacuate my bowels.

"The parole board sent it to the victim's family as a courtesy." Her voice has gone scarily sweet, like the hostess of a party you don't want to attend.

"What are you going to do?" I lean forward and face her. Melody told on me for saying my first swear word when I was seven. Her tattling ways can get me in much more trouble this time.

"What would you do, Cass?"

"It's over, Melody. I'd be pissed as hell. But I'd know that it's over. I certainly wouldn't send you to jail over it. It's just sex." As I say the words, I know it's not true. Sex is rarely just sex.

Tears well in her eyes. "If it was just sex, why couldn't it have been with someone else?"

I sigh. "I guess a part of me still loves of him. Not like you do. But I missed him." I shrug again because I don't know what else to do. "I really am sorry."

"He doesn't love you like he loves me. You're just a memory."

"Why did you marry him, Melody? Why did you marry the only man that ever meant something to me and hurt me so badly?"

She sits down across from me, slowly like it's sort of painful. "We became friends. I got to know the kids. It seems awful to you, I know. But it was a natural progression. It felt like it was meant to be."

"I wish it could have been 'meant to be' with anyone else."

Melody nods and says, "My mom might die." The tears start to fall.

"Shit. I'm so sorry." I start to put my arms around her, then remember why she's here. She won't welcome my affection. "Where's Tiffany during all this?" Tiffany—Melody's little sister, the shame of her family because she's a lesbian. A real one, not a fake one like me. She's ten years younger than me, so I barely know her.

Melody sighs and says, "She lives in St. Louis now. She's coming home tomorrow to see mom. Hopefully she'll look like a woman this time and not send mom to her grave even earlier."

"Oh, come on. She never was one to dress very feminine. I'm sure your mom is used to it."

Tears stream quietly down Melody's cheeks. It's dignified crying. "All this has me thinking about when your mom died. You stayed with us for what, a month? Two months?"

"I don't really remember. That whole time is blurry." I'm holding her against me, trying to remember my childhood, but only coming up with fuzzy pieces of memory. I run my fingers through her thick brown hair, a little more coarse now that she's older.

Our fights are more serious now, but they've always been there. We've never had an easy relationship. I guess Wayne took the place of the Barbie we used to wrestle over.

"The thing is, I thought Wayne was better than this. Better than you," she says.

Her words make my stomach curdle. I want to punch her in the face to make myself feel better. But she's allowed her anger.

"Look, you're not dead or an ex-con. You're not doing as bad as the other women he's been with."

Melody sits up and wipes her face with the backs of her hands. She folds up the parole agreement and puts it in her pocket. "This doesn't mean I forgive you."

"Okay," I say.

"You can't bend the rules of society just because you want something, or somebody."

There's only so many times I can apologize before the words lose their meaning. So I change the subject.

"Look. I have to find out who killed Judith." I pause as Melody rolls her eyes. "Do you know anything that can help me?"

She says, "You were high on pills. You did it, even if you don't remember. You admitted it when you pleaded guilty."

Her ignorance enrages me. I want to punch her, but she'll have me arrested.

"I had to take the deal so I didn't spend my life in prison or get lethal injection. And that's not how pain pills work. I would remember shooting someone, dumbass."

The door creaks open behind me and Tilly walks out with a square of cloth in her hands. The blue fabric looks familiar, and I jump up as she unfolds it into a pair of cotton boxer shorts.

"Who do these belong to, hussy?" She's wearing a wide grin and holding an edge of the underwear in each hand.

Melody jumps up and grabs Wayne's boxer shorts from Tilly's grip. She looks at me with her teeth clenched and stomps down the stairs.

Melody turns and says, "You deserve what you got."

"Uh oh," Tilly says. She turns her head slowly and puts her hands to her mouth. "I'm sorry." The apology comes out muffled by her palm.

"Me, too," I say as Melody tears down the street in her white sports car.

Chapter 16

Even though I'm probably going back to prison for screwing Wayne, I decide to keep trying to get information out of Tilly. Other than Sonya, I don't know who can help me with finding weed and I can't ask anyone else. I just have to make Tilly like me.

"Tilly, want to go for a walk?" I ask.

She eyes me as if I had asked her if she'd like to go build a deck. "Why?"

"You can smoke cigarettes."

"Sure," she says. She pops up from her bed and throws aside the dog-eared romance novel she was reading. There's a long-haired man on the cover wearing a pirate shirt. He looks ridiculous. He's staring longingly at an equally ridiculous woman with huge boobs. She's wearing a peasant dress and a lot of makeup. I'm fairly certain that a peasant wouldn't be able to afford makeup.

It's sunny outside, a little too hot. It feels great to walk with no particular destination, and I don't know why I don't do it every day. It occurs to me that Tabitha would love this, to feel the sidewalk beneath her shoes and the warm breeze against her skin. Sadness threatens to ruin my goal. I push it far down so I can deal with it later.

"Do you ever think of people from your past and get really depressed?" I ask Tilly.

"Who doesn't?" She lights a cigarette and pollutes the fresh air.

"Who do you think of the most? Matt or someone else?"

She looks off into the distance, squinting. "I wasn't with Matt all that long. A lot went down in a short time with him. We were only together for a few months." She takes a deep drag. The sunlight highlights her wrinkles, not deep, but plentiful. "It's worse to think about my parents. How much I let them down. They had high hopes for me. My dad worked hard to make sure he had enough money to send me to college. I blew most of that money on drugs. He wised up and cut me off before it was *all* gone."

"How old are you, Tilly?" I ask, finally tired of my guessing game.

"I just turned thirty. I thought I would have a real job and be married by now, and I don't even have a boyfriend." She smirks and tiny smoker's wrinkles appear around her lips.

"Welcome to the club." I skip a step to avoid a tree root. "I thought I would have children by now. Once I got to prison, not having kids was one of the best things about my situation. The prisoners who were moms had it the worst. I missed Wayne's kids for a long time, but I was able to get over it."

"Yeah. I get that."

I've gotten off track. It's so easy to do. "How well did you know Judith?"

"We did drugs together a few times." She throws her cigarette on the ground and steps on it, grinding it out with her shoe like it might catch the concrete on fire. "Do you have any gum?"

"No." We keep walking toward nowhere.

"What was it like? Finding her dead?"

The brazen question would take me by surprise if I hadn't been asked so many times by other inmates. "It was awful, sickening. Such a shock that it didn't seem real. But it was. Are you asking because you cared about her, or because you're nosy?" There was a lot of blood and a terrible smell, but the pain pills I swallowed before going to her apartment softened the scene for me. TJ's face stuck in my memory the most. The way he looked when he walked in and saw me standing over his mother's bloody body.

"A little of both." Her voice sounds more mature than normal. "I'm not giving you any information unless you have my weed."

"I'm not doing anything. Just talking." I try to play innocent, though it's never been my strong suite.

"You've already done the time. You'll never get it back no matter what." She sighs and shakes her head, bobbing her cotton candy ponytail back and forth. "Nothing good can come from digging in the past."

We're still walking. She won't look at me. I'm staring, willing her to turn her head.

"It's what I have to do."

She stops and finally turns toward me. "I know you think you're tough because you've been to jail. But women's prison is nothing compared to meth cooks. They'll kill you and no one will find your body." She starts walking again. "They'll say you deserved it for poking around. There won't be any justice because you'll just disappear. Someone will start a rumor that you skipped out on your parole. Left town with some man or some woman. It's a small town. The rumor will convince enough people, and the cops won't give a shit about some ex-con murderer."

"Help me, Tilly. It's not just for me. It's for Blankenship House, too." I'm looking at her face, hoping she'll turn toward me again. We walk past houses. Some are beautiful. Lived in and loved, with unbroken windows and flower gardens. Porch swings and trimmed bushes.

"Get me the weed. Didn't you learn about trading in prison?"

"Yeah," I say. But knowing how to barter doesn't mean I know how to find weed. "What if I pay you? I can get money."

"I'll tell you what I know for a bag of weed. That's it." She stops walking and looks at me. "I don't want to be seen outside with you. I don't want anyone you piss off thinking that we're friends." She turns away from me and runs toward the House. She runs faster than a smoker should be able to. If anyone saw her as they drove past, they'd think there was some kind of emergency.

I walk slowly and enjoy a few more minutes of fresh air. There's no reason to hurry. The conversation is over.

* * *

When I drag myself back to the House, Mack Brown is sitting on the porch. His eyes are narrowed into a wrinkly frown. I'm glad he's catching me while my hair is still lustrous and I'm wearing one of my new cotton sundresses. Oh, yes. It's not perfection, but not bad for a middle-aged broad who just got out of the joint.

"Cass," he says and stands. He looks surprised.

"Hey, Mack." I climb up the stairs.

"You're wearing a dress," he says.

"Yes, I am." I wait for him to comment further, but he doesn't. He sits down instead and averts his gaze to the street. He doesn't even mention my shiny hair. I sit down, tired of waiting for praise. "No chaperone again?"

All this time I thought it was me. I thought I didn't look good enough. But I forgot that men are dumbasses.

"No. Still short-staffed. And we have private things to discuss." He clinches his jaw and says, "You saw Wayne."

"Oh, shit." I fall back onto a one of the chairs, my favorite one. It has a red gingham cushion, reminds me of a picnic.

"What the hell were you thinking?" He sits down in the chair next to me. His chair has a floral cushion, kind of silly for his manly butt.

"I wanted him to admit he killed Judith so I could get my money."

"Then why did you have sex with him?" He leans toward me. I can smell the coffee on his breath.

"He didn't kill Judith." I shrug. "I can't believe Melody called you. What a bitch."

"Well, she's angry. Can't say that I blame her."

"I was in jail ten years, Mack. Ten years. It's easy to give in to urges after that amount of time." I cross my arms over my chest.

"Use your head to think, not your crotch. I'm supposed to report you. You could go back to prison." He sits back in his chair and stares off into the street.

"Are you going to do it? Report me?"

He shakes his head. "No. Not this time. But if you contact him again, I will."

I take a deep breath. "Might as well come clean. Did she tell you it happened twice?"

"Yes, dumbass, she did. She would have told me the positions if she knew them. Never again, okay?" He looks at me with his jaw still clenched. Reminds me of one time in high school when I got in trouble for cheating on an exam even though I could have passed.

"Okay. I'm sorry, Mack." I look down at my shoes and then back at his face.

"This is getting too messy. I checked to see if I could pass you off to another probation officer."

"No!" I had never considered that he might give up on me.

"There's no one available right now. So I'm stuck with you. But I'm not playing this game anymore."

"You won't help me?"

"Matt Morgan is dead. I can't help you with him anyway."

"He's dead? Why wouldn't Tilly just say so?" A lump forms in my throat but I choke it down.

"She might not know." He leans toward me again, puts his hand on my arm, and removes it quickly.

"I tried to get information out of her just now. She told me to let it go. Said there are meth cooks who will kill us both." I watch his expression go from anger to concern. I wonder how much he cares. I need a friend.

"Well, that's probably true."

"Do you think he told anyone else what he saw that night?" I ask, even though I know it's pointless.

He shrugs. "No way to know." Mack stands up and looks at me. "You need to be careful."

"Thanks, Mack."

He steps off the porch. "Remember, don't visit Wayne. I'm serious."

"I promise I won't." Regret grips my guts, but I don't want to beg.

I watch him leave, knowing I've blown it with the only person who could really help me. I walk into the House and Vangie Ann is in the kitchen. She has managed to avoid me since I accused her of murder two days ago. Leaving the room when I enter. Being on the phone. Being in a hurry. But now I have her trapped.

Vangie Ann doesn't look up, so I know she's still angry with me. She's stirring a pot at the stove, smells like chili.

"I'm really sorry, V. I was out of line."

She stirs the chili faster in response.

"You were really messed up back then, and you were really angry when Judith showed up at my place. When I couldn't find you, my mind jumped to the worst place."

"So you went to prison instead of asking me?" She stops stirring and stares into the pot.

"There were other reasons, too. Things were looking really bad for me. I had to take the deal." I sigh. "After I had time to think, I knew it wasn't you. But it was too late by then."

"It didn't help that you were high off your face during that time. But that's something I can understand."

I sit down in front of the yearbook; it's in the exact same spot where I left it. I open it to my senior picture. My skin was pretty but blemished, and my hair was flat even though I teased it for ten minutes that morning. Sometimes I'm sad for the girl I was, the one whose future was stolen. But I don't have time for that right now.

"My cellmate had dark eyes and skin, so different from mine in a way that I loved. She smelled like prison soap and sweat, never quite clean or dirty. I guess that's the way we all smelled in there since we were packed in so tight. No one could go without sweating long. Her hair was coarse like the rope we used to climb in gym. You remember that, don't you?"

Vangie Ann turns to look at me but doesn't speak, so I continue. "The way we used to have to ring the bell when we got to the top. Ding, ding, ding. I would touch her braids and make the bell sound sometimes. She'd just roll her eyes and smile. 'Cass,' she'd say, 'I ain't no rope.' I miss her, you know. I'll never have a friend like that on the outside. Someone forced to put up with me twenty-four hours a day, to work it out no matter how mad she got. Unconditional love is beautiful, even if the law forces it on you." I release a long held breath when I'm finished with my monologue.

Vangie Ann stops stirring and puts her hands on my face. "You know I love you unconditionally, Cass. I just wish you were trying harder to keep your ass out of jail. I can't lose you again."

I stand and wrap my arms around my sister. "I'm so sorry for everything. I don't know how many more times I can say it."

"I know," she says. "Now I got to get back to the stove before my chili scorches."

"Can I help with anything?" I ask.

"Yes," she says as she resumes her post at the stove. She points to the cupboard across the room. "See how much rice we have, would you? And then start grating cheese. You didn't get enough shredded on your last grocery run."

I lose myself in the pace of the kitchen, pretending that I'm a normal woman doing proper woman things.

Chapter 17

I walk upstairs to talk with Tilly and tell her the chili is ready. Her side of the room is vacant. No cheesy romance novel, no sheets on the bed, no crumpled pack of cigarettes on the bedside table. I know she didn't go anywhere, I would have seen her leave.

I go down the hall to Sonya's room and knock on the door.

"Come in," Sonya says.

Sonya sits on one bed, and Tilly sits on the other, reading that stupid book. Sonya's hair looks great. I stop for a second to admire my handiwork. Still a little dry, but the color is really good.

"What the fuck, Tilly?" I ask, back to the task at hand.

She gets up and comes out into the hallway. "I can't keep doing this with you. I'm going to stay with Sonya. She isn't bugging the shit out of me about anything."

"I'll leave you alone. Okay? You don't have to move out of our room." I'm whining, begging like a child. I didn't want her in my room, but now I don't want to be alone.

"It's for the best, Cass. I'm just down the hall." She frowns and sighs.

"There's something I need to tell you," I say and put a hand on her shoulder.

"Don't you dare say the name Matt Morgan. We're done talking about him." Her teeth clench.

"He's dead, Tilly." Part of the reason for telling is selfish. Maybe her grief will make her need me.

Her face softens and goes blank. Her knees buckle and she crouches against the wall.

"What? When?" She doesn't look at me. She doesn't look at anything. It's the blank stare of loss.

"I don't know." I bend down to face Tilly. "A friend of mine tried to find out what prison he was in so I could ask him what he saw that night. All he told me was that he's dead. I'm sorry I don't have more information for you."

She nods and a single tear rolls down her cheek. "I thought once he went to prison he would be safe, you know? Kind of stupid of me, I guess."

"That's not stupid, Tilly. Don't say that." I rub my palm against her back. The cotton of her pale pink t-shirt is soft and comforting.

"It's my fault he was there. I got busted and ratted him out. I had to." She looks up at me. Her face is splotchy and red. "I'm a snitch."

"Hey." Sonya sticks her head out of the bedroom door. "Did Vangie Ann make chili?" She sniffs the air like a dog.

"Yeah. Sorry, that's what I came to tell you guys." I stand up and my knees crack in protest.

"What did you do to her?" She points at Tilly.

"Nothing. I had some bad news."

"Could you two please stop talking about me like I'm not here?" Tilly asks. She stands up and wipes her face.

"You okay?" I ask Tilly.

"Yeah. It was just a shock."

"Sorry, Tilly." I wrap my arms around her and squeeze her short, bony frame. The top of her bleached head smells like cigarettes, dust, and grapefruit.

"What is it?" Sonya walks out into the hallway.

"Dead ex-boyfriend," Tilly answers.

"Ah. I have a couple of those myself. More than a couple if you count Johns. I usually don't though. Count them, I mean." Sonya hugs Tilly after I back away. Tilly doesn't cringe. I'm pretty sure I would, especially after the talk of dead Johns.

Sonya moves to my side and whispers, "I need that pee today."

I look at her and nod. I want to ask her about the weed but not here in the hallway. I walk to Dana's door and knock softly.

She jerks the door open with a "What?" The black eye is almost gone. There is just a slight tinge of yellow remaining. I start to comment, but decide against it.

"Vangie Ann made chili, Sunshine." I smile so broadly it feels like my face might split. I dig deep, remembering how my mom used to tell me to kill people with kindness. Sometimes it would just be easier to kill them.

I lead the way down the stairs with Tilly, Sonya, Dana, and Troy following. We all gather in the kitchen. No one mentions that it's much too hot of a day to eat chili.

* * *

There's a knock on the door after lunch, and I see a ghost through the peephole. More of a pixie than a ghost, really. Short with short hair, with Judith's delicate features and soft skin. I unlock all three locks quickly.

"Danielle?"

She smiles and nods. I pull her into my chest and squeeze her tightly. She's an adult, a miniature remnant of Judith.

"Hi, Cass." She pulls away and looks at me.

"Come in, please."

"Actually, I was wondering if you could come somewhere with me?" She steps back on the porch. She eyes the House nervously, as if it might swallow her.

"Yeah. I guess that's okay. As long as we stay in town."

"Sure. I just want to take you out for a cup of coffee." She smiles delicately.

"Just let me get my shoes," I say. "I can't believe you're old enough to drive. That's so weird."

We go to the street and climb into her car, a baby blue Jeep with no top. She looks like a child driving a Big Wheel.

Danielle's feet barely reach the pedals. She has to point her toes to shift the gears. It's cute, but I don't know if she thinks so. It's probably one of those things every boy comments on and makes her feel young and silly, like she can't defend herself. So I don't say anything.

We pull into a coffee shop, which in West Plains is really just a churched-up café. I stand head and shoulders above Danielle, and have to fight the urge to bend my knees when I stand beside her.

She leads the way to the counter and orders a latte. I do the same and she pays for both. I thank her, and I'm a little embarrassed by her charity. I can't argue with her, though, since I spent all my money on hair dye and clothes.

"I've missed you," I say as we sit down. I want to stroke her face. To kiss her, hold her like a child. She's a beautiful young childlike woman who was nearly my daughter.

"You could have called." Her lip trembles.

"No, Danielle. I couldn't." I place my hand over hers.

"I know you didn't kill my mom."

"Thank you." I remove my hand and grab my coffee mug. Maybe there's hope here. Maybe the truth didn't die with Matt Morgan. But my best bet is to stay calm.

"Did you know she named me after Danielle Steele?" Her lips stretch in a closed-lipped smile. "She left tons of her books behind. Do you read her stuff?"

"I read a few of her books in prison." I nod. "TJ came to see me."

Danielle's eyes fill up immediately, and she shakes her head back and forth. "TJ's not doing too good. He's mixed up in all kinds of bad stuff."

"I didn't think he looked too good." My heart aches. It's not quite longing, not quite stabbing pain.

"He took after mom, I guess." She sips her latte and looks down into her mug, as if it will yield an answer to her problems.

"I saw your dad and he didn't say anything."

"He's in denial. He's afraid if he confronts TJ like he did mom, history will repeat itself. That's my theory anyway."

I take a sip of coffee. "How about Melody?"

"She'll say stuff to TJ about it, but not much. I'm the only one who will call him out, but he doesn't get angry with me like he does other people. He tried to kill himself a few years back. Now everyone is careful with him." She says it like she's telling me he went to a concert.

"I'm sorry, Danielle. Things should have turned out better for you two."

"Well, things didn't turn out great for you, did they?" She smiles slightly. "Melody told me you slept with my dad."

I choke on a swallow of latte. Hot, frothed milk gets stuck between my throat and my mouth and I cough for about thirty seconds. My eyes water, destroying my makeup efforts.

"Why did she tell you that?" I ask once I finally regain my composure.

"She's kind of spiteful that way." Danielle shrugs and hands me a napkin for my face. "It's not like I care. When your mom is dead and your brother's on meth, something like your dad having sex with his ex-con ex-girlfriend really isn't a big deal."

"Well, that's good, I guess."

"I think she's going to tell your parole officer."

"Thanks for letting me know, but you're a little too late."

Danielle sucks in a deep gust of air and her little-girl eyes go wide like a baby doll's. "Are you going back to jail?"

"Nah. Not yet anyway. He was pissed at me, though." My coffee is starting to cool, so I take a large gulp. I realize quickly that I miscalculated the temperature. My throat and tongue burn for punctuation. Prison coffee was only as hot as bath water if we were lucky.

"Sorry. She only just told me yesterday. I would have come to tell you earlier."

"It wouldn't have mattered, Danielle. There's nothing you could have done. My PO is giving me a second chance. I have to stay away from your dad and stay away from Pleasant Fields." I push my hair behind my ears. "Is Melody giving Wayne a hard time?"

Danielle laughs and says, "God, yes. It's awful. He's sleeping on the couch. She makes dinner for me and her, TJ if he shows up, but makes Dad eat out of the fridge. She won't wash his clothes." She smiles at me. "I think they'll be fine, though. She only made him sleep at his shop for one night."

I look at Danielle's face. The miniature version of her mother's face. "How do you know I didn't kill your mother?"

"I'd rather not talk about it, Cass." She puts her hands flat on the table and stares at them. "It's all very rough for me. I loved you both so much." She keeps staring like she's reading the newspaper on the back of her hands. "People talk about how awful it is when bad shit happens to kids, but if I hadn't been so young, I think her dying and you going to jail would have killed me. I definitely couldn't take something like that now."

"It's very important that I find out who did it. If there's anything you can do to help, you have to."

I place my hands over hers. She looks up at me slowly, deliberately, with narrowed eyes. There's something hateful and foreign in her gaze. I remove my hands and place them in my lap.

"Danielle, are you okay?"

She glares at me that way for one beat, two beats, three beats, and then her face relaxes.

"Yeah. I'm fine." She picks up her coffee mug and takes a sip of her latte. She smiles softly over the top of the cup. She puts the cup down. "Cass, promise me you stay in touch now. I don't want to lose you again. Give me your cell number."

"I don't know how to work cell phones. No buttons. You don't have to press anything to hang up. I don't get it." A flip phone, that's the last cell phone I had. I wonder if those still exist.

"Well, I'll call you at the House, then. Call me if you need anything."

I'm not sure how to maintain a relationship with this girl, but I don't know how to tell her that. "Sure, Danielle."

She was so special to me at one time. Someone I thought I would watch grow, to help learn about life, to help get ready for prom. But now she's a stranger.

Chapter 18

"What if it was TJ?" I have to talk to Vangie Ann about this. Nobody else will listen to me at this point.

Vangie Ann's eyes are like golf balls and her mouth is wide open. "You really think it could have been him?"

"Well, I don't know for sure, but it makes sense. It was probably just an accident, but he's been covering so long and feeling guilty, the poor kid."

She lights a cigarette and leans against the peeling porch rail. "I don't know. Maybe. Are you really sure it wasn't Wayne?"

"Yeah, I'm sure."

"Why? Just because you screwed him?" She takes a drag and cocks her head, perfecting a smirk.

"I'm just sure. I thought it was him because I saw him leaving her parking lot. But it could have been TJ. What if he was in there with his mom and found the gun? Kids do that kind of shit all the time. And that's why Wayne didn't stick up for me." I lean forward in the rocking chair and lower my voice, "Danielle got this creepy look on her face when I asked for help. It's hard to describe, but something weird is definitely going on. Maybe she accidentally did it."

Vangie Ann shudders and any trace of her smirk disappears. "Both of those kids are messed up. I bet TJ's been doing meth since before puberty took hold."

"What should I do, Sis?" I rub my hands on my face.

"We need the money real bad. But I don't want you to get hurt."

"But we need the money. A homeless shelter isn't a place for us."

"You won't get the money if you're dead, Cass. I used to know folks like TJ. Trust me. You can't take any chances. Give up for a while." She smiles a smile that reminds me of the way she looked when she was younger and softer. "Maybe he'll sober up and become a reasonable person. It happens. In the meantime, we'll hold the fundraiser for a Band-Aid."

"He's just a kid, V." I lean back in the rocking chair and stretch my legs out in front of me. I'm not interested in waiting for TJ to get clean. I can't stay here indefinitely.

"He's what, twenty? Twenty-one, now?" She looks away toward the street or the sky, as if she's remembering something that happened in a story she read. "He probably started drinking beer at thirteen or fourteen. Then smoking pot about fourteen or fifteen. I'd say judging by the company he keeps, he was snorting meth before he was driving a car." She takes a drag and snubs her cigarette into the ashtray. "The point I'm trying to make is: don't act like he's a normal young man. But I don't think he killed his mama. And whatever he knows, he ain't telling."

"Fuck!" I slam my palms on the chair arms. A half-a-million dollars is slipping away. "Even if he wouldn't kill me, I'm not sure I could roll over on him. He was almost my stepkid."

"You're awfully sentimental about someone who might be standing between you and a half-million dollars." The smirk is back.

"I don't have much on the outside. Can't blame me for hanging on to what I can."

"Yes, I can blame you. Sentimentality is what landed you in jail in the first place." She pulls the pink scrunchie from her wrist and piles her curly hair on top of her head.

"Now I just feel like you're giving me mixed messages. You are so much like Mom." I realize Vangie Ann even looks like our mother. A trashier, bleached, and smoke-wrinkled version.

"I'm not giving you mixed messages. Don't say anything else to anyone about TJ Talbot because you don't want to be spreading rumors about a meth-head. If the possibility of a miserable death wasn't an issue, I would say go for it because the boy needs some discipline. But that's not your problem to deal with." She picks at the flaking paint on the post.

"Should we paint the porch if we make enough money off the party?" I can't take another second talking about the possibility of my miserable death.

"That's exactly what I was thinking. What do you think of pink? Not too bright, like a pale pink, barely pink." She strokes the post with her open palm.

I want to tell her it's a terrible idea. Pink will make the place stand out when we need to blend in with the neighborhood. The neighbors will hate it. But I can tell that she's in love with the idea.

"Do you mean like a white that is just sort of pink when the light hits it just right? Because I think that would be perfect."

Vangie Ann smiles. "Yeah. Just like that." She stands up and dusts off the back of her dress. "Let's go in. Sonya is going to take the car to town and try to get some more donations for the party. Dana's going to cook supper. You and Tilly can clean the windows, and I'll do the floors."

"When did you get so organized?" I ask as I stand.

"I have to be. The focus helps me live clean." She puts her hand on my back as we walk back into the House. "Can't take care of you reprobates if I'm distracted by drugs."

I turn to her as a shadow crosses her face so quickly I'm not sure if I imagined it.

* * *

The police show up early in the evening as the aroma of meatloaf starts to radiate from the oven. Vangie Ann opens the door and lets them in while I remain seated at the kitchen table. I don't panic. I just sit. I didn't expect them to show up, but it's not a surprise.

"Hey there, Evangeline."

"Officer Flores. Officer Johnson." She smiles softly, warmly like a mother. "What can I do for you?"

"We're here for Cass. Parole violation," Officer Johnson says. Both men remove their hats as they walk in.

I hear their words but my mind doesn't know what to do with them. So I don't move.

"Cass," Vangie Ann says over her shoulder.

I push away from the table and stand. My feet shuffle to the door, taking the rest of me with them. Vangie Ann looks at the floor.

Officer Flores grabs handcuffs from his belt. His first name is Mike. I know this because we went to school together. We snuck out during a high school assembly one time to make out in the janitor's closet. Time has been kind to him, but it wouldn't be appropriate to mention it.

"It that necessary?" I ask.

"Afraid so, Cass. Sorry." He wraps the cuffs around my wrist. I feel the click in my stomach. I've been on the bricks for two weeks, and I'm already in handcuffs.

They lead me to the car. When I look back at the House, Tilly and Sonya have joined Vangie Ann on the porch. They're watching us like some kind of morbid parade.

We pull away from the curb. I think the officers are talking to me, but I'm not sure. The only clear sound is my heart beating in my ears. *Thump, thump, thump.* The last time I was in the back of a police car felt sort of the same, except I had the benefit of my senses being slightly dulled by opiates. I didn't know yet that I had thrown my life away. This time it's much clearer.

We arrive at the police station in less than five minutes.

"Mike," I say as he's taking the cuffs off, "why, exactly, am I here?"

The first stop is a shiny new mug shot. Since they already have my prints on file, I don't have to suffer that indignation again. Silver linings. Ha.

"Well. It seems that you, um, had relations with Wayne Talbot. That's a direct violation of your parole agreement." He unlocks the cell and motions for me to walk in. It's empty. I should be relieved that I'm not about to be locked in with other criminals, but instead the emptiness feels cold.

"Who told you that?"

"Mr. Talbot's son. He said he feels threatened by your proximity to his family." He locks the cell door. "I know that kid has been in some trouble, but he has feelings, you know." Officer Flores points at me as if I don't know it's me he's talking to and turns away.

I sit on the cold metal bench for lack of anything else to do. Part of me wants to strangle both Wayne and TJ for their big mouths, but most of me knows this is my fault. Unlike last time, I'm actually guilty.

The cell is over air conditioned. I wrap my arms around myself and shiver. I wish I had thought to grab a jacket. The cold air smells of mildew and Lysol. I'm sure Wayne and Melody are home and warm, even if they're fighting about me.

I don't remember if the cell was cold the last time I was here. It was winter, so the air conditioner wouldn't have been running overtime. Even if the room was cold, the drugs would have warmed me up.

Officer Flores reappears a few minutes later. He has a woman with him. I think she's about sixty-five, but it's hard to tell. Hard drugs have scarred her face and dried out her hair. She might only be forty. She's wearing short jogging shorts, but I'm certain she hasn't been jogging.

I start to ask him for a blanket, but think better of it. If he says "yes," the other woman will hate me.

"Hello, cutie," she says to me as Flores nudges her into the cell.

"Hi."

I could ask her to cuddle for warmth, but she's too thin and smells like Lucinda.

"He's a hot piece of ass, huh?" She points her thumb at Flores as he walks away. He's close enough to hear her, but pretends he can't.

"We made out once in high school." High school. Back when I had my whole life in front of me.

She sits down beside me. "Why only once?"

"Don't remember," I say.

"I'm Rhoda," she says and extends her boney hand.

"Cass," I say.

Rhoda jumps up and goes to the cell door. She wraps her hands around the bars and yells, "It's freezing in here. You're violating my human rights."

"Shut up in there," a man yells from somewhere.

"Bite me," Rhoda yells in response.

Officer Johnson appears a few minutes later with two scratchy-looking blankets.

"Is it clean?" Rhoda asks.

"Clean enough for you," he says. He looks at both of us for a beat and his face softens. "Yes, they're both clean."

"Can't be too careful. Don't want you bringing us smallbox blankets or nothin'."

"Smallpox," I say.

"Huh?"

"It was smallpox." I stand and take a blanket from Johnson. "Thank you."

Officer Johnson nods his head once and walks away, securing the door behind him.

"Thanks for speaking up, Rhoda." I take my place on the bench and wrap the scratchy gray blanket around my shoulders. "I was freezing my ass off."

Rhoda sits next to me and asks, "Solicitation?"

"Nope. Parole violation."

"Assault for me. Again." She crosses her arms and leans against the wall. "A girl's gotta defend herself, right?"

I nod and lean my head against the cold concrete wall. I can feel tears forming, but I can't cry here. If I've learned anything from my years with the penal system, it's that there's a time and place for crying.

"You okay, hun?" Rhoda asks.

I nod and squeeze my eyes tight to keep the crying at bay.

"I just don't know why I'm such a fuck-up," I say.

Rhoda wraps her boney arm around my shoulders and says, "I have a girl about your age. She's got four kids and three baby daddies. Poor thing never stood a chance."

But I did stand a chance. And I blew it. Over and over. And once again, I stand to lose my freedom over a man. The same man as last time.

"Well, well. What do we have going on in here?" The voice is manly but high-pitched. I open my eyes to see a female officer bringing in a black man dressed like 1980s Cher. It's a busy night in West Plains.

Rhoda and I both sit up straight.

"Unique! How the hell have you been?" Rhoda stands and greets the newcomer with open arms.

"Oh, you know. Just shaking what the good Lord gave me!" Unique shakes her ass at the cop as she locks the cell.

"What brings you by?" Rhoda holds out her hand and sweeps it around as if to say, "welcome to my home."

Unique smiles and says, "Got caught with something dirty in my mouth." She sticks her thumb out toward her cheek and does the international sign for blow job. She looks at me and says, "Never seen you here before."

"I haven't been in this particular facility in about eleven years." The police station banter is a relief. It feels good to pretend this is normal and okay.

"I assume Rhoda showed you around."

I nod and say, "And secured a blanket for me."

"Good job, Rhoda." Unique sits across from me and crosses her legs. "Guess I should settle in."

Rhoda sits next to her and they start to discuss the finer points of oral sex in cars. I wad up the blanket into a pillow and lay down on the cold bench. I curl into a ball in an effort to warm up my body. I can't decide what I need more: a pillow or blanket.

Unique wakes me up some time later by tapping me repeatedly on the arm. "Hey, girl. Does this shirt smell weird to you?"

I sit up and sniff at the air. "I don't think so."

"No. You have to really smell it." She holds out her black lace scoop collar and bends closer to my face. Her Adam's apple is sharp enough to put an eye out but I lean forward anyway. It's not the time to be impolite.

"I smell cologne. That's all." I do my best to smile.

"It smells weird to me. Kind of like butt." She releases her shirt and runs her palm down her curly wig.

"I told you it didn't smell like butt," Rhoda says. I notice that she has three teeth on the top and four on bottom. "Now shut up about it already."

"She's cranky." Cher smiles broadly and says, "Get it? Cranky? Crank?"

"Yeah. Good one." I curl back up and squeeze my eyes closed. Hopefully my roommates won't have any more debates that need settling tonight.

I hope they at least put me back with Tabitha. It wouldn't make it okay that I fucked up my parole, but it would at least bring a degree of comfort. Sort of like finding a five-dollar bill in a pair of pants that have become too small.

* * *

"Blankenship." Officer Johnson is standing at the door of the cell. His belly is pushed against the bars so segments of fat are pressing through.

I stand up and stretch.

"It's your lucky day." He unlocks the door and steps to the side.

My new friends Unique and Rhoda shout "bye, girl," and "good luck," and I nod and smile in response.

Lucinda is waiting for me when I get to the end of the hallway with Officer Johnson.

"You're being released to Lucinda's custody. Don't get in any trouble."

"Thanks, Toby," Lucinda says to Officer Johnson.

"Don't forget that you owe me a pecan pie," he says and crosses his arms over his chest, his elbows resting on his belly.

"You got it." She squeezes his shoulder. "In fact, I'll bring you two."

We get outside. It's dark now, my day wasted on the floor of a city jail cell.

"Thanks, Lucinda." I look up to the navy-blue sky. "Where were you when I was arrested the first time?" I chuckle, hoping the joke will break the tension between us.

"I was able to help you, but you have to watch yourself." She lights a cigarette. "I won't do this again. It's my name on the line, my reputation."

"Okay."

"And you're not out of trouble yet. I just made it to where you can go home. You still have to face the music."

I nod and open the door to Lucinda's car. The nicotine-stained upholstery smells like comfort, and I'm afraid I'll miss it when I go back to prison.

Chapter 19

It's almost seven-thirty and I'm still in bed. Vangie Ann will be banging on my door any minute, demanding that I get my lazy ass up and start with the chores. I'm surprised she hasn't started in already. Maybe she's too pissed at me to make me clean the House. She didn't speak to me when I got back from jail last night. She went to her room as soon as I got back and didn't come out again.

I'll get up and shower and then talk to Vangie Ann. I can't imagine how disappointed in me she must be.

But when I emerge from the shower, Vangie Ann is still in bed. Her face is pressed against the pillow, and her hair is tangled in knots.

"V, you okay?" I ask the words softly.

Vangie Ann lifts her head. There are bags under her eyes.

"Why are you up?" Vangie Ann pulls the covers up to her chin and rolls over to her side.

"Because it's almost eight." I sit on the foot of her bed.

"Shit." Vangie Ann sits up. "I'll get up. What's my problem?"

"Don't know. I'll go start some coffee." I stand up. "You need anything else, V?"

Vangie Ann hesitates a second. "No, thanks. I'll be up in a minute."

"It was TJ. He told the cops about me seeing Wayne," I say, hoping it will make a difference for some reason.

"I guess it doesn't really matter. Does it?"

"No. Guess not. I'll see you in the kitchen."

She reaches for her phone as I leave the room, and I catch a glimpse of someone from the past. The Vangie Ann I knew before I went to prison. Someone I hoped to never see again.

* * *

Two hours later, Vangie Ann's phone rings when we're in the kitchen making the week's menu. She grabs it and runs to the porch. It's the first time she's smiled all day.

I go to the sitting room and crack a window slightly. It's wrong, sure, but I have to know what's going on with my sister. Her voice is quiet but clear.

"I'm good, Gabe. Yeah. Good. Cass is here. She's out of jail."

Gabe, the boyfriend from her druggie days. Last I'd heard, he was clean and wanted nothing to do with V or anything else that reminded him of those days.

She takes a drag from a cigarette and smoke billows through the window screen.

"Yeah. Mostly. Can we meet for coffee?"

Vangie Ann laughs. It doesn't sound like her, though. She sounds more girlish, fake.

"Sounds good. See you tomorrow."

Maybe he's still clean, and she's seeing him to stay on the straight and narrow. When folks get sober they're supposed to go to each other for help, right?

I go back to the kitchen table where I've been working on a grocery list. Vangie Ann comes in still smiling.

"Who was that?" I tap the table with my pencil.

"That was Paul. He was checking to see if the toilet was running okay." She sits at the table.

"That was nice of him."

"Sure was." She looks right at me, daring me to say she's lying.

I should be able to tell her I eavesdropped, and that I'm worried about her. But it's easier to change the subject. "Are you going to the grocery store with me?"

"Sure. Tell you what: I'll treat us to manicures on the way. Your cuticles look like shit."

I hold my hands up to survey my nails. She's right. "Okay. Thanks."

"Let's go then, Cass. We're burning daylight." She grabs her cheap purse and seems normal again. I relax and head out of the door toward better fingernails with my sister.

Chapter 20

There's a letter from Tabitha on the kitchen table. I see her handwriting in pencil on the envelope before I read the name. I pick up the envelope and run my fingers along the edges, knowing her fingers were there. This isn't right, I should have written to her first.

I open it slowly and unfold the paper.

Dear Cass,

I miss you. Life hasn't changed much for me.

I have a new cellmate. Her name is Maria. She's short. We don't carry-on together. At least not yet. I don't know if we ever will. She's nice enough, but it's not the same. She's in for forging checks, too boring. You should have seen her face when I told her why I'm here. I thought she was going to pee her pants!

I hope you can visit some time. I can understand why you would want to stay away, but please don't forget what it's like to be trapped in here. I also have a favor to ask and I can only do it in person. So if you can, please visit.

I don't know what else to say.

Love always,
Tabitha

Tears form in my eyes and pour down my cheeks. I sit on a kitchen chair and let the tears flow freely. I think of my best friend still sitting in prison without me. And I have done nothing but ignore her, couldn't even be bothered to finish a letter to her. Some friend I turned out to be. It's not that I don't miss her, because I do. It's just so easy to move on with my own problems and dramas which are always so abundant. My life is separate from her now.

Vangie Ann walks in and asks, "What now, Cass?"

"That's not very nice." I fold the letter and place it back in the envelope.

"Sorry. What's troubling your highness now? Is that better?"

"No." I put the envelope in my back pocket and stand. I notice that Vangie Ann is wearing heels with her stripper dress. "Where are you going?"

"I'm meeting a friend for coffee." She grins.

"A male friend, I presume?"

"Yep." She fishes her keys out of her tacky purse. "Sorry about what I said, okay? Been a bit on edge lately."

"It's okay. I understand." That's a lie. I don't really understand, but I don't feel like fighting with her. Maybe she needs to get laid. That *is* something I can understand. And I can't really be mad at her for being a bitch to me. After all, I did sort of accuse her of murder.

"Have you decided to hold off on the inheritance investigation?" Her keys are gripped by her left hand. She tugs the purse up to her shoulder.

"No. I get what you're saying about TJ, but I don't want to put this off." I pause and Vangie Ann stares at me thoughtfully. It's nice to have her attention when she's not angry with me. "So far I know that Wayne, TJ, and Danielle are all hiding something. And Melody. Tilly's holding something back, too."

"Well," she sighs, "maybe I can talk to Tilly for you. I'll do it when I get back."

"Thanks, V. Need me to do anything for you while you're gone?"

"Sure. Can you please start supper? I have some hamburger thawing in the fridge. Do you know how to make lasagna?" She's grinning. It's a little creepy.

"I can probably figure it out. Do you have a cookbook anywhere if I get lost?"

She opens a drawer and throws a cookbook on the table. "Here you go. Back in a bit." Her heels click and clack all the way out the door.

I open the cookbook and start looking for a lasagna recipe. I've never made it before, and I don't think I've eaten homemade lasagna since I was a teenager. It's another one of those foods that is just as good frozen. But it seems like I need to get it right.

"Need any help?" It's Sonya. I don't have to turn around. I can tell by the smell of stale cigarettes and Vanilla Fields.

"You know how to make lasagna?"

"Yeah. It's just cheese and meat and shit." She shrugs.

The hooker knows how to make lasagna and I don't. This is my life.

Sonya hands me a paper cup and raises her eyebrows.

"Oh. Okay. Just do it in this cup?"

"Yep." She smiles and nods her head toward the bathroom.

I sigh and go to the bathroom. I've given enough urine samples that I don't have to worry about peeing on my hand.

Sonya is waiting for me when I emerge from the bathroom. She's holding her hand out like a nurse.

I guess to make a friend, sometimes you have to pee for a prostitute.

***

We're all sitting at the table when Vangie Ann slinks in. Her hair is messy and she's stumbling on her heels. Her skin has lost its healthy glow in favor of a sticky pale sheen.

"Oh, great. You made supper." She drops her purse on the floor and joins us at the table.

"Yeah," I say. I start to cut a slice for her.

"Not much for me, okay?"

"Sure." I cut a small square and put it on a plate.

"This looks great, Cass."

"Sonya did most of the work."

"Well, good work." Vangie Ann cuts a bite with her fork and pushes it around her plate. She smiles at us and puts in her mouth. She gags a little.

"It's not that bad," I say. We've all almost finished ours, and I thought it was pretty damn good.

"Sorry. I don't feel very well. I think I should go to my room." She puts her fork down and bolts down the hall to her room. I follow her.

She tries to close the door between us but I'm too close behind. I stop the door with my palm.

"You're high," I say.

"Only a little. I tried to eat. I just couldn't do it." She peels off her dress and throws it on the floor.

"What the fuck, V?" I sit on her bed and stare at her, even though she's only in her underwear.

"I don't know, Cass. I don't know. I just couldn't fight anymore. I saw Gabe today. He was holding. I was weak." She pulls a ratty t-shirt and cut-off sweatpants from her chest of drawers and pulls them on. "It was just a little bit. It had been a long time so it hit me pretty hard."

I look at her face and then jump up. I rush through the door and run down the stairs. I hear her follow me. I find her purse on the floor next to the front door. I grab it and dump it on the floor.

"No, Cass!" she screams.

The ladies in the kitchen have all stood at attention. This is the most excitement to happen here in days. I find the tiny baggy and run toward the bathroom. Vangie Ann intercepts me in the hall. She balls up her fist and punches me square in the nose.

Pain jolts across my face into my eyes and cheeks but I don't let go. She grabs at my hand, her fake nails scratching ruts into my skin. I taste the metallic warmth as blood from my nose runs down to my lips.

"That's mine!" she says like we're children fighting over a Barbie.

I push her to the floor, flat on her ass. She jumps up as I make it into the hall bathroom. I lock the door and dump the bag of powder into the toilet. I flush, watching the contents swirl into the watery oblivion.

My reflection in the mirror is shocking. There's blood smeared from my nose to my lips, chin, and cheeks. I fill my cupped hands with water and splash it on my face, then dab it dry with the pink hand towel. That's when I notice the scratches on my arms, bumpy and raw, with blood rising to the surface.

When I open the door, Vangie Ann is sitting with her back against the wall. Her jaw is set.

"You owe me fifty dollars," she says.

"Fuck you," I say. I march up the stairs and slam my bedroom door.

Chapter 21

When I emerge from my room an hour later, there's no sign of Vangie Ann. I know she's gone back to Gabe and his drugs. There's nothing I can do about it.

My face hurts. My arm hurts. My heart is broken and all I want is a fistful of pain pills. Medicine to reward my pain with euphoria. But one of us has to stay strong.

I call her cell phone and it goes straight to voicemail. "Hello, you've reached Evangeline Blankenship. Please leave a message, and I'll call you back as soon as possible." Her voice on the message is professional and calm, not like when I saw her an hour ago. She has morphed into someone else within the span of one day.

Sonya appears before my face. "What are we going to do?"

"The same shit we do all the time," I say. I place the phone on the wall charger.

Tilly slides behind her. "You know this is bad." She crosses her arms over her chest. "Do you know how to take care of stuff? There's a lot to do around here. She might be gone a while."

"Don't overreact. She's only been gone an hour."

I don't want these women looking to me for answers, but that's what will happen if she doesn't come home. I'll become her replacement, the surrogate leader when I don't know how to take care of myself.

"We'll help you if you don't know what to do," Tilly says softly.

I look at Tilly and then to Sonya. They're both waiting for some sort of answer. We all know things are probably dire. None of us want it to fall apart.

"Thank you," I say. "We'll take care of things. Don't worry. She'll probably come back soon anyway. It's a relapse, sure. But Vangie Ann loves this place. She's not going to throw her life away."

"You're acting like it's a choice, Cass. You're living in a dream world." Sonya pulls a soda from the refrigerator and pulls the tab. She slurps from the top. "Things are happening to her now. Her life isn't her own."

"What can we do?" I ask.

Tilly pulls a chair from the table and sits. "We just have to be here for her."

"I can't wait around and do nothing, can I?" I pull out the chair across from Tilly and sit down.

"She ain't thinking about you or any of the rest of us right now. This is about her. You can't fix it." Tilly pulls a banana from the fruit bowl in the center of the table, but doesn't peel it.

Sonya puts her can of soda on the table and sits down. "Seriously, a girl like you ain't never done drugs?"

"Not meth." Pills. So many pills. But never meth.

Dana walks in. "No sign of our leader?" She grabs a glass from the cabinet and fills it from the tap.

"No," Sonya says.

"Well," she shrugs. "Shit happens." She stomps up the stairs.

"I don't like her," I say.

"Duh," Tilly says. She peels the banana without looking up.

I wonder if my sister's okay. If she's going to stay okay. If she'll be healthy. If she'll make it through this alive. She made it through last time, but how many times can she tempt fate? And I wonder what pushed her over the edge. She was doing fine until I came back. Wasn't she? Maybe I should have tried to go straight to California. Then I wouldn't be dealing with a parole violation or dealing with Vangie Ann's drama.

And just like that, I have made Vangie Ann's relapse about me.

A knock on the door brings me out of my narcissism. My stomach lurches. I hope it's nothing I can't deal with. I stand and walk to the door. It's Mack Brown. My body braces for a lecture.

"Hi. What brings you by?" The open door brings a wall of heat inside.

"You have a hearing in the morning." He's wearing a short-sleeved button-down shirt and slacks. It's too hot for anything more formal. "What the hell happened to your face?"

"Vangie Ann." I walk out onto the porch. We take our normal seats. "Can I tell you something in confidence?"

"Yeah. I guess." He raises his eyebrows.

"Vangie Ann took off today. I think she's back on meth." I don't commit to the truth of her relapse.

"Oh." He pulls my manila folder from beneath his arm and a pen from his shirt pocket.

"You can't write that down," I say.

"Not going to," he says. "I'm just saying you've picked up extra responsibilities." He scribbles some notes and then says, "The one upside to this is that you have a little more freedom of movement. If you're running things for her, you can go out on your own more. That is, of course, if you aren't sent back to prison."

"Thanks." If only that made her absence worth it.

"Do you know where she went?" Mack asks.

"I think she's hanging out with a guy named Gabe."

He nods and squints into the street.

"Do you know him?"

"Doesn't ring a bell." He puts my folder in his lap and looks at me. "I had an uncle who cooked meth. He was my dad's little brother." Mack gazes into the street again, but he's not looking at anything. "He lived out in the backwoods off of Highway 56."

"Yeah?" I'm surprised to learn that he had trouble in his family. I know I shouldn't be. Everybody does.

Mack turns to look at me again. "When I was in high school he blew himself up. My dad was never the same after."

"I'm sorry, Mack. That's terrible."

"Meth is a terrible thing. It ruins people. Ruins families." He sighs and looks down the notebook in his lap. "Call the therapist yet?"

"Are you serious right now?"

"Yep." He clicks his pen and sticks it in his pocket. "I have a responsibility. Stop making my job difficult."

"I'm having a really shit day. Okay?"

Mack sighs and shakes his head. "I'll pick you up at eight o'clock. Dress modestly. And try to make your face look better." He gets up and walks off the porch and to his car.

Chapter 22

The next morning I wake to stomping noises on the stairs. It sounds like someone walking with cinder blocks for shoes. I look out and see Troy stomping with huge boots on his feet.

"Yo, Troy. Can you keep it down?" I say.

He looks at me and proceeds to stomp. Dana peeks out of their room.

"Can you do something about Frankenstein here?" I ask.

"Knock it off, Troy," she says and closes the door.

Troy stops and sits down on the stairs. He puts his chin in hands. I walk down a few stairs and sit down beside him.

"You okay?"

He looks up at me. "Yep. Just felt like stompin'."

"Maybe you could stomp outside."

"Can I ask you somethin'?" His chin quivers.

"Sure, Troy." I take a deep breath. I really hope he doesn't want to talk about his dad.

"Do you ever have too many boogers?"

A chuckle escapes my throat. "Yeah. I guess so." I look at my watch. It's seven thirty. "I have to get ready."

Modest. My only clothes are jeans and sundresses. I check Vangie Ann's closet.

Our mom used to take us to the mall once a month for new dresses. Dad would complain about her spending the money, but not enough to make her stop. He only complained out of habit, out of obligation. He liked seeing our faces when we came downstairs in our new dresses. The way we smiled when we twirled. Sometimes we would hold hands, sometimes we wouldn't. It depended on what kind of mood Vangie Ann was in.

The only dress that isn't in the stripper motif is pink and floral. I guess it will have to do. I pancake foundation under my eyes and over my nose. The purple shows through, but only if someone looks really close. My nose is swollen, but I can't do anything about that.

Mack arrives promptly at eight. "That's what you're wearing?"

"You have something better for me?"

"Nope. Let's go." He opens the sedan door for me and I get in. My nerves have gone numb.

"Lucinda is going to meet us there. She was a dispatcher here in town, so hopefully having her there will help."

"Can't hurt," he says. He looks straight ahead and drives us to the courthouse.

The courtroom is a giant wooden casket just like they all are. I don't remember walking inside from the parking lot, but I know I must have. I take a seat at a table next to the attorney that Lucinda selected. She smells like tangy perfume, and she's wearing a black suit. We've never spoken.

The judge is an old white man with a gray handlebar mustache. He nods in Lucinda's direction as he sits down. There are words said by several people, but I don't hear anything until the judge says, "Cass Blankenship."

I stand up and he continues, "You violated your parole agreement by contacting Wayne Talbot. I understand that you recently filed a parole transfer agreement."

"Yes, sir," I say.

"Your application is denied, and I'm adding two years to your parole. You are not going back to prison at this time thanks to overcrowding. But if you commit another violation, you will return to prison without delay. Do you understand?"

"Yes, sir."

"You have been in contact with Mr. Talbot's daughter. She contacted the court to say that she wants you to be allowed to spend time with her. If she changes her mind, you leave her alone."

"Yes, sir."

After he says a few more things I forget to hear, I walk outside with Lucinda and Mack.

"When can I apply for a transfer again?" I ask Mack.

"Really, Cass?" Lucinda asks. "You just narrowly avoided prison and you're worried about moving right now?"

"I need to get away from here, Lucinda. If I leave, I'll never see Wayne again. I won't see his kids again. I won't see his wife again." I face her and put my hands on her shoulders. "Thank you for your help. I'm so glad that I'm not going back to prison. I don't mean to seem ungrateful." I let my hands drop.

Lucinda nods at says, "Stay out of trouble and you'll get to go eventually."

"She's right, Cass," Mack says. He opens the car door for me.

"I think I'll walk back." I slip off the high heels I borrowed from Vangie Ann's closet and take off down the sidewalk before Mack or Lucinda can say anything else.

* * *

I've been in my room ten minutes when the phone rings in the kitchen. I jump up and take the stairs two at a time. I hope more than anything that it's Vangie Ann on the other end.

"Hello." I remember that there is more to say. "Blankenship House."

"Hi. This is Wanda from Wanda's Salon. Evangeline stopped by last week to pick up a gift certificate and I wasn't in. I have it ready now, though. Can she come by today?" She sounds old, like the type of hairdresser who uses a lot of permanent solution and tiny curlers on the same customers week after week.

It occurs to me that the fundraiser is two weeks away. I don't know how to do this.

"This is Evangeline's sister, Cass. I don't know if Evangeline will be available today. If she's not, I'll come by myself. What's your address?" I pull a piece of paper and pencil from the drawer beneath the phone and scribble down the address she gives me.

"Okay, thanks. I'll be by in a couple of hours."

It's not until I hang up the phone that I remember that I have no car. I'm stuck in a house with a junkie, a hooker, a miserable bitch, and a little boy. Vangie Ann has officially screwed us all over to go get high with her old boyfriend.

My fingertips run over the countertop. It's smooth and warm. I feel grounded, and though I'm trapped in this House, I remind myself I'm not in prison. I will figure this out. This is not the worst thing that has happened to me. Really, it's not even happening to me. This is Vangie Ann's breakdown. I'm just here for it.

"Sonya!" I yell up the stairs, too shell-shocked to walk my ass up the lavender trail.

"Yeah?" She appears at the top. The light from the window behind her makes her skin appear alabaster, her hair smooth; she looks angelic. It's a crazy illusion, the kind of thing that people do drugs to experience. The bend in reality that turns a hooker into an angel.

"Do you know where we can find a car?"

Sonya purses her lips together and cocks her head to the side. "I'm not sure. I can make some calls."

"Thanks. Will you ask Tilly, too?"

"Yeah." She turns to walk away, and her backlighting disappears. She's wearing cut-offs so short that the pockets are hanging below the bottom seam.

I go back to the kitchen and start a pot of coffee. I try to think of people who can help me. The list is short.

I don't want to call Lucinda because I'm not prepared to be a middle-aged tattletale. It might come to that, but not yet. Vangie Ann hasn't knocked me off my bike, hasn't stolen my favorite dress and thrown it in the garbage. Anyway, Lucinda has done enough for me today.

I've already asked enough of Mack Brown. I can't ask to borrow his truck to chase down my strung-out sister's gift certificates.

Wayne, of course not. Melody, hell no.

There are friends from before prison—the other teachers I would go for margaritas with in the evenings. We would make fun of students and parents. Laugh at the ones who were the biggest jerks, all the while certain we would make better parents than those assholes. I don't think any of them will help me now. None of them have made any move to contact me since I've been out. None of them supported me during the trial. A couple of my friends showed up as tourists. I know it wasn't for support because neither of them would make eye contact with me. None of those people are a part of my life now. I'm not allowed to sit at their table.

Tilly bounds down the stairs. "Sonya said you're looking for a car."

"Yeah. Do you have any ideas?"

She puts an unlit cigarette between her lips and shakes her head. "Nope," she says between her teeth. Tilly walks out, and the thought enters my brain that she won't come back. My heart starts to pound. I'm not sure why I care so much.

The countertop supports me as I panic. One name enters my brain. One person has offered to help and sworn to stand by me.

Just then, the door opens and Tilly walks back in. "Forgot my lighter."

My breathing steadies and I start the search for Danielle Talbot's phone number.

Chapter 23

Danielle shows up on the doorstep an hour later. She's wearing a big, friendly smile. But I'm still taken aback by how much she looks like Judith. I wonder how long it will take to get used to her as an adult, this small person with the dead woman's face. Haunting me, reminding me of my stolen years. But maybe if she's my friend, she can help me with the rest of the family.

"I'm so glad you called me!" She stands on her tiptoes and throws her arms around my neck. I almost want to push little Judith away, but I can't do that. For some reason she craves my acceptance. I pat Danielle on the back. "I'm so sorry about TJ turning you in. I can't believe he did that. I told the cops that I still want to see you."

"Thanks for doing that," I said. "I didn't know where to turn."

"Well, you have me. What do we need to do?"

"We have to pick up a gift certificate for the fundraiser. And I need to run a few errands for the House. Grocery store, hardware store, stuff like that."

"Let's go then." She's still smiling with her entire face.

The phone rings from the kitchen as we reach the front door. I turn back and grab the receiver from the wall.

"Blankenship House." *Please be Vangie Ann.*

"This is Cheryl Pipkins from County. May I speak to Evangeline, please?"

My mind races. County Hospital? County lockup? What? I don't want this woman to know that I don't know what's going on.

"Evangeline isn't available. This is her sister, Cass. Can I help you?"

"Sure. We're sending a young woman. Her name is Margaret Willis. She's being released today. I'd rather discuss this with Evangeline. Can she call me back?"

"She, well, she's on vacation."

"Vacation?" Cheryl Pipkins sighs loudly, and I feel like I'm being chastised by a teacher in school. "When will she be back?"

"Next Tuesday." *I'll gladly pay you Tuesday for a hamburger today.* Don't know, maybe I'm hungry, but it's the first thought that pops into my head. "I'm here to take care of things in her absence."

"Okay. Well. Miss Willis will be there today at two o'clock. I'm not really comfortable sending her without Evangeline there, but I don't really have another place for her to go."

"It's fine, really." Fine. Like I'm capable of taking care of anybody. Please send me your young delinquents.

"All right." She hangs up.

"Let's go, Danielle. I need to get back sooner than I thought."

Danielle's waiting for me at the door, wearing the same grin. She keeps that grin the entire time we run errands.

* * *

When we return to Blankenship House in the early afternoon, there's a teenager and a police officer on the porch.

The police officer is tall and wiry. He's standing with his arms crossed over his chest and a cigar between his teeth. He's puffing his chest out, trying to appear larger than his size.

The teenaged girl is sitting in the rocking chair. She's wearing jeans and a baggy black t-shirt. Her hair is dyed black with several inches of dusty brown roots. What is it with all of us and neglected dye jobs? She's looking down at her beat-up tennis shoes and rocking slowly.

"Hi," I say as we walk up the steps. "I'm Cass. Have you been waiting long?" It makes me nervous to talk to the cop, but I try not to let on.

I put down my shopping bags. Groceries mostly. I've never had to feed other people before. It's another milestone I should have reached much earlier in life.

"Nah. About five minutes." He says. "I'm Officer Stead. This here is Maggie. She'll be staying with y'all for a while." He hands me a manila envelope: the life of Margaret Willis. "Sign here, please." He hands me a clipboard with a form. I have to sign a piece of paper that places Maggie in my possession. A special delivery. She's no longer in jail, she's nowhere else but right here. Maggie is still staring at her shoes like they contain information. I don't know what color her eyes are.

I hand the clipboard back to the cop. "Thank you," he says and then leaves without another word. I want to tell him he forgot his grumpy teenager, but that would be inappropriate and I'm trying to be better than that.

I crouch down. "Hi, Maggie. I'm Cass and that's Danielle. Want to go inside?"

Maggie looks up. Her eyes are the color of root beer in a glass of ice. She glares at Danielle and says, "I know her."

"Hi, Maggie." Danielle smiles tentatively like she's waiting for permission.

Maggie responds with a nod and stands, picking up her duffle bag in the process. Danielle and I gather all the bags, and Maggie follows us inside. Danielle is scowling like someone just took her favorite toy.

We dump the bags in the kitchen. I feel slightly overwhelmed. Plastic bags and young women in a small room. I want to be alone but can't.

"Thanks, Danielle. You really saved my ass today," I say, then wish I was more eloquent. I really need to work on sounding like I didn't just get out of prison.

"No problem. Please call me anytime. I mean it." She hugs me again, and she cuts her eyes at Maggie.

"See you soon." I close the door behind her.

Maggie is still staring at her shoes, but now from the standing position.

"You're going to be sharing my room," I say. "Come on up."

She follows me up the lavender stairs, still not looking up.

"That's your bed."

Maggie puts her duffle bag on the bed and sits down. I sit on my bed and look at her. I feel her silence in my neck and shoulders.

"How old are you, Maggie?"

"You can look in my file." Her voice is soft. I didn't expect that.

"I'd rather you told me. I'm not your enemy, you know. I live here, too."

She looks up. Her face is pale, pimply with freckles. "I'm eighteen."

I could be her mother. My hands have gone to my stomach without my knowledge or permission. My body aching over something I don't even want.

"We all help each other here. Well, mostly anyway. None of us are here to judge. We've all been in trouble." I move my hands to my lap and then stand. "I'm going to go put the groceries away. Come down when you feel like it."

Maggie says nothing. She takes off her shoes, those beat-up, stare-worthy shoes, and curls up on her bed.

Chapter 24

When we were little, Vangie Ann and I would camp outside in the backyard with Dad in tents right when summer hit. It was before it was too hot, before the bugs moved in for the season. Mom would bring snacks and juice outside then go inside by herself. I have dreams of watching her walk back inside the house, fiddling with the sliding screen door that would get off track. She would use PG-rated swear words like "crap" and jiggle it until she got the door back where it was supposed to go.

I'm reaching out to touch the back of her head, her long, thick hair, when I wake up to the sound of coughing. It's Maggie Willis.

"You okay?" I ask.

"Yeah," she says between coughs. "I didn't smoke at all in county. I just had my first cigarette since I got out. I should have left them alone."

I sit up and look at her. "How long have you been smoking?"

"About three years." She's curled up, looking toward the wall.

"Jesus. Don't you have parents?" The words spill out and I wish I could shove them back in.

"I have a mom. When she feels like it."

"Sorry. None of my business."

"Yeah," she says and turns toward me.

"Let's go downstairs and make breakfast. You haven't eaten since you've been here." I get up and stretch. "You haven't even left this room."

I wonder if she's afraid of freedom or too depressed to care that she's free. She's still locked up like I was those first few days.

Vangie Ann would know what to do. I have to find her. Maybe knowing that she's needed will give her a reason to get sober again. Surely V doesn't trust me with all her business.

"Okay," she says, but doesn't move. "I'll be down in a minute."

I sit on the edge of her bed. "Maggie, I know it's rough at first. It will do you some good to get up and take a nice warm shower. All by yourself without the worry of anyone bothering you. You'll be surprised by how much better that makes you feel."

She sits up and looks at me, really looks at me for the first time. "Okay." She swings around and puts her feet on the floor. "Where are the towels?"

* * *

"Do you know this Gabe somebody who Vangie Ann might be shacked up with?" I'm sitting at the table with Tilly, sipping coffee and waiting for the canned cinnamon rolls to bake.

"I don't know everybody who does meth, you know." She smirks over the top of her cup and takes a sip. She raises her eyebrows and puts the cup down. "Wait. Does he have a goatee?"

"I don't know."

"I might know this guy. I think I was in rehab with a Gabe a few years ago. Real hot thing, gorgeous face and a body like Marky Mark." She picks the cup up again. "That doesn't help you, though."

Maggie walks in. Her hair is dripping onto her dingy white, shapeless t-shirt. Bruised legs stick out of her cut-offs.

"Hi. I'm Tilly." Tilly gives a little wave.

Maggie nods at her and says, "Maggie."

"Do you drink coffee, Maggie?" I ask.

"No." She shakes her head and tiny droplets of water fall to the floor. "Do you have any Cokes?"

"Yeah. Regular or diet?" I stand and open the refrigerator door.

"Regular," then, "please," as an afterthought. She sits at the table across from Tilly.

I put the can in front of her and pull the cinnamon rolls out of the oven. They're done, almost too much, but I caught them before they were too far gone. I did it: I made breakfast. My markers of success are pitiful.

There's a banging at the door before I can give it too much thought. I have a moment of panic: is it the police to tell me Vangie Ann is dead? Is it Dana's nasty-ass husband again?

No need to stay in suspense. I look out the peephole to see Lucinda. Oh, shit. I open the door.

"Where is she?" Lucinda pushes past me and shouts up the stairs. "Vangie Ann!"

"She's not here, Lucinda."

"I know it was her. You tell her when you see her." Lucinda is pointing at my face. Her nostrils are flared like a horse's.

"I don't know what you're talking about." I speak slowly, evenly, hoping to calm her down and not get myself riled up.

Lucinda's jaw softens and she lowers her hand. "I saw your sister last night. She tried to break in to my house. She didn't know I was home. She tried to steal from me."

"I'm sorry," I say. It's not that I don't believe Lucinda, but I can't imagine my sister stealing from her. "She left two days ago."

"She's back on the crystal, isn't she?" Lucinda's nodding as she asks.

"Yeah. Do you know where I can find her? I think she's with a guy named Gabe."

Lucinda nods and says, "Come on, let's go."

I run upstairs for a pair of flip-flops and follow Lucinda's hairspray-and-nicotine cloud outside. We climb into her Cadillac. Even though it's only mid-morning, her car already feels like an oven.

Lucinda opens the glove box and pulls out a small pistol. "Do you remember how to shoot?"

My stomach lurches as she places the pistol in my palm. It's warm and hard, and much heavier than it looks. "What the hell are you doing, Lucinda? I'm in enough trouble already. I can't have a gun."

"Well, don't tell anyone else that, and we'll be fine." She lights a cigarette and starts the car. "Geez. You'll screw Wayne but you flip out about holding a gun for a second. Pretty choosey about what you'll avoid for jail."

My dad taught me and Vangie Ann how to shoot before we were in the double-digits. It's a rite of passage around here. But I haven't touched a gun since high school.

"I don't even remember how to use one of these things. It's been too long." I check the safety, wipe my prints from the gun and let it rest on my lap. "Do you know where we're going?"

"Of course." She flicks ashes out the window. "That fucker lives in those shitty apartments by the railroad tracks. He moved away after he got clean. He came back a few months ago. I've been keeping tabs on him in case something like this happened."

I don't know how to respond. Lucinda had been watching out for Vangie Ann all this time, even though she doesn't owe us anything. She's not our blood kin, and she's not responsible to our dad anymore.

I look down at her pistol resting in my lap. It's silver and shiny. It probably hasn't been fired very many times.

Lucinda doesn't have time to finish her cigarette before we arrive at the sad little apartment complex. The outside is covered in wood siding, painted brown decades ago, neglected not long after. The roof is missing tiles and the yard is overgrown. The cars in the parking lot are either very old with faded paint, or new with dark tinted windows and gold rims. Lucinda grabs the pistol from my lap after I make no move to pick it up.

I follow Lucinda up a chipped cement stairwell. My nerves are jumping, and I remind myself that I've been through worse. But this isn't just about me. This is my entire family.

"Here we are," she says as she leads me to a small breezeway. I can smell marijuana and fried food. I can't identify which apartment the smells are coming from, or even if they're both coming from the same one.

Lucinda balls up her fist and bangs on a door that has the letter "H" fastened at eye level. A surprisingly handsome man jerks the door open. He's wearing a gray t-shirt and long khaki shorts. Tattoos cover his arms and he has a neatly trimmed beard. He leans against the open door and doesn't invite us in.

"Where is she, Gabe?" Lucinda asks.

"She left." His eyes dart to me. "Who are you?"

"I'm Vangie Ann's sister."

"Cass?" he asks.

"Yeah."

He nods like he knows everything about me, and maybe he does. I imagine the two of them up all night talking, the talk migrating to family, maybe even childhood. Conversations go everywhere when the hours are endless.

His eyes are dark and piercing. Those eyes that look through people like they see more than most. I can understand why Vangie Ann would keep going back to him. Even though he's a tweaker, he has a sexual intensity in his gaze mixed with a kindness in his face that makes him irresistible. Or maybe I'm just horny again already. I really need to get a boyfriend before I do something else stupid.

I look past him into the living room. The shades are drawn, and the sparse sunlight peeking through only highlights the cigarette smoke and dust in the small, dingy room. A huge overflowing ceramic ashtray sits on a squat glass coffee table on the threadbare carpet. Other than more remote controls than I can bother counting, a brown velour couch leftover from another decade, and a TV, there doesn't seem to be much else in the room.

"I don't know where she went. I ran out of drugs." He shrugs. "She left last night. Said she knew somewhere to get more."

Lucinda takes the pistol from her purse and points it at Gabe. I jump back a few steps but he doesn't flinch, he just rolls his eyes.

"If you're lying," she stares at him in those eyes for a couple of beats, "I'll shoot your nuts off."

Gabe sighs like they've been through this before. "I'm not lying, Lucinda. Now leave before I call the cops. I'm sure this is a parole violation for Cass, so get out of here."

She relaxes her arm so the pistol points at the ground. "Let us in. I want to look around."

"Hell no."

"We won't leave until we know she's not here." The thought of leaving when my sister could be only a few feet away in his bedroom forces my feet to plant firmly in front of this man, this handsome meth-head, and I cut my eyes purposefully toward Lucinda's silver pistol.

Gabe looks at me. His expression doesn't change.

"Please," I say.

He opens the door all the way. "Fine. Make it quick and don't touch anything."

"Thank you," I say.

Lucinda charges in and I follow, both of us knocking against Gabe as we enter. He closes the door behind us and I feel trapped inside the tiny, dirty apartment.

I glance into the kitchen. There's no need to investigate, as there's no closet or any other place to hide. It's a standard apartment galley kitchen with beige countertops. There are dirty dishes in the sink and beer bottles on the countertops. The garbage is overflowing and the floor is covered in a film of dirt and crumbs.

"I thought tweakers got bored and cleaned stuff," I say even though I don't mean to.

"They start that way, all energized and happy. But then it goes wrong," Lucinda says, shaking her head.

"Hey. It's not like I knew I would have two women barging in demanding to look around today," Gabe says. He motions for us to keep moving. "And I'm not a tweaker. I relapsed for a couple of days. I'm done."

"Whatever," Lucinda says under her breath. The gun is still dangling in her hand in case she decides she still might want to shoot him.

We walk down a short hallway. I turn left into a bathroom, while Lucinda and Gabe turn right into a bedroom. I open a mildewed shower curtain to a bathtub that holds a few wet towels, but not my sister. The countertop holds evidence of her recent presence: a small pink hairbrush she always keeps in her purse. I can't imagine how messed up she must be to leave without it. I grab the brush and squeeze it against my palms. Some of V's blond hairs are wrapped around the plastic spokes.

I close my eyes, hoping to catch some glimpse of Vangie Ann. Of course I don't. I hold the hairbrush in my left hand and walk out into the breezeway. Lucinda comes out about thirty seconds later.

Gabe stands against the doorframe, waiting for us to walk away.

"Nice to meet you," I say and then my cheeks turn red. Why would I say that in this situation?

He winks and says, "You, too." Gabe closes the door. I can hear two locks click into place.

"What now?" I ask as we walk back to the car.

"I don't know. The last time she got mixed up in drugs it was only Gabe." She lights another cigarette. "Want to get something to eat?"

"No, thanks. I need to get back to the House. I have to take care of things with V out."

Lucinda nods and starts the car.

"Wait!" I say and open the door. "I forgot something."

"What?"

Instead of answering I dash up the stairs. I knock on Gabe's door.

"Go away," he says from behind the closed door.

"It's Cass. Let me in."

"I know it's Cass. Go the fuck away." His voice comes out as a muffled yell.

"Lucinda's in the car. I just need to ask you one thing." I feel like a dipshit talking to a closed door.

"What?" He jerks the door open and I stumble in. I hadn't realized I was leaning on the door.

"Can you get me some weed?"

"Are you fucking serious?" He's smiling like I brought him a present.

"Yeah. I need to get it for a friend and I don't know who to ask." I'm trying my best to look charming, but I probably look crazy with my eyes wide and smile broad.

"Get the fuck out of here, Cass." He grabs my shoulders and nudges me out the door. Not quite a push but just enough that I can feel the pressure from his hands on my shoulders. It feels good.

Before I have time to say anything else, he closes the door behind me.

Chapter 25

My dad drove an old GMC pickup until the day he died. Lucinda doesn't have the heart to sell it, so I get to borrow it for a while. I never realized what a relief it would be to have Lucinda in my corner. And she wouldn't even know I needed her if Vangie Ann hadn't tried to rip her off. I'm not sure if it's irony or dumb luck.

I park the white truck in the driveway of the Blankenship House and make my way to the front door. I stop at the mailbox first. I don't have to open the envelopes to know they hold bad news. Past due notices are menacing even on the envelopes.

The grass needs to be mowed, and I'm not sure if I need to do that or if V has someone she calls for that.

I find Sonya and Maggie in the living room watching TV. "Hey Sonya, who mows the lawn?" I ask.

She looks up from the soap opera. "We take turns. I'll do it in the morning when it's not so hot. Okay?"

Maggie doesn't look away from the television, but at least she's not holed up in the bedroom.

"That'd be great. Thanks."

"Any luck?" Sonya asks.

"No," I say and shake my head. "She left the guy's house last night."

"Sorry," she says, and I can tell she means it.

I walk in into the kitchen. There's a note on the countertop. "Cass—Melody called. Come to the hospital. Room 2471." Tilly's name is scribbled at the bottom.

The paper is small and square and terrifying. I don't want to face Melody and my dying Aunt Rita. But I know I have to. Melody is giving me a chance to do right by the family, and I can't let her down.

"Sonya, Maggie," I say as I go back into the living room.

"Yeah?" Sonya asks. Maggie looks up this time and I find it more comforting than I probably should. I remember that I haven't read her file yet. I don't even know why she's here.

"Can you guys start dinner if I'm not back in a couple of hours? I have to go see my aunt in the hospital."

"Sure. What do you want us to do?" Sonya asks.

"Well, there's some chicken if you know how to fry it or something. There's also stuff to make tacos. It's up to you."

Sonya responds with a blank stare. Maybe it's having a choice that's putting her off.

"I can fry chicken," Maggie says quietly. "Do we have any potatoes to mash?"

"Yeah. They're in the pantry." I smile at her and she smiles back before turning her attention back to the TV. Warmth spreads through my stomach, and my worries dissipate for a beat. "Are the others here?"

"Yeah. Dana and Troy are in the backyard and Tilly's upstairs," Sonya says.

"Okay. I'll be back as soon as I can." I survey the two women sitting in the tatty velour recliners. The hooker with wiry hair and the juvenile delinquent, both with the never-mending broken heart that comes from a bad childhood. The pain we share widens the lens and puts us all in the same frame. These are my people now.

***

The hospital smells like every other damned hospital I've ever been to. Disinfectant and illness, babies and old people. Orange tape lines the green tiled floor. Nurses and doctors move around the space, some with urgency, others languidly while reading charts. I make my way to room 2471 slowly, delaying the inevitable.

The door is open a few inches. I open it the rest of the way and walk in. Aunt Rita is alone and asleep. She looks frail and ghostly white. Aunt Rita's not young, but she's not old enough to be in this bed.

I stand beside the bed and touch her hand. Her skin feels too thin. Her face is much older than I remember. I'm not sure if it's because it's been so long or because she's so sick. Probably both.

"You're here," Melody says as she walks in.

"How's she doing?"

"Really bad," she whispers. "The doctors don't reckon she'll make it through the night." Melody pulls the edge of the blanket around her mother's feet and tucks it beneath them.

"Thank you for calling me," I say.

"We're family." She doesn't look at me. "I feel bad about you getting arrested."

"It's okay. I guess I deserved it."

"Yeah. You did." Melody crosses the room and sits in the chair at the window.

"Did you put TJ up to it?"

"Nobody puts TJ up to anything." She looks down at her mother and looks back to me. "I thought Vangie Ann would be with you."

I look down at Aunt Rita. Her hair needs to be smoothed but I don't know if I should do it in front of Melody.

"She's been gone a couple of days. Don't know where."

"Oh."

The judgment on her face is evident. Melody's never been in trouble, never struggled with terrible decisions that change lives forever. Right and wrong have always been as clear to her as night and day, and she doesn't get hung up in twilight like some of us.

"I don't suppose you'd know where she is?" It's a long shot, but there's nothing to lose.

"You think she's back on meth?"

Maybe if I don't say the words it won't be so bad, so I only nod.

"Have you checked with TJ?" She looks out the window and then turns back toward me.

"No. They barely know each other."

"If she's looking for drugs, they may have crossed paths. Want me to call him?"

My sister being with TJ wasn't a possibility that had crossed my mind. He has nothing to do with her life. She didn't even want him on her porch.

"Mel—dy," Aunt Rita says. Her voice is coarse and her eyes are only open in slits.

Melody stands and walks to the bed.

"Hi, Aunt Rita," I say and touch her thin-skinned hand once again.

She opens her eyes all the way. "Cass? When did you get out?" It takes a while for her to get the words out.

"A few weeks ago."

"You look good." Aunt Rita tries to smile, but it's too much work.

"You do, too."

"Don't lie to a dying woman, Cass." Her words are becoming more fluid. "It's bad karma."

Melody strokes Aunt Rita's hair with her palm, and I release a breath I didn't realize I was holding. "Mama, do you need anything?"

Aunt Rita answers with a cough and closes her eyes again. Melody and I remain silent for a minute, waiting to see if she's asleep.

"She does that a lot," Melody says. Her eyes fill with tears and she goes back to her window seat.

"I'm sorry, Melody." I join her on the window.

"I'm losing everything." She stares into the parking lot. "My mom, my husband."

"You don't have to lose Wayne." I put my hand on her shoulder and she doesn't pull away. "Don't let what we did ruin your marriage. It shouldn't have happened. You guys can move on from this."

"He's different now, Cass. It's not just about having sex with you." Melody looks at me as a tear falls from her left eye and cuts a path through her makeup. She wipes the tear with her thumb. "There's a division between us. There's been a shift. I don't know if we can fix this."

"You can. I'm sure of it." I'm not sure. I know nothing about long-term relationships in the real world, but I had to say something.

"Well, at least you're out of prison. Right?" She turns back to the parking lot and falls silent.

The only sound in the room is Aunt Rita breathing heavily in and out, in and out.

Chapter 26

Margaret Amber Willis: the manila envelope is thin. The system hasn't defined her yet.

She's a high school dropout who was raised by her grandmother. Maggie served four months in county for weed and ecstasy before joining us at the Blankenship House. Her psych evaluation is longer than I would have expected at her age.

"What are you doing?" Maggie's standing in front me. I didn't hear her walk into the bedroom. No one could sneak up on me in prison. I'm losing my edge.

"I'm reading your file. I was supposed to do it right away, but I forgot." I put the papers back on the bed. "Do you want to read it?"

Maggie sits down on the bed and grabs one of the papers. Her bottom lip trembles as she reads. I put my arm around her shoulders and pull her close. She relaxes against me.

"They weren't my drugs. Danielle stuck them in my purse when we got pulled over." She wipes a tear. "No one believed me. She could afford a lawyer, and I couldn't."

"Danielle Talbot?"

"Yeah. We were best friends. Some friend she turned out to be."

"That's crazy," I say. But really it's not. It's just small-town dynamics.

"I dated her brother, too."

"Gross. I mean, really?"

Maggie starts to shake and shudder. Her tears soak through my shirt to my skin. I squeeze her tighter. She wipes her eyes with both hands and pulls away.

"She was my best friend. It still sucks that she'd do that to me." She wipes her palms on her jeans shorts.

"I'm sorry, Maggie. You're so young. You can get past this."

"Can I, Cass? I'm a dropout with a record. My mom ain't worth a shit, and I don't even know where my dad lives. Girls like me, we're fucked before we're fourteen." Maggie looks at the wall and shakes her head. "I'm never going to get out of this shit town."

"It happens. People fuck us over." I grab her hand, and she turns to look at me. "You have to decide you want to pull yourself up."

Maggie smiles and nods. "I know. GED, right?"

"Well, yeah. But other stuff, too. We can help each other out. I'm trying to get my shit together, too. You help me, and I'll help you."

"Oh!" She raises her eyebrows and sits up straight. "I came up here because Danielle is downstairs to see you."

I gather Maggie's papers and put them in the envelope. "Do you want to look at any more of this?" I make a mental note to finish reading the papers later.

"No. I think it will just make me sad." She smiles and gets up. "I'm going to go for a walk. I think I need some fresh air."

We walk down the stairs together. Maggie's moving slow like she's packing a heavy burden.

Danielle's sitting in the front room. Her feet are curled up beneath her, and she's pushing buttons on her cell phone.

"Hi, Danielle." I sit on the velour sofa.

She drops the phone in her lap, puts her feet on the floor and clasps her hands together. "Hi. Did Melody call you yet?"

"You put your drugs in Maggie's purse." It's not a question. I don't want to give her the chance to deny it.

Danielle sighs and leans forward. "Grandma Rita died early this morning." She kind of smiles, kind of frowns. It turns out to be an accidental smirk.

"I'm sorry, Danielle." A knot forms in my throat, but choke it down. I put my hands over Danielle's. It's the wrong time to hurl accusations at her.

"Do you know that I never hear from my Mom's mom?" She pulls a tissue from her back shorts pocket. "I shouldn't say 'never.' She sends a birthday card every year. She calls every six months or so. But she only lives a couple of hours away. I haven't seen her in five years."

"That's…well, I don't know what to say." And I don't. There's not enough of my family left to make me feel rejected.

"Grandma Rita's at peace now, right?" Danielle dabs the tissue under her eyes. Black specs of mascara appear on the white paper.

"Yeah. She's at peace." I hope I'm not lying to the poor girl. But if I am lying, I suppose it's a low risk lie.

* * *

Our aunt is dead and my sister is still missing. Aunt Rita's death proposed the possibility that Vangie Ann would find her way home to mourn and to be with me, but so far there hasn't been hide nor hair of her. Maybe if I can get my inheritance she'll rush home to claim the money I promised her.

Her absence is becoming more frightening. Southern folks love death. Well, maybe not love it, but it gives us reason to gather in fellowship. We mourn and grieve, cry and wail. Then we pray, dab our eyes, and eat until we pass out. It's a social event that works only on God's timing. Nothing short of prison can keep us from funerals and the accompanying festivities.

Three days after Aunt Rita died, I'm standing at the back of the church as we pray and cry over the "charitable, God-fearing woman." By the time I arrived at the church, the only available seat close to the front was too near Wayne and Melody, so I figured far away was the only option. Danielle is wedged under her dad's arm, but TJ is absent. Tiffany is with them, her hair just as short as Melody had feared.

Rows of sobbing women and stoic men line the chronically musty church. It looks and smells like every funeral for a man or woman of a certain age who died of natural causes. Peaceful prayers and light sobbing. Men softly saying "amen" along with the pastor.

The younger the dead person, the louder the sobs. A baby will bring wails. The more violent or unexpected the cause of death, the more spectacular the show of grief that is allowed. White Christian folk only grieve loudly when it's appropriate. Too much grieving questions God's will, and even a funeral isn't the time for that.

But this death was just a white-bread, natural-cause death in advancing age. Sure Aunt Rita wasn't nursing home old, but she certainly wasn't young. The oldest of this bunch probably envy her for getting out before things really started breaking down.

When we make our way to the graveside, I hide behind a big tree to avoid the people I'm not prepared to deal with. Distant family who want to invite me to church, who'll pray away my iniquities if I only give them a chance. Folks I avoided long before prison and folks I'll continue to avoid.

The sun is nearly unbearable and I'm so thankful for the tree that I have commandeered as my own.

When the place has cleared out, I approach the grave and kneel beside it. I'm wearing one of Vangie Ann's dresses: a black tube dress that's too short for me. I found a white shrug to put over it so I don't look completely slutty. But bending down is a struggle. I get to my knees and the sun beats down on the back of my neck, laid bare because my hair is thrown on top of my head in my effort to look presentable.

"I can almost see your snatch." Melody is standing beside me, looking down at me like I'm homeless. I've let someone else sneak up on me. My focus is fading too fast.

"Well, lucky you." I stand up and put my arm around her. It's a normal funeral gesture, but it feels foreign and stupid. "I thought I was the only one here."

"I came back to be alone." She looks into the hole at the lavish casket. Roses cover the lacquered top.

"Sorry." My arm drops to my side. "I can leave if you want."

"It's okay." Melody crosses her arms and turns to me. "I need to talk to you anyway. Vangie Ann's with TJ. I talked to him this morning."

I don't know why exactly, but my stomach turns and leaps to my throat. "Thanks for letting me know. Are they at his house?"

"Yeah, but not a house. He lives in a trailer." Her eyes go down to my borrowed black platform sandals and back up to the white shrug. She's judging me, even here at her mother's grave, probably wondering if Wayne saw me in this too-short dress. "It's so weird, isn't it? I hope they're not screwin'. Vangie Ann's old enough to be his mother."

"That hadn't crossed my mind. Nasty." I should be glad to know she's alive and where she is. This should be a relief. But if feels like doom. It feels like she's lost to an unknown force.

"He lives off Highway 5, just past the chicken plant. There's a small trailer park there. TJ's place is the fourth on the right. You know where to look?"

I nod. "I just want my sister." A tear rolls down my cheek. I'm selfish to leach off her grief. "I'm sorry. I'm so sorry." I shake my head and more tears fall.

Melody wraps her arms around me and it feels so perfect for two beats, then she rips her arms away. She glares at me for a second before turning on her heel.

I drop back to my knees and let the tears fall. They form tiny puddles in the dry, hot dirt.

Get it out, all of it. This is the last of the tears. It's time to be strong. No one else is going to do it for me.

Chapter 27

Tilly's on the porch smoking a cigarette. She narrows her eyes when she sees me walk up the steps.

"Where you been?"

"My aunt's funeral."

"Oh, right. Sorry." She looks down and takes a deep drag of her smoke. "Was Vangie Ann there?"

I shake my head slowly and sit in the wicker chair next to Tilly. "I know where she is, though."

"Yeah. I do, too." She exhales a billow of smoke and puts the cigarette butt in a soda can that sits at her feet. "Heard about it today."

"How did you hear about it?"

"Word in the yard." Tilly winks at me. "I still talk to some of my friends from the druggie days. I know I shouldn't. I'm trying to cut them out of my life, but it's hard to dump everyone at once."

"How well do you actually know TJ?"

She shakes her head and lets out one loud laugh, a resounding "Ha!" Then she lights another cigarette. "We've met a time or two. But really, I only know him by reputation. And his reputation ain't nothing good."

"I wouldn't think so after seeing him. That kid is messed up."

She takes a drag and looks at me. "It's more than that. There's been a rumor for years that TJ killed his mama. And if he did, he'll kill you for trying to find the truth."

"Why didn't you tell me about the rumor before?"

"Because it's just a rumor." Tilly squints through her cigarette smoke. "But he might have, and he's fucking your sister right now."

The thought sends a shudder through my stomach. "Gross, Tilly." I cross my arms and lean forward.

Tilly stares toward the street for a minute, the cigarette perched between her lips the entire time. She takes a drag and removes the cigarette. "He's trying to get at you."

Frustration rolls in my bones and grips my nerves. I need to take up smoking. "It's working."

Tilly raises her eyebrows, and she chuckles a little.

I stand up and walk toward the door. "I have to go to the trailer park and find my sister. But first, I have to change out of this fucking tube dress."

* * *

The smell of death fills the cab of the truck as I pull into the trailer park. That stench is rotten, filthy, and profitable. The plant turns out hundreds of thousands of chickens a week, bigger and fatter every year so they're worth more money. And these people live in the hormone-laden runoff from the death plant.

The trailer is unlocked, so I let myself in after knocking a couple of times. A spoon and needle are on the coffee table, but the trailer is void of human life. TJ and Vangie Ann have vanished. Maybe they've gone to buy cigarettes, maybe they've left for Mexico. But the window air conditioning unit is on, so they probably haven't gone far.

An overwhelming helplessness weighs me down, and I sit on the filthy couch that smells like a dive bar early in the morning. A cockroach greets my thigh, and I jump to my feet. Between the rotten smell of the nearby chicken plant, the couch, and the roach, I would probably throw up if I had eaten anything yet today.

Vangie Ann's tolerance for filth when she is using shocks and scares me.

I walk outside and sit on the cinder blocks that serve as front steps. The sun beats down on my arms and legs, and I wish I had put on sunscreen.

Sweat pours down my face and back for forty-five minutes. My skin bakes, and I'm ready to give up.

I'm digging for a piece of paper and pen in my purse when a white Honda Civic pulls up. I stand up as Tiffany gets out of the car.

"Cass!" She smiles as she walks toward me.

"Hey, Tiffany." I pull her in a hug that's not quite awkward, yet not quite warm. "Sorry about your mom."

She pulls away and I can see that there are tears in her eyes. Tiffany sniffs and blinks, and the tears disappear.

"Thanks." She shrugs. "I should have been to visit her more. I just thought we had more time."

Her words make me think of my dad, and the goodbye we'll never have. I push the memory of his face down, far away.

"What are you doing here?" she asks.

"I'm looking for Vangie Ann."

"Oh." She sits down on the cinderblock steps, and I sit beside her. "I'm looking for TJ. I want to give him shit for not showing up to Mom's funeral."

My face must register confusion, because she adds, "I used to babysit him and Danielle. Up until I came out and Melody decided I was a bad influence."

I roll my eyes at the last statement. "I didn't know. Makes sense that you would have, though."

"What a mess that kid turned out to be. I promise none of that was my fault." Tiffany smiles with half her mouth. "Nobody's home?"

"Nope. I'm about to give up." I stand up. "Are you sticking around town for a while?"

"Hell no. I'm hitting the road right now." She stands and we share another weird hug. "It was good to see you. I'm glad you're free."

Free. Sure the fuck doesn't feel like it. "Thanks, Tiffany. Keep in touch."

"You bet." She waves as she gets in the car.

We both know we won't keep in touch. We never have before. Why start now? I take the pen and paper inside and get to work.

Dear V,

We buried Aunt Rita today. You weren't there and you should have been. Don't turn your back on what little family we have left. I know, I know, hypocritical coming from me. But that's what you're for. You're better at family things.

The fundraiser is coming up and we need you. The Blankenship House is your baby. Don't let us do this without you.

There's a new girl at the House. Her name is Maggie. She's only eighteen. I'm trying my best with her, but I need your help.

Come home. We'll get you the help you need and you can put this behind you. This isn't you. It's not too late. This isn't the life you want. We all miss you.

I love you, but you're being a selfish cunt.

Cass

I put the letter on the coffee table. I grab the needle and spoon and throw them in the trash. Just like when I was little and threw away my dad's cigarettes.

Wayne pulls up in his pickup just as I'm walking out of the trailer door. He's still in his funeral clothes: a button-down shirt and slacks. He's even wearing a tie. It's the most dressed up I've ever seen him.

"Hi," I say.

"Hey." He walks toward me, but stops about six feet away.

I walk down the cinder block steps, but maintain my distance.

"Nobody's home." I pull my sunglasses from the front of my t-shirt and put them on my face.

"Figures." He crosses his arms and looks from side to side. "Sorry that TJ turned you in. Are you in trouble?"

"My parole has been extended, and I can't leave the state like I planned."

"I really am sorry."

"Well, I shouldn't have slept with you. Lesson learned." My face is sweating, and my sunglasses are starting to slide down my nose.

"Don't give up on Vangie Ann. You have to keep trying to save her."

"I'll do everything I can."

"It's easier to give up than you think. It's tiring to love someone who's an addict." His arms drop to his sides. "I tried to save Judith. I really did. But I pushed her away and now she's dead. So I didn't try so hard to save TJ. And he's a mess. Danielle ain't doing too great, either. There's no way to win."

"I won't give up on her, Wayne. I couldn't if I wanted to."

Wayne steps toward me with his arms out. I shake my head and he backs up.

"Sorry," he says.

"It's okay. I just can't touch you. It'll hurt too much." I push my sunglasses up on my nose.

"Lately everything hurts too much." Wayne turns around and walks to his truck. "Take care of yourself, Cass."

"You, too." I stand with my feet planted until he's out of the driveway.

All the way back to the House I look for TJ's truck. But I don't see him or my sister. It's a half-hour drive, a long time to worry about whether or not I should have waited a little longer. What if it was my last chance to see my sister? If she's using needles, she's playing with her life.

I dismiss the thought as quickly as it comes. I can't let the fear of what might happen to her take over. It will become all-consuming if I let it.

Chapter 28

Sonya and Tilly are smoking on the porch when I get back to the House. There's always somebody on the porch, just like an old-timey brothel.

"Did you find her?" Tilly squints at me, and I wonder why she's not wearing sunglasses.

"No. They weren't there."

"Well, you know what they say. Two tears in a bucket, motherfuck it," Sonya says and brings a cigarette to her lips.

"Who says that?" Tilly asks.

"They do," Sonya says through a plume of smoke.

"I've never heard that," I say.

Sonya shrugs. "Your PO came around looking for you. He's sure a good-looking fella. My probation officer looks like Don Rickles."

"Mine looks like that big black woman from *Gimme a Break*. Remember that show?" Tilly chuckles and takes a drag.

It's not really that funny, but I laugh anyway. And once I start, I can't stop. The laughter takes over and my body convulses for at least two minutes. It feels wonderful, orgasmic.

"That was a good show," I say with a sigh once I'm able to speak.

"Sure was," Tilly says. Her smile is huge.

"Where's Maggie?" I ask, suddenly noticing her absence.

"Napping. That girl naps a lot." Tilly shrugs and adds, "Teenagers."

The door flies open and Dana emerges with her brown tweed suitcase. Troy trails her, trying his best to haul a fake leather blue suitcase. He has his elbows pulled up to his chin for leverage.

Dana drops her suitcase on the porch with a thud and wipes the sweat from her forehead with the back of her hand. She squints into the street.

"Anybody seen Elijah?" she asks.

"Not had the pleasure today," Tilly says.

Dana turns to me. "Me and Troy're leaving. Elijah needs help with the house and he's over his little hissy fit about what I did."

"Hissy fit? Half of your face was bruised." I know I should tone down my words for Troy's sake, but there's no time. And a boy like him deserves honesty anyway.

"Well. We're going home no matter what your opinion is. Without Evangeline here, it just feels like we're hanging out at a cheap hotel and I don't see the point." She moves her head from side to side as she says the words. I know it's supposed to punctuate the words as an insult, but it just makes her look like a dipshit.

"Just make sure to keep Troy out of the line of fire, okay?" I say. Sonya raises her eyebrows at me like I've crossed the line. But my words are of little consequence in this situation.

Dana takes a step toward me and a car horn blows from the street. The bastard doesn't even bother getting his greasy ass out of the car.

She grunts as she picks up her brown suitcase and turns toward the rusty beige car that was probably a luxury ride fifteen years ago.

I turn to Troy and bend down. "Take care of yourself, kid. You call me if you need help."

He nods and smiles before wobbling down the steps with the suitcase pulled up to his neck.

A heavy blanket of sadness covers me as the car pulls away from the curb. Their leaving feels like a failure, and I'm afraid of what will happen to them with Elijah. Of course, they were with him a long time before he punched her in the face. And I only knew her a couple of days before almost hitting her.

"It's just us, girls. How the hell are we going to pull off this fundraiser?" Tilly asks.

"We can postpone," I say. Nothing would make me happier. Well, nothing other than my sister coming home safe and my inheritance coming through.

"I don't think we can," Sonya says. "I have the caterer booked at a special charity rate. I hate to screw that up by moving it around. Plus I got a bluegrass band that's playing for free because they'll be in town playing a gig later that night at Slick's."

The words seem like a foreign language coming from her mouth. It takes a second for me to process everything. But as the longest resident, she has the most invested. This has become her home.

"How did you manage all that?" I ask.

"I've been staying busy while you've been dealing with your drama." Sonya smiles and winks. "Plus, I have connections. If you could learn guitar from fucking musicians, I'd be goddamn virtuoso."

"Well, we won't postpone then. Maybe we can pull this off." And I almost believe it.

Chapter 29

Dear Tabitha,

Everything's gone to shit. I can't find my sister. She's on drugs again. I could have gone back to prison for sleeping with that asshole Wayne, but instead I'm stuck here when I should be on my way to California. By the way—he didn't kill Judith. It's a regular whodunit around here.

I'm running the House without Vangie Ann, and one of the ladies returned to her abusive husband over staying here today.

I'm fucking everything up.

Love,
Cass

I read the letter and tear it up. It's not fair to dump on Tabitha like that. There's a crisp sheet of paper in front of me, and I'm ready to tell her I miss her and keep my whining to myself, when someone knocks on the bedroom door. The door opens two seconds later and Tilly barges in.

"What's up with Maggie?" Tilly plops down on Maggie's bed.

"What do you mean?"

"She's getting fat but she doesn't eat much." Tilly crosses her arms. Her face reflects excitement—that damned glow of gossip. "I swear she's put on five pounds in the last two days."

"Maybe she's eating in private. People do that." The page in my lap is still empty, and I want to be alone for a few more minutes. I tilt my head toward the door, and Tilly stomps out.

Dear Tabitha,

I've destroyed everything in my wake, a regular tsunami of fuckupedness.

I wad the paper up and throw it on the floor. Why is this so difficult? I pull a deep breath into my lungs and think about Tabitha's smile. How do I put that into words?

Before the words can form, Maggie bursts through the door and flops down on the bed. She looks puffy and miserable.

"Are you okay, Maggie?"

"No. I don't feel good." She curls up into the fetal position and turns away from me. "It's too hot."

"Do you need anything?"

"Do we have any ginger ale?" Her voice is a whimper.

"I'll go check."

Tilly and Sonya are huddled in the hallway. They follow me down to the kitchen.

"Something's going on with that girl," Sonya says and raises her eyebrows, which are four shades darker than her hair. "She looks ten pounds heavier since she got here."

"So? She's stressed. Leave her alone." The cabinets and refrigerator offer a variety of sodas, but no ginger ale. "She said she's too hot."

"Think, Cass. Little Maggie is about to become a little mama." Tilly crosses her arms and stands in front of me. "What did her file say?"

"Her file didn't say anything about her being pregnant. Or at least the part I read didn't." Ice cubes in a big plastic cup and four different cans of soda. Surely something will work for her.

"You can't be that naïve." Sonya grabs two of the cans from me. "It's August and she's pregnant. Of course she's too hot."

"Shit. What if she is pregnant? I don't know what to do with that." A baby in the House. I didn't sign up for this.

"She'll have to move on. We don't need a baby here." Tilly takes a cloth from the drawer and wets it under the tap. "Let's take this up, too. It's cold."

"Maggie's not here by choice, Tilly. It was court-ordered." Looks like we have everything we need to take care of an overheated girl. I start walking up the stairs and the other two follow. I knock gently when we get to the top even though it's my room, too.

"Come in," Maggie answers. Her voice is weak.

We enter the room in a single file, all of us bearing gifts like a distorted version of the three wise men. Maggie sits up and looks at us as if we're interrupting something.

"There's no ginger ale, so I brought you some other choices and some ice." I display everything gently on the bed like I'm making an offering to an angry god.

"We also have a cold rag. Want me to run you a bath?" Tilly's voice is creepily sweet.

Maggie looks at her and slowly shakes her head "no."

Sonya sits on the bed. "Look, Maggie. We need to ask you something. We're not being nosy. But if you need our help you have to be honest with us."

"What?" Maggie asks. Her eyes are narrowed to slits.

"Are you pregnant?" The words tumble from my mouth, as words have a habit of doing.

The room is quiet and still for a second, then Maggie begins to sob like a young child. "Nobody else knows, not even my grandma." The words come out between gasps.

"Oh shit," Tilly says. "Is it too late to take care of it?"

Maggie nods and her cries grow louder.

The three of us gather around Maggie and hug her. When we pull away, her crying has become quiet tears.

"I had some prenatal care in County. But now I don't even have a doctor. And I've felt like shit the entire time."

"How far along are you, sweetie?" My voice is even and calm, the complete opposite of the way my insides feel.

"About eight months." She rubs her face with the wet rag. The motion has to feel too rough against her young skin.

"What? Eight months? You could have a baby any day now!" Tilly's eyes are huge as she stares at Maggie like she's an alien. She turns to me and says, "I went to high school with a girl who hid her pregnancy from her parents. Didn't tell them about it until she was in labor."

"I didn't mean to hide it. I just didn't know how to talk about it," Maggie says.

"You have to go to the doctor, Maggie." I rub her hair gently, trying to ignore the sweat that has left it damp.

"I don't have insurance."

"Doesn't matter when you're pregnant." Sonya's smiling at her and holding her hand. "They'll take care of you. We'll take you to get signed up for WIC. I think that's where we start."

The sobs take Maggie over again. "Nobody's ever been so nice to me before." Tears and snot roll down her face.

Tilly puts her hand on Maggie's shoulder. "You're a mess, girl."

"I'll go make some calls." Sonya stands up. "We need to get you scheduled for a doctor's appointment on the double."

"Thanks, Sonya." I know this should be my job, but I have no idea where to start. "Do you need anything else right now, Maggie?"

Maggie shakes her head. "I'm going to take a nap. I always feel better after I rest."

"Okay." I stand up and Tilly follows. We leave the room and walk down the stairs.

"Told you," Tilly says.

"How did I miss it?"

"You've kind of got some stuff going on."

"True." The clock on the wall grabs my attention. "Shit. I haven't even showered yet today."

"You need to start taking better care of yourself. When is the last time you shaved your legs? You're starting to look kind of butch." Tilly puts her hand over her mouth and then quickly removes it. "No offense, I mean. I know you used to bump tacos with that girl in prison."

I sigh loudly. "No offense taken." Being in the bathroom alone suddenly seems like a welcome reprieve.

***

"Lucinda, can you teach me how to make pancakes today?" I don't say please, can't say please. It's too draining.

"I'll be over in an hour. I'm watching my stories." She hangs up.

The doorbell rings a half hour later. I'm surprised that Lucinda is early, until I see Danielle on the porch.

"Hey," I say when I open the door.

"Hi." She smiles. "I just wanted to come over and visit. Is that okay?"

"Sure, yeah." I stand aside so she can walk in.

We're sitting at the table drinking coffee when Lucinda arrives, as promised, an hour after I called her. She floats into the Blankenship House on her Lucinda-scented cloud.

"Let's get with it. Tonight's bowling league."

"Sure."

"Any word from V?" Lucinda pulls bowls from the cabinets, at least six. She settles on two and puts the others back.

"No." Lucinda knows I wouldn't bother learning how to make pancakes if Vangie Ann was home.

"Don't just stand there." She eyes me like I'm covered in filth. "We need eggs, milk, oil, flour, sugar, baking powder, and salt. You're probably the only adult in America who doesn't know how to make pancakes."

I move around the kitchen gathering ingredients and dumping them on the counter. "I like the frozen ones. Never saw the need to make them."

"Need any help?" Danielle asks. She's flipping through a magazine at the table.

"No, thanks. I need to figure this out on my own," I say, then look at Lucinda. "Well, not completely on my own."

Lucinda gathers measuring cups. "Start with dry ingredients." She measures flour in a cup and dumps into the larger bowl.

"Should I be writing this down?"

"No. I brought you a cookbook. I left in the car, but I'll get it before I leave." She measures baking power in a tiny spoon. "Can you crack an egg?"

"Yeah."

Lucinda points to the smaller bowl. "Crack it in there and beat it with a fork. What you need to remember about Vangie Ann and all druggies is that they lose track of time like regular people do car keys or pieces of mail." She measures the sugar and hands me a small cup. "Put the oil in here and mix it with the egg."

"There's a new girl here. Her name is Maggie. She's only eighteen and she's eight months pregnant. We need Vangie Ann." There are a couple of shards of eggshell, not too difficult to pick out.

"Maggie's pregnant?" Danielle asks. "I thought she had gotten fat."

I look at Danielle, but don't respond.

"Vangie Ann isn't thinking of you right now. She probably doesn't even know it's been a week since she's been gone." Lucinda stirs the powdered mixture together. "When you first went to jail, things got really bad. Your sister was bad on drugs and decided a kitten would make her more responsible. You know, having something to take care of? That poor kitten had her full attention for about one week." Lucinda is speaking quietly, I assume to keep Danielle from hearing the entire conversation. "It was a white fluff ball of a thing and she named him Cotton. About a month or so after she got Cotton, Vangie Ann found his carcass in the laundry room."

I look up from my bowl. A gasp seems to be in order, but it doesn't materialize. Instead my jaw just hangs silently like a door on a broken hinge.

"She accidentally left him alone for two weeks. She didn't mean to leave her apartment that long, but a friend came by with some meth. They did some drugs then went to visit a friend another town over. They decided to spend the night then went to visit another friend. She simply lost track of time. And that poor kitten starved to death."

"That's terrible." I can't imagine the guilt associated with a death of a kitten. Poor V.

"Point is: bad shit happens. Did you hear about that murdered girl in Detroit? She was just working a shift at a gas station and some jerk came in and killed her." Lucinda takes my bowl and dumps it into the dried mixture.

"That sucks, but I don't see that what has to do with my sister."

"Vangie Ann is making her own choices right now. If she dies, she chose that death. Hopefully she'll come back to us safe and sound any day, any minute now." Lucinda stirs the bowl vigorously. "The batter will be lumpy. That's okay. Now put a nonstick skillet on the stove. Put some butter in it and turn on the heat."

The pans are stuffed in a cabinet next to the oven. I find what I think she's asking for and put it on the stovetop.

"Any luck figuring out who killed Judith? There's a lot of money just sitting around." Lucinda keeps stirring.

"Not really. I'm staying pretty busy trying to keep everything together around here." I grab a tub of butter from the second shelf of the refrigerator.

"That's not butter, it's margarine. Look for a stick."

A stick. There's a yellow butter stick under a glass case on the top shelf. "This?"

"Yep."

"Why does it need its own glass case? It's butter, not a museum exhibit."

"Do you feel any better about your sister? Did I make my point?" Lucinda's hands are on her hips.

"It's better that she's on meth than murdered in a Detroit gas station?" The butter knife slides off the hard stick of butter, leaving me only a chip to put into the pan.

"Well, yeah. But that's not the point. Vangie Ann is making her own choices. She's out of control right now. But even that was her choice."

Lucinda grabs a steak knife and hacks off a chunk of butter. After she turns on the heat, it starts melting in the pan immediately. "You don't want to turn the heat up too much. The butter will scorch."

"Isn't Vangie Ann even thinking about us?"

"Remember how you keep saying prison was about your life and not ours? Well, welcome to the other side of that."

Lucinda pours batter into the skillet. "You'll wait until the top starts to bubble, and then you'll flip it."

Maggie waddles into the room. The waddle that I never noticed before now. "Do I smell pancakes?"

"Yes, you do. Have a seat, young lady." Lucinda smiles at her. "I'm teaching Cass here how to make breakfast for you reprobates," she croaks.

"Lucinda!"

"Sorry. What should I have said?" The question is genuine.

"Do you want something to drink, Maggie?" There's a cup in my hand before I finish asking the question.

"Sure, thanks. A Sprite or something." Maggie yawns deeply. Now that the pregnancy is no longer a secret, it's obvious in every movement and gesture. "Sonya scheduled an appointment for me tomorrow morning at nine. Can you give me a ride?"

"I'd be happy to." I put the drink in front of Maggie and she smiles.

"Hi," Danielle says. She's staring at Maggie. "Just heard the good news."

Maggie nods at her and looks down.

"This is ready to flip. Care to do the honors?" Lucinda thrusts the spatula at me.

I nod and slide the spatula under the pancake. Lucinda stands too close, breathing on my shoulder.

"Good. Now just flip it over."

My wrist twists and the pancake lands on the other side. "It worked." Again, my markers of success mirror those of a child.

"See. Easy as can be. Pancakes are simple and delicious any time of day." She turns to the table. "Right, Maddy?"

"It's Maggie," I say.

"Right, Maggie?"

"Right." Maggie's rubbing her lower back with her palms.

"You okay, shug?" Lucinda asks.

"Yeah, just feeling a little crampy." Maggie's face scrunches a little then smooths out again.

"Do you mind letting me look at your belly?" she asks.

"Is this done, Lucinda?" I ask and grab a plate from the cabinet.

"Probably." She puts her hand on Maggie's stomach as Maggie lifts her shirt. "Are you sure you're only eight months?"

Maggie sighs. "Well, not really. I couldn't remember the date of my last period and my first ultrasound was too late to be accurate. Eight months is about right, though."

"You hid it well. Maybe because you were already a little thick. I've heard that helps a girl to not show so fast." Danielle is looking at the magazine when she speaks.

"Danielle!" I'm surprised at her rudeness, though I don't know her well enough these days to know if she's rude or not.

"I'm going to kick your ass once this baby is out of me." Maggie pulls her eyebrows together.

"Does the daddy know about this little miracle?" Danielle cocks her head to the side.

"None of your business," Maggie says.

Lucinda frowns and turns back to me. "Get that pancake on the plate."

The spatula is under the pancake again, and the pancake is on the plate. I can do this.

"You look worried," I say.

Lucinda puts her arm around my shoulders and leans into my ear. "I think she might be going into labor." She looks at Maggie and then back to me. At normal volume, she says, "Put some more butter in the pan."

My skin prickles with anxious sweat as the butter spits in the pan. "What?" I mouth to Lucinda.

"Don't worry," she whispers, "first babies usually take a really long time. If she starts hurting really bad just take her to the ER. Otherwise, just take her to the appointment in the morning. It's only sixteen hours from now. And really, what do I know?"

This is a big fucking deal. Why is Lucinda acting like it's not?

"Pour some batter in the pan, Cass. This one's all you."

Chapter 30

My sister's room smells of nicotine from the smoke that clings to her hair and attaches itself to her pillow while she sleeps. This is only the second time I've been in her room since she left, abandoning us to do drugs in whatever hovel she's found. The first time was to borrow the black dress and shoes for Aunt Rita's funeral. Sure, I looked like a hooker, but a hooker in the appropriate color for mourning.

Her bedspread is peach, a crisp cotton she must have tended to carefully to keep so spotless. It's same color as Vangie Ann's prom dress from senior year, all taffeta and bows. She looked so beautiful that night with her giant hair and blue eye shadow. I watched from the stairs as my big sister left with her date and all I could think about was what it must be like to be so glamorous. My big sister, the blonde beauty in some boy's Trans Am on the way to a dance with a theme like "Stairway to Heaven" or "A Night to Remember."

It would be great to open a window, to release the stale air that smells like Joe Camel's balls. But it's almost a hundred degrees outside today. I pull the chain that starts the lazy motion of her ceiling fan, and look around for anything that will connect me to her.

Instead of connection, I feel sweaty and light-headed. My breath starts fighting to get out. I force myself to take three deep breaths. To remind myself no matter what, I will be okay.

A jewelry box on Vangie Ann's dresser, pink and out of place in an adult's room, seems like a great place to start. I open the lid to a tiny ballerina that doesn't bother to spin. A necklace, more of a medallion with praying hands and the words "one day at a time," sits at the ballerina's feet. I pull it from the box, trace the hands with my fingertips, slide the chain around my neck, and fasten the clasp. The hands in prayer for my sister. *Please God, if you've ever cared about me at all, keep my sister alive and bring her home.*

***

"You in recovery now?" Mack points at the medallion around my neck.

My fingers wrap around it and I shake my head. "It's Vangie Ann's."

He nods. "I need you to come with me for a little bit."

I turn my head to Maggie. She's lying on the couch with her feet up, but not complaining of pain or throwing up.

"Just a sec."

Sonya and Tilly are at the kitchen table, making a list of items we need for the fundraiser that I wish wasn't happening.

"Ladies, I need to go somewhere with Mack."

Both of them raise their eyebrows.

"Can I go, too?" Sonya asks.

"It's not like that. Just keep an eye on Maggie, okay? Lucinda was worried that she could already be in labor."

"We'll be here. Leave me your truck keys just in case, but I think she's fine." Sonya turns her attention back to her list, like pregnant teenagers should cause the same amount of worry as the possibility of not having enough chips for the party. Her attitude somehow puts me at ease, as if I'm overreacting to the situation.

Mack's waiting for me on the porch, sweating in his button-down short-sleeved shirt. "Ready?"

"Yeah. I just had to let the girls know I'm leaving."

He opens the door for me when we get to his truck. No one has done that for me in more years than I care to remember.

"No fancy sedan today?" I ask.

"Nope. This is an off-the-record visit." He closes the door and walks to the driver's side.

"Where are we going?" My palms are sweating. I don't know when that started.

"There's a place out past Pleasant Fields I think you should see."

"I thought you were through with me and my drama." I'm surprised to hear those words come out in front of Mack.

He puts one of his giant hands on my leg. My heart jumps and I'm afraid to move. Before I can analyze the meaning any further, his hand is gone.

"Turns out that I really need the money."

"So you are helping me?" I ask.

"Yes." He gives me a lazy smile. "But you're getting a new parole officer in a couple of weeks. Things have crossed the line with us."

I open my mouth to argue but stop myself. It would be a waste of energy at this point, and I'm grateful for what he's giving me.

144

"Sorry, the air conditioner doesn't work." He nods toward my window, so I crank it down.

"Bad time of year for your air conditioner to break." I pull a ponytail holder from my pocket. The wind will leave my hair a tangled mess if I don't take care of it now.

"Sure is. I'm starting to realize that maybe you are innocent and did get a raw deal." Mack's looking at the road and it feels like maybe he's not talking to me. "Did you realize that the prosecuting attorney who sent you to jail was Wayne's cousin?"

"No." Why didn't I know that? Wayne and I dated for close to two years. I knew his family. Of course, a lot of folks around here have more cousins than they can count on their fingers and toes.

"Well, he was. There's nothing that can be done about that now. But I'm sure he helped push your conviction through." He turns to me and makes sure I'm looking at him. "Consider that fact when you're doing your own digging into Judith's death."

"Do you think if I can prove that someone else did it, I'll have a chance of getting my parole transferred?"

"I'm sure it would help." Mack looks straight ahead into the night sky. "Especially since you wouldn't be on parole anymore if you prove your innocence."

"I hadn't thought of that." That's an exciting revelation. "Mack, I know this is inappropriate, but I'm just curious. You never talk about your private life at all. Are you married?"

"No."

There's a little tickle of excitement in my belly. I didn't expect that. But I guess I should have.

"But I live with a woman."

"Oh." My happy tickle disappears.

He glances at me. "A lot of women attach themselves to the first man they meet out of prison. You don't have to do that with me."

I'm insulted, but I realize he knows what he's talking about. Time to move on.

"Do you have anybody close to you mixed up in drugs, now that your uncle's gone?" I immediately regret asking such a personal question, then remember that Mack knows everything about me, so I don't apologize. And hopefully it will take his mind off of my previous question.

"No. I don't have a lot of family. Just one brother. But he lives in Colorado with his wife and kids." Mack grins, damn the dimples. "He's a lawyer and made my parents grandparents. So, I'm the bad kid."

Mack's the bad kid. That rolls around in my brain, and I can't help but laugh. "Jesus, Mack. Are you serious? You're the bad kid? Your parents should spend five minutes with me or Vangie Ann. They'd have you sainted."

"It's just my mom now. Dad died a couple years ago. Heart attack." He smiles softly in a way that tells me he's dealt with it. "You're not so bad, Cass. You just have to shed this convict thing. You'll get there."

"Dad was so proud when I graduated college. Of course, he didn't say so. But I knew it. He glowed on my graduation day." An education degree. Just what Dad wanted me to get.

I don't want to continue with these thoughts that can go from happy to sad so quickly. We ride in silence for a few minutes. Mack opens his mouth to speak several times, but he can't seem to get the words out.

Then, he finally does. "When Judith died, Wayne was still the beneficiary of her life insurance."

"Well, it would make sense that he would be. He was raising their kids. She wasn't remarried." I shift in the seat so I can get a full view of him.

"When it was all said and done, Wayne and his kids inherited seven hundred and fifty thousand dollars."

"How did she have that kind of life insurance?" An unemployed tweaker had a massive policy, and I don't even have health insurance.

"Her boss at the bank never cancelled it. He paid the premium himself because he felt bad for her. I'm sorry." He glances at me.

"Why?"

"Because it must hurt to know your freedom had a cash value."

I don't know what to say, so I remain silent with my mouth open.

Chapter 31

We've been driving almost an hour, and I get tenser with each passing minute. It would be great if I could convince myself I was on a leisurely ride with a good-looking man, maybe going parking or to a bar. Just like the old me, carefree and enjoying life. Ready for the next dance, drink, pill, kiss, the next thrill. Not worried about what comes next because I have nothing to worry about. But instead I'm going to parts unknown in search of my lost sister with my parole officer.

The radio plays a Willie Nelson tune and any other time I'd turn it up and sing along. But I'm too nervous to move. What if Vangie Ann's body has been found and he doesn't have the heart to tell me? What if my sister was found with her curly blond hair matted in blood and vomit on some dingy floor? My sister who tries so hard to take care of everyone else but somehow forgot to take care of herself.

"I went to college at Ole Miss. That's the only time I've ever lived out of Arkansas." Mack is trying to fill the silence, and I'm thankful. "I used to think I'd go somewhere exciting after college and go to law school. California or New York. But my dad died, and I had to come back for my mom."

"I know a thing or two about derailed plans." I look out into the darkness and imagine an alternate life for both of us. Lives that don't lead us on a search to find my drugged-up sister. "When I was in high school I wanted to be an actress. My dad said I had to go to college first. College led to teaching. I met a boy and decided to stay put. Then another boy. Then Wayne. Then I lost my freedom." I sound like a loser. "California's my big chance."

"I used to think everything happens for a reason. But I'm starting to think that's a crock of shit." His smile appears, and warmth spreads in my belly.

Mack pulls the car onto a gravel road, pocked and bumpy, long since ignored by the county. "There's a cabin down here. That's where we going."

"Why?"

"TJ Talbot and some of his buddies hang out here with they're hiding out. I think Vangie Ann might be here, but I'm not sure. I didn't tell you before because I didn't want to get your hopes up too much." Again his large, thick hand finds his way to me. This time on my shoulder, resting gently for just a second.

I realize his logic was just like any man's, I guess. Let her think the worst instead of getting her hopes up over the best.

My hands come together in my lap and squeeze each other tightly.

"Are you packing?" I ask.

"Yeah, but I can't let you use one of my guns." He turns the headlights off before I can see a cabin, and steers the truck into a spot between two pine trees. "Let's get out here and walk the rest of the way. Can't spook them or they'll just run into the woods."

The trees appear black against the dark blue sky. The stars haven't found their way out yet. But the night is alive with cicadas and crickets. I take Mack's thick arm and he leads the way toward a distant light, a light from the cabin.

I want to be better than this, but I really wish he'd kiss me. Just once. Just to make me forget for a second that this is my life now. If he'd wrap me in his large arms, such safety and warmth, tell me I'm pretty and place his lips over mine. His large hand on the small of my back and this whole mess with my sister would disappear. I could have a break, if only for one minute.

"We have to proceed carefully, Cass. If it's just TJ and Vangie Ann, it should be fine. If it's a whole nest of tweakers, it's a different story. Some of them are real paranoid and a big guy like me won't do anything to make them feel better." He walks deliberately through the woods, careful to keep my hand on his arm. He steps gracefully, like a man half his size.

"Okay. I'll do what you tell me to do." Sweat dots my forehead, but I make no move to wipe it clean.

"Even if it means leaving without her?"

The question hangs in the night air, absorbed by a cicada's song, and we continue our path.

The cabin comes into view and my stomach jumps. When I think of drug dens, abandoned buildings with boarded up windows and piss in the corners always come to mind. Or maybe trailers like TJ's with roaches and the smell of rotting chickens. Not a cabin in the woods with a porch swing and a welcome mat. But that's where we are.

"Do we knock?" I whisper.

He's close enough that his breath hits my face. It sends a chill against my skin, dampened from sweat. My hand is still wrapped around his arm. My breath quickens, and I remind myself where I am, why I'm here.

"Yeah. The best move would be for me to wait at the back door in case anyone runs out while you knock at the front. But we shouldn't do that since you're unarmed." Mack looks at my face and starts to walk forward again, the gravel shifting lightly beneath his feet.

We walk up the wooden front steps and onto the porch, and I release Mack's arm even though I don't want to. The blue curtains are pulled shut. There's no way to preview the contents of the cabin. Mack looks at me and nods.

I'm nervous. More nervous than I remember being in a long time, maybe since my parole hearing. My balled fist raps on the door. *Knock, knock, knock.* I can feel the sweat from my armpits trickle down my sides.

"Should I let her know it's me?" My voice is a whisper so quiet I'm not sure I'm actually speaking.

"Better you than the cops," he says quietly and shrugs.

"Vangie Ann, I don't know if you're in there. But it's me, Cass. I need to see you." My words go directly into the door. I knock again for punctuation.

The door creaks open like I'm in a horror movie. But the monster on the other side is my own flesh and blood.

A gasp escapes my lips when I see her. She's lost at least ten pounds and there are dark circles beneath her puffy eyes. Her face, usually made up even to go to the gas station, is bare, and the discoloration of hard drug abuse is obvious. Her hair is tangled and matted, and pulled into pigtails she should have outgrown three decades ago. She's wearing cut-offs and a loose t-shirt. Her boobs dangle freely beneath the shirt. A cigarette hangs from her lips, so at least something about her is the same.

"What do you want?" Her jaw is tight. It looks painful.

"I want you to come home." I remember that Mack is beside me, and put my hand back on his reassuring bicep.

Vangie Ann lets out a "pfft" and takes a drag from her cigarette.

"We need you. There's a pregnant teenager there. She's going to have a baby any day now. The fundraiser's in less than two weeks. Dana took off. The past due notices are rolling in." I stare at her and search for any movement in her face, any clues that she gives a shit. She's giving me nothing. "Please, V. Please."

TJ appears from within the cabin. He drapes his arm over Vangie Ann's shoulders.

"She ain't goin' nowhere." He's only wearing cut-offs, no shirt. His ribs are visible through his pale skin. There's a razorback tattoo where he should have a right pectoral muscle.

"TJ. Got any warrants right now?" Mack folds his arms across his chest. The look works for him, but I hate to lose the place for my hand.

"You ain't got nothin' on me." TJ grins, revealing his yellowed teeth.

"You're right. But I'm sure I could find something. Who's your PO? McBride, right? Does he know where you are?"

"Fuck you." TJ lets go of Vangie Ann and crosses his arms over his chest.

Mack moves in front of him. TJ opens his mouth to speak, but before any words come out Mack pushes him backward. TJ falls against the coffee table.

Vangie Ann lets out a scream that's more anger than fear.

Mack walks into the cabin, and I follow close behind. There's a bag of powder on the coffee table. It's surrounded by overflowing ashtrays. One ashtray fell with TJ and emptied onto the carpet. The room is sparsely decorated, and only a couch serves for furniture.

"You can't do this. You can't just barge in here like this and push TJ. What the fuck?" She's yelling like someone from a trashy talk show.

"Yes, we can." I start to close the door, but decide to leave it open to air the place out.

TJ stands up, brushing ashes from his shorts. "You're an asshole, man."

Vangie Ann stands with her feet planted. She takes a drag from her cigarette and flicks the butt out of the front door. "You can handle the House for a while, Cass. Get used to some responsibility. It will do you some good."

"Like it's done you?" My anger grows every time she grinds her teeth.

"Fuck you, you spoiled cunt."

Rage boils in my gut and before I realize what I'm doing, my open palm strikes Vangie Ann across the face.

She grabs her cheek and stares at me with her mouth open. "It's my life. You barged in and took the fuck over. And guess what? You can just have it."

"What are even talking about?" I ask.

"You! I'm talking about you. Your amazing ability to fuck up everything in your path." She's flailing her arms as she speaks.

I gasp and open my mouth to retaliate. Mack jumps in before I have the chance.

"Evangeline, there's a real good rehab center in Little Rock. You can go in and decide if you need inpatient or outpatient. I can arrange everything for you." Mack's voice is calm, soothing.

Vangie Ann looks at him, but her eyes don't seem to focus. It's like she can't really see him. "I want you both to get the fuck out of here."

Mack grabs my arm and pulls me toward the door. "You heard her."

"No. I'm not leaving." I pull away from his grasp.

"You are leaving, Cass." Vangie Ann stands in front of me with her arms crossed. "I don't need to be saved."

Mack wraps his hand around mine and nods his head once. He starts walking out and I follow.

I turn around and say, "I love you, V."

TJ steps in front of Vangie Ann. He smiles at me as he closes the door.

We're thirty feet or so away from the cabin when I realize I'm holding my breath. Gasps escape my throat, and I sway back in forth where I stand. Mack stops walking and turns toward me.

"Are you okay?" He wraps his arms around me so I don't fall over.

I can see his face, but that's the only thing in my vision. No trees, no stars, just Mack's face. I concentrate on his features and try to breathe deep. He pulls me close and I breathe at his neck: sweat and adrenaline.

I don't know how long it goes on. Maybe only a couple of minutes, but I start breathing again. The trees are back in my view.

"You okay now?" he asks.

"Yeah," I whisper. We start walking. I didn't think I had the ability to panic after going to prison. The worst possible thing has already happened to me.

"We could have kidnapped her or something. Made her come with us and detox." I speak the words slowly, unsure of my ability to talk.

He grabs my hand in his as we continue toward the car. "No. That's not the answer. It has to be her decision."

Even though I don't want to, I pull my hand away from his. He belongs to someone else, and it's foolish to get used to leaning on someone all the time.

Once we're on the road, the seriousness of the situation hits me hard. My sister is lost, maybe completely.

"Cass," Mack says but doesn't look at me.

"Yeah?"

"Sometimes I think about kissing you." He grips the wheel with both hands. "But it's just not right."

My response sticks in my throat. It probably would have been the wrong thing to say anyway. And after a few minutes, I'm not even sure he really said it.

Chapter 32

We ride the rest of the way to the House in silence. It's completely dark now, and stars freckle the sky. The windows are open and the humid night air whips my hair against my face. It would normally be annoying, but the fatigue of seeing Vangie Ann has pushed me into lethargy. My thoughts roam to Maggie, and I remember that things could be urgent. I shouldn't be out chasing someone who doesn't want to be chased.

Mack pulls to the curb in front of the House. He puts his arm on the back of the seat and turns to me.

"Need anything?" he asks.

What I would like is for him to stay the night with me. Envelop me in his muscular arms and hold me until I fall asleep. I haven't slept in the same bed with a man in so long, and it would be therapeutic. But I can't ask for that. He'd certainly say no, and then I'd hurt more. If he didn't say no, I'd just be adding chronic home-wrecker to my list of sins.

So I say, "No, thank you." I try to smile, but it doesn't really work. "Thanks for taking me to her. At least I know she's alive." I open the door and it creaks in response.

"She isn't hopeless, okay?" Mack looks at me and gives a half smile. Then he opens his door. "I'll walk you in."

I start to protest. Sure, it's dark, but I'm right in front of my home. But his chivalry warms me.

We walk up the sidewalk, and I unlock all three locks on the door. Sonya is standing on the other side.

"Thank God you're back!"

"Is it Maggie?" Panic spreads from my stomach to my scalp.

"Yeah. She's in a lot of pain but she won't go to the hospital."

Sonya grabs my hand and pulls me up the stairs. Mack follows.

Maggie's in her bed, groaning and crying. Tilly is wiping Maggie's sweaty forehead with a wet rag.

"Did your water break yet?" Mack pushes past us and bends down to face Maggie.

"No," Maggie says. Tears are streaming down her face. "It hurts so bad."

"We're going to the hospital, Maggie." I grab her hand and try to pull her up.

"I'm scared. I'm not ready." She pulls her hand away and clutches the sheets. Maggie releases a scream from her chest.

"Staying here won't keep the baby from coming," Sonya says.

Mack puts his arms under her and picks her up with a grunt. "Come on," he says.

Maggie relaxes against him as we move out their way. She looks tiny in his grasp, like a strange doll with a round tummy.

He maneuvers her down the stairs, quickly but carefully, and Sonya opens the front door.

"Does she have a hospital bag or anything?" I ask Tilly.

"I don't think so. She really ain't ready for this baby at all." Tilly shrugs and follows me to the front door.

"I'm going with them. Keep an eye on things, ladies. I'll call you when I know something." The front door closes behind me, and I have to fight the impulse to run back in. I'm not ready for this baby, either.

Mack places Maggie gently in his truck. I sit down beside her, she groans as she scoots over to make room for me.

"I hope her water doesn't break now," I say. "Your truck would never be the same."

Mack shakes his head. "That'd be gross."

"Would you two please shut up?" Maggie says.

We get in the car and Maggie cries loudly all the way to the hospital. Fortunately, it's only a ten-minute drive. My ears are splitting and my head hurts by the time we get there.

"Wait here." Mack gets out of the truck at the emergency room door.

"You okay, Maggie?" I have to speak loudly so she can hear me over her own sobs.

"Fuck no!" She probably would have slapped me if she wasn't too busy holding her stomach.

Two men in hospital uniforms appear quickly with a wheelchair. I get out of the truck and they lift her out.

"I'll go with her," I say.

"I'll be there after I park the pickup." Mack pulls his eyebrows together as he speaks.

Maggie is whisked into a room immediately and surrounded by nurses.

"Is this your mother?" a nurse with a butt the size of two watermelons asks her.

"No," Maggie answers.

For a second, I'm appalled that Nurse Big Butt could think I was Maggie's mom. But this is the South. I graduated high school with folks who are grandmothers by now.

"Do you want her to stay?" another nurse asks Maggie.

Maggie looks at me and nods her head. "Yes, please."

I'm terrified and pleased. Seeing a baby born has never been on my to-do list, but it's sweet that she wants me with her. Nobody's ever asked for anything like that.

"If I die, promise to take care of my baby." She's squeezing my hand so hard, it feels like something inside of it will break.

"You're not going to die." *Please, God. Don't let her die. I can't take of a baby. I mean, I wouldn't want her to die anyway. You know what I mean, right? Amen.*

"Don't worry, sweetie. Women give birth all the time," another nurse says. This one has mocha skin and wire-rimmed glasses. Her tag reads "Sharon Levin, RN." She pats Maggie on the head. "We don't have any records for you. Who's your doctor, sweetie?"

A fresh pool of tears rushes down Maggie's face as she says, "I don't have one."

"She has an appointment set for tomorrow morning. It would have been her first one." My words stop the activity in the room, except for Maggie's crying.

Nurse Levin turns her full attention to me. "You haven't taken this girl to a doctor yet?"

My words stick in my throat. I start to make excuses, but really I have no right. I should have paid attention to Maggie, should have known what was going on. At least she would have been to the doctor by now.

"It's not her fault," Maggie says quietly. The tears are slowing down, though she still has a death-grip on my hand. "I saw a doctor when I was in the county lockup. He didn't do much, though…"

Movement in the room stops for a second at the words "lockup."

Nurse Big Butt hands me a gown. "Help her get into this."

The thin cotton gown feels soft. The texture grounds me for a second, takes me out of this room I don't really want to be in anymore.

"Maggie, can you take off your clothes?" I ask.

Maggie nods and raises up. She pulls off her t-shirt, revealing a tatty cotton bra. She pulls off her cut-offs that weren't buttoned at the top, leaving behind cotton panties that sit below her belly.

"You have to take off your bra and panties, too," I say before one of the nurses does.

I hold the gown in front of her as she pulls off her bra and panties, the last of her armor. She slips her arms into the gown.

"Cass, I've never even been to a real gynecologist. How am I going to do this?"

"You don't have a choice. Anyway, you'll forget your modesty once that baby is pushing out." Nurse Levin has returned to her side. "The doctor will be with you in a minute. Don't worry."

"Yeah, right." The tears start flowing from Maggie's eyes once again. "Don't worry. Ha!" Then another scream, deep from her gut, emerges from her mouth. I've never heard a more terrifying sound, even in prison.

Mack bursts through the door. "How's she doing?"

"Who are you?" Nurse Levin asks.

"He's my parole officer," I say, and once again movement in the room stops.

"Do you want him here?" Nurse Big Butt asks. I realize she has a nametag. It reads "Janet Collins, BSN," but I'm still angry with her so my mind hasn't transitioned to using her name yet.

"Will he see my cooter?" Maggie asks, her eyes darting to each person in the room. "Y'all are all going to see my cooter, aren't you?"

Mack pushes toward her just like when he was in our bedroom. "Maggie, I'll stay if you want me to. I won't look at," he gestures toward her crotch with his head, "your business."

"He can stay," she says.

I release a sigh of relief. And before I realize it, my free hand is wrapped around his arm.

A doctor rushes in and pulls the stirrups out at the end of the bed. "Hello there, Maggie. Let's see where we are with this." He's older than any of the doctors I saw in prison. Probably close to seventy. He has a relaxed smile that showcases his dentures. "Scoot to the edge of the bed, please."

Fear fills her eyes, but she does it anyway.

"Just relax and let your knees fall to the sides," the doctor says.

Maggie looks at me, her eyes pleading for a way out of this situation. All I can do is offer an uneasy smile.

"Well, young lady, this baby is on its way out."

"I need drugs," she says. "I can't do this without drugs."

"I'm sorry. But there's no time." The doctor stands up and gives orders to the nurses.

I don't hear any of it. I can only focus on Maggie's face. Her pure, raw terror that makes me thankful I've never gone through this and never will.

Chapter 33

It's morning when Mack drops me off at the House. My knowledge of the human body has expanded to places it didn't need to go. I'm exhausted, and completely in love. I have no idea how doctors and nurses avoid falling in love with every nasty little baby they see get born.

I want to respond to what he said earlier. It's a conversation that we should have, but neither of us have the energy. I leave his truck and go into the House without speaking, only a nod for goodbye.

Sonya and Tilly are in the kitchen drinking coffee.

"It's a girl." I plop down at the table and Sonya puts a cup of coffee in front of me.

"Is she healthy?" Sonya asks.

"Yeah. Somehow she is." I take a sip of coffee. "They're keeping Maggie there a couple of days so she can learn all the stuff she should have learned already."

"What's her name?" Tilly stands up to take cinnamon rolls out of the oven.

"No word on that yet." I had to talk her out of naming the girl Gypsy Rose or Destiny. No reason to start the baby off on a stripper's path. Maggie agreed to think it over for a day. She was too tired to make any big decisions anyway.

The girls are looking at me, waiting for more. My overwhelming fatigue makes it difficult to stay on topic, so I shift gears.

"I saw Vangie Ann last night. She doesn't want to come back."

My words hang in the air and both women drop their jaws.

"Well, that's bullshit." Tilly crosses her arms over her chest.

"I know." Exhaustion suddenly gathers in my head and stomach like the flu. "Ladies, I need some sleep." I push away from the table and stand.

"I need your truck. I have some last minute fundraiser stuff to pick up," Sonya says.

"Fuck. The fundraiser." My shoulders drop. "We can't pull this off."

"Yes, we can. We can't give everything back," Tilly says. "Go get some rest."

I nod and turn away. The stairs greet my feet and the bed envelopes me in its warmth. This place is killing me faster than prison.

***

Sleep offers no rest for my racing mind. Dreams of Maggie's childbirth, TJ, and Vangie Ann cause me to toss and turn, waking frequently, covered in sweat. I wake up thinking about the damn fundraiser and rise to pace around the room. It's hard to have shit to do.

We're going to need a crib if Maggie stays. I don't know where else she'll go, and this place isn't set up for a baby. Children, sure. We have a swing set. But a baby?

As I pace with my racing brain, I realize something. This room isn't big enough for Maggie, her baby, and me. She could move across the hall to Dana's old room, but there is a better alternative. And it's just downstairs.

The door to Vangie Ann's room opens with a slow groan. The cigarette stink is still prevalent, but washing the sheets will take care of most of that. I turn the fan on and start pulling the sheets from the double bed. The thought of sleeping in the larger bed gives me a spark of happiness that slows down the panic.

"What are you doing?" Sonya appears in the doorway. She's holding a broom, and her hair is pulled into a tight ponytail.

"Moving down here. Maggie's going to need our room for the baby." Shaking the pillows from their cases releases more stale nicotine.

"What about Evangeline?" Sonya's mouth turns down at the corners as she leans against the door frame.

"She can have it back when she decides to come home. Until then, it's mine." I grab the pile of sheets from the floor. "Did you get your errands done?"

"Yeah. We'll be ready. Don't worry."

"I can't help it. I'm worried about fucking everything." The sheets against my chest smell of my sister: cigarettes and flowery perfume. My anger toward her starts to wane, but I need it to keep moving. It's the only thing giving me energy at this point. "How do we know people will even show up to this shindig?"

Sonya shrugs. "We don't for sure. But we have fliers all over town."

"We have eight days." I wad the sheets into a tighter ball, squeezing them like gold might come out.

Sonya steps closer and puts a hand on my shoulder. "It will be fine. If nothing else, we'll have a bluegrass band to ourselves. At least two of them are cute, a third if you're into really long beards."

"Can I tell you a secret?" I sit down on the bed, the sheets still squished against my chest.

"Yes!" Sonya's eyes get wide and she smiles.

"I have a crush on my PO, and I think it's mutual."

"Oh girl, everybody crushes on their PO. Unless they look like mine, of course." She sits next to me. "How could you not have a crush on that man? Did you see the way he carried Maggie down the stairs like Kevin Costner carried Whitney Houston in *The Bodyguard*?"

"He's living with somebody. He never talks about her, though."

"Then he doesn't care that much about her."

"We don't know that." I lean my head forward and rest it on the ball of sheets.

Tilly walks in. "What's going on in here?"

"I'm moving in here until Vangie Ann sees it fit to come home." My head lifts from the sheets.

"You guys want to go to Goodwill and look for costumes? Gotta get started on finding something for our party." Her indifference to my move reassures me of my decision. This is not a big deal. "I'm not sure about the slutty zombie thing anymore."

"Yeah. Just let me get these sheets in the wash." I stand up and arch my back to stretch.

I carry the sheets down the hall and dump them into washing machine. After prison there's one thing I can be confident in: my ability to do laundry.

Chapter 34

If a stranger saw us pulling up to the curb, we'd just look like three friends in a pickup truck. Not a trio of women who've been beaten down by life and our own bad decisions.

That's what I'm thinking as I park. Then I see a visitor on our porch: TJ Talbot. The sight of him makes my blood boil and my skin crawl at the same time. He's like a bad virus.

I tear out of the truck and charge toward him. "What the fuck do you want, TJ?"

"It's about Vangie Ann."

"What is it?" My fear is swelling, but I try to push it down.

TJ lights a cigarette and watches Sonya and Tilly walk up the steps.

"Hey, ladies. How's it going?"

Tilly lifts her middle finger in the air and walks past him into the House with Sonya behind her. Sonya doesn't look at him.

"I guess they don't want to see you."

"Guess not." TJ sits down in a chair, my favorite one with the gingham cushion. "I know you're upset with me. Sorry about having you arrested. I just wanted to remind you that I'm the one in control here."

I sit across from him and look for a trace of the boy I once knew. Instead, I only see a tweaker who's trying to bully me.

"What do you want, TJ?"

Humidity squeezes my chest. I want to be in the air-conditioned House, but I won't invite this asshole in.

"I have more than one way to hurt you." He takes a deep drag from his cigarette. "But for now I'm willing to call a truce."

"Oh, really?"

"Danielle told me about Maggie. That baby is mine. If you can convince her to come back to me, I'll trade you Vangie Ann."

"They aren't football players. We can't trade them." I wish I could send Maggie far away instead, somewhere he could never find her or the baby.

"You know, you've done nothing but stir up shit since you've been home." TJ grinds his teeth and stares at me, his eyes in slits like a reptile. "All you have to do is get Maggie to give me another chance and I'll convince Vangie Ann to come home. It won't be hard if I stop giving her drugs. She'll have no reason to stay with me."

Do I want this bad enough to throw Maggie under the drug-addled hillbilly bus?

"Would you clean up and be a father?" I return his gaze, challenging him to tell me the truth.

"Of course."

Maggie saw something in him. Enough to get sleep with him, anyway. Maybe giving him another chance wouldn't be a big deal to her. Maybe it's not the worst thing I could do.

"I'll see what I can do." The words taste like rotten milk.

TJ stands up. "Better get with it. Vangie Ann has a taste for needles now. Sure is a nasty habit that can have really bad results." He shakes his head and walks down the steps.

"Why are you doing this, TJ?"

"It's what I have to do for my family." He doesn't turn around. He just goes straight to his truck.

I go in the House with my bag of useless shit from Goodwill and find Tilly at the table, flipping through a trashy magazine.

"I can't figure out why he's so hell-bent on me not finding out who killed his mom if it wasn't him or Danielle. What's his problem?" I sit at the table and crack open a soda, wishing it was a beer.

"Beats me." Tilly looks up. "Maybe he just wants things to stay the same and not have to go through the whole trial process again. That had to have been hard on him. Or he's lying and it was him."

She turns her attention back to the magazine, and I don't understand why everyone isn't as worried about Vangie Ann as I am.

* * *

Danielle's staring at me like there's an extra nose growing out of my forehead. "Are they, well, doing it?"

"I don't know." I put a cup of coffee in front of her at the kitchen table.

"Thanks." She looks down at the table and takes a sip. "That's gross." Her eyebrows lift and she puts her coffee cup down. "Them doing it, I mean. Not the coffee."

Danielle came by to bring a baby gift for Maggie. I'm not sure it will be welcome, but I accepted it anyway.

"Yeah." I sit down across from her. "TJ said he'd try to get her to come home if I can talk Maggie into giving him another chance."

"Do you think you can do that?" She smiles with her entire face.

"I don't know. Should I even try?" I know I shouldn't. But I want something that will make it okay to try.

"Yes, you should. It's partly my fault they broke up. She got so mad at me over that weed thing," Danielle says.

"It was weed and ecstasy and she was arrested."

"The drugs belonged to both of us. I was just able to get out of it." Danielle takes a sip of coffee. "It's fine now, right?"

"Not really. Maggie's still on probation and she has a record now."

"Yeah. I guess it sucks." Danielle reaches out and puts her hands over mine. "She really has you fooled, doesn't she?"

"What do you mean?"

"That girl isn't so sweet and innocent. She's only out for herself. Trust me. Plus, she's on lots of medications. Makes me look sane." She rubs her thumb over my hand in a back and forth motion. "But even so, TJ was at his best when he was with Maggie. And he'll be even better this time because there's a baby involved."

"Okay. But why doesn't he want me to know who killed your mom?"

Danielle opens her mouth to speak, closes it, then starts again. "I can't pretend to understand why he does the things he does. He's never talked about that night, not even to me or Dad." She moves her hands to her lap.

"But he *does* know who did it?"

"Goddammit, Cass!" She slams her hands on the table, and I jump in my seat. "You're out of jail. Isn't that enough for you?" Her temper makes her look more like Judith, the angry way she looked the last time I saw her alive.

I lean forward and narrow my eyes. "No. And it shouldn't be enough for you, either."

She takes a deep breath and slumps in her chair. "I know." Danielle sits up straight. "But our family has been through enough. Dredging up all those memories of our mom is rough. She's gone. She would have died from the drugs anyway."

"Do you really believe that? That she would have died anyway, so it's okay to let this go?"

She spreads her lips in a sweet smile that makes her look like a creepy doll. "I've been in a lot of therapy. I know myself pretty well by now. And yes, that's what I believe. I had to realize that her death was inevitable."

A sigh escapes my throat. There's nothing more to say.

She holds her hands out in the middle of the table. Even though I don't want to, I reach and take her hands. "I can't believe I'm an aunt. It's so exciting."

"I guess it must be."

"Thanks for the coffee." She pulls her hands from mine and stands up.

"Sure."

She crosses her hands over her chest. "I wish I could tell you not to worry, but I know what it's like to have a junkie for a sibling."

"Vangie Ann has recovered before. She can do it again." I push away from the table and stand. "We just need to get her…"

"Away from my loser brother?" She glares at me, daring me to respond.

"That would be a great start."

She gazes at me, then pulls me into an embrace. I remain stiff for a beat then return her hug.

"If you can't tell me what really happened to your mom, I don't want to see you again." My words are steady and clear.

She flashes me a blank look and turns toward the door.

I walk her out and check the mail. There's a foreclosure notice waiting for me.

Chapter 35

"TJ and Danielle were both here yesterday at different times." I'm in the sitting room with Mack, not talking about feelings. "TJ said he'd get Vangie Ann to come home if I get Maggie to give him another chance."

"I hope that girl has more sense than that. You didn't agree to it, did you?" Mack leans forward.

"No. Not really." Well, sort of. "I still think TJ or Danielle might have killed Judith. Kids accidentally shoot people all the time."

Mack sighs and rubs his hands on his face. "It was a gunshot wound to the chest at close range. It's not likely that it was an accidental shooting by a kid."

"She was involved with drug dealers and other lowlifes. It could have been anybody." Could it have been *anybody*? All the evidence pointed to me. "If only Matt Morgan wasn't dead."

"Well, he is."

"What would you do if you were me?"

He sighs again and looks at my face. "I don't know, Cass." His face softens. "You have a lot going on right now. I think maybe you should wait a little while."

"I don't have a little while. The bank is going to take Blankenship House." My voice is louder than I intended. "Maybe I should talk to Wayne again. Maybe he'll give me some sort of clue."

"No. You can't." His tone reminds me of the way Tabitha would speak when another inmate thought she could make me her prison wife.

"I can't talk to him, or you just don't want me to sleep with him?"

Mack looks up at me. "No, I don't want you to sleep with him." He looks down again as his cheeks turn pink. "I'm still your parole officer for now. You can't see him because you will go back to prison. I'm pretty sure his wife will make sure of it." He looks up and holds out one of his hands. I slip my hand into his before he has time to change his mind. "You shouldn't even be seeing his kids. But since they've been coming here, I guess it's not a big deal."

We sit in silence for a minute. It's like my first boyfriend in middle school. He'd ride his bike over and we would hold hands on the couch under my father's half-assed watch.

There's too much to say and too much to think about. His touch is comforting, but not much, since this isn't a real possibility. He's with someone and he's my parole officer. We could sleep together a time or two in secret, but he doesn't seem like that type of guy. Just like that relationship in middle school, holding hands may be as far as this ever goes.

"I can't stop trying." I run my free hand down the velour arm rest of the chair. "I have to save this place."

Mack nods and smiles slightly. "We're going to figure this out, then."

"Thank you." I don't know if he believes it. It doesn't matter right now, I just need comfort.

"When are Maggie and the baby coming home?" he asks.

"I think tomorrow, but I'm not sure." Maggie and the baby, a tangible and immediate issue.

He pulls his hand away and stands up. "I should be going."

"I'm just about to make coffee. Do you want to stay for a little while?" When he leaves I'll be alone with my thoughts, forced to deal with everything around me.

"No. But thanks. I have a lot of work to do." He steps toward the door as I rise from the chair. "I'll check in with you soon."

I stand with my feet planted and nod, unsure of what I'm supposed to do. Is a hug appropriate, a handshake?

"Okay. Thanks, Mack."

I lean forward and close my eyes. Instead of meeting me halfway for a kiss, he walks out of the door without another word. I watch him walk away, and I want to whisper the words "I could love you" into the breeze so they will be out of my lungs and in his ears and he will drive home wondering where they came from.

***

"Tell him I'll try, okay?" I wrap the phone cord around my fingers, watching it cut into my skin. My sister is lost and my only hope is little Judith. And I'm not sure I'm telling her the truth.

"I'll talk to him today." Danielle responds like we are talking about going to a movie. "In fact, I'll call him when we hang up."

"Thanks, Danielle. I really need Vangie Ann to come home."

"You're doing the right thing. Talk to you soon."

Just like when I declared my innocence eleven years ago, I'm speaking in vain. This won't bring my sister home.

Sonya walks in as I hang up.

"Do you have any weed yet?" I ask. No time to beat around the bush.

Sonya shakes her head. "Nope. It's dry right now. No idea why."

"You mean I peed for you for nothing?" I grab my keys from the countertop and slip into my flip-flops.

"Not for nothing. That was super helpful." Her face registers hurt, but I don't have time to deal with it.

"I'll be back in a bit." I charge out of the door and climb into the pickup.

The drive is longer than I remember, giving me plenty of time to consider how stupid this idea is. But it's all I've got.

I bang on door "H" and Gabe opens it. He's wearing a white t-shirt that showcases his bulging muscles and tattoos.

"What?" He's trying to come off angry, but he's smiling.

"I need your help."

He lets out an exaggerated sigh and takes a step back. "Come in."

"Thanks." The apartment is cleaner this time. It still smells like cigarettes and dust, but the beer bottles are gone from the countertops and the garbage isn't overflowing.

"Have a seat." He motions to the brown velour couch.

I nod and sit down with my hands in my lap. "I really need some weed."

"You can't smoke weed. You're on parole." He pulls a wooden chair from the kitchen table and pulls it caddy-corner to the couch.

"It's a long story."

"So, you're out on parole and you're trying to get me to sell weed to you?" He puts his hands behind his head and leans back. I try not to stare at his arms.

"Or you could just give it to me." I smile and shrug like this is a completely normal situation.

"You should do meth instead. It gets out of your system faster." He reaches under the coffee table and pulls out a mirror with one fat line of powder on it.

"No, thank you." I shake my head.

"Have you ever tried it?" he asks and puts the mirror on the coffee table.

"No. And I don't want to." I'm keeping my smile so I don't come off impolite. "I thought you ran out of meth. Isn't that why V left?"

"I was done. This is the end for real, though. I'm moving away from here. Should have never come back." He nods toward the coffee table. "Don't you want to know what all the fuss is about?" It's a question I've never been asked, and it gives me pause.

There was meth circulating in prison. We all knew it. There were plenty of women who would degrade themselves just to escape the pain of where they were. The pain of what they did that brought them there and what they had to do to get the drugs. Not me. Not after that one time during the first week. I guess Tabitha and books were my escape after that.

But here and now, the drugs are offered to me for the cost of zero BJs.

Gabe returns my smile. He has the devil's grin and it makes my panties moist. I hope he can't tell that my cheeks are flushing.

"I haven't slept with Vangie Ann in years. We didn't mess around this last time. She just wanted the drugs."

It's like he's in my head, watching me bounce up and down on him. There are so many things wrong with this scenario, and I can't seem to move.

Gabe stands and walks over to the couch. He sits down beside me, close enough that I can feel the heat from his skin.

"It's no fun to get high alone."

My heart is racing. And it's not in the panic sort of way. It's just that everything in this moment is so exciting and scary I can hardly stand it.

In prison, I sat with the other druggies in the rec room, our chairs in a circle. Each of us were asked repeatedly, "What are you trying to escape?" All I could say was "everything," all the while knowing that if I could just get another chance at real life, I would embrace it and not seek out a chemical escape. But I want it more than anything.

"I can't." I jump up and head for the door like my ass is on fire.

"Wait." He stands up. "I'll give you a little weed."

"You will?" It comes out overly enthusiastic and squeaky.

"Sure." Gabe goes to the galley kitchen and opens a drawer. He pulls out a small plastic bag and walks over to me. He holds out the baggie. "It's not much."

"Thank you," I say and grab the bag.

Gabe lets go of the weed and grabs my wrist. He pulls me close and puts his lips to mine. He kisses me like we're on the cover of one of Tilly's cheesy romance novels. My legs go numb but I manage to remain standing.

"I'm only here for another week. Come by if you want to give me some company." He smiles like the devil again.

I nod and walk out, even though my body wants to stay.

Chapter 36

Tilly's in the kitchen when I get home.

"Follow me," I say and charge up the stairs.

"What's up?" We go into my room and she closes the door.

I pull the baggie of weed from my pocket and hold it. She smiles as she reaches for it, but I put it back in my pocket.

"Not yet, sweetie. Give me what you've got first."

Tilly sits down on her old bed. "Okay. I don't know if it will help, but you should know anyway."

"Tell me." I sit on my bed.

She purses her lips and sweeps her bleached bangs away from her brown eyes. "I can't believe you scored some pot. Where'd you get it?"

"Tell me what you know." I fight the urge to shake the words out of her.

"Okay. That night. When Matt came home from Judith's." She looks down. "It was rough, you know? She and I were starting to kind of bond." She shakes her head. "Matt came home with a gun that night."

"What are you telling me?" Heat prickles beneath my skin, not quite anger but more than anxiety.

"He found the gun at Judith's and he wanted to keep it." She shrugs like it makes sense. "It was a free pistol."

"What happened to it after that?"

"I don't know. I was coming down, and he offered me some heroin, and I didn't ask any more questions." She shrugs. "Them not finding the weapon helped you, right?"

"Tilly." I take a deep breath. "The gun would have had fingerprints on it. None of which would have been mine. The gun would have saved my ass. There was an open window. They thought I tossed it out into the woods. The fact that they didn't find it didn't help me."

She shrugs again. "I'm sorry."

"Fuck!" I jump from my bed and Tilly stands in response. I toss the weed at her. She fumbles it, and it drops to the floor. "Don't follow me."

I take the stairs two at a time. The humidity hits me in the chest as soon as I open the front door. I try to sit, but my anger keeps me on my feet. I walk to the edge of the porch and stare out into the street.

The door groans as Tilly walks out, one foot in front of the other like she's waiting for me to yell at her.

"Some junkie drug dealer could have saved me from jail, but didn't because he wanted a free gun." I'm facing the street as I speak. Looking at her creates an unwelcome rage.

"How were we supposed to know that you would go down for killing her?" She closes the door and walks two paces toward me.

"You both knew I was arrested, right? He could have come forward then."

"And admit that he was on the scene and that he stole the gun? Think about what you're saying."

"No, you think!" I turn to face her. "Your tweaker boyfriend put me in jail."

Tears gather in her eyes. She wipes them away with palms before they make it to her cheeks. "It was wrong. It was awful. But it's done."

Her words hit me in the stomach. There's a good chance I'll never know what happened to Judith. I'll always be guilty. And now we'll all be homeless.

"It's not done."

Thinking about Judith has brought me nothing but grief. It's only money, lots of money, and a home. But is it worth it?

Tilly lights a cigarette and sits down. "Accept it, Cass. You pled guilty. It's done."

I turn back to the street. The pavement sends the air boiling in waves away from it. A cicada sings from a nearby tree. I guess I can take Tilly off the list. Only Wayne and his family remain.

Chapter 37

"I named her Samantha Dyan. Samantha because I love that name, and Dyan after Dyan Cannon. My grandma used to show me her movies." Maggie holds the baby out to me.

She's swaddled in a hospital blanket, white with a pink and blue stripe. I pull her close so I don't drop her.

"I like that name." The face peeking out from the blanket is perfect. Pink and soft, with blue eyes and heart-shaped lips. I thought all newborn babies looked the same, but this one is more beautiful than any I've ever seen. "There's a crib upstairs. We found it at the Salvation Army store, but the mattress and sheets are new."

"Thank you." Maggie's bottom lip trembles. "I know I should have planned ahead. I guess I thought if I pretended I wasn't pregnant, it wouldn't be true."

"Don't worry about that now." The baby is sleeping against my chest. She's warm and soft, and her presence relaxes me.

"My turn!" And like that, Sonya snatches her away from me.

"Don't wake her up," I say.

Sonya pulls her close and smells the top of her head. "I always thought I'd be a mom someday. But it just wasn't meant to be."

Tilly opens her mouth to speak, then closes it again before any words escape. She shakes her head and looks down at the magazine in her lap.

I know it's not the right time, maybe it will never be the right time. But there's a foreclosure notice on the kitchen table, and like having my own toilet, waiting is a luxury I don't have.

"TJ thinks the baby is his," I say.

Maggie glares at me. "So?"

"He wants you to give him another chance." Poor girl. I should never be responsible for anybody.

Tilly is shaking her head. "Just because he has a trust fund doesn't make him a good choice for a baby daddy."

"TJ has a trust fund?" Maggie turns to Tilly.

"That's what I heard. It's from his mama dying. He gets it when he turns twenty-one," Tilly says.

"His birthday is next month." Maggie is looking at her baby now, safely cradled in Sonya's arms.

"Are you breastfeeding?" Sonya asks.

"Gross." Tilly speaks barely above a whisper, but loud enough for us to hear.

"Yeah. I can't afford not to." Maggie cuts her eyes at Tilly, but Tilly doesn't look up. "I'm supposed to be on medication, but I can skip it for a little while longer. Shouldn't hurt."

"Breastfeeding's best for the baby, they say. You have antibodies and nutrients designed just for little Samantha here." Sonya looks down at the baby's face and smiles.

"The party is this weekend, Maggie. Do you want to stay at Lucinda's while that's going on?" I ask.

"No. I don't want to miss the party. We'll be fine here. Hopefully she'll sleep the whole time."

According to Lucinda, the party is the only hope we have of keeping this place afloat. Vangie Ann had the place running on a shoestring budget, and what little reserve she had has dwindled since she took off. If the fundraiser isn't a success, Blankenship House will close. We'll all be homeless.

"I'm going to take Samantha upstairs so she can get used to our new home." Maggie lifts the baby from Sonya.

"Do you think they'll stay?" Tilly asks once Maggie is out of earshot.

"Sounds like it. At least for now." Sonya says with a smile. "It's just a baby. Not a rabid stray dog."

"Babies cry all the time. Just wait." Tilly crinkles her nose up.

"What do you know about babies?" I ask.

"Well nothing, really. But they do cry a lot. Everybody knows that." She turns her attention back to her magazine.

"I think it will do us all some good to have a baby around. Too bad Dana and Troy left when they did. I bet she would have enjoyed it, too," Sonya says.

"Dana didn't seem like she enjoyed anything," I say.

"She was only like that with you," Tilly says without looking up. "She was nice around us. Kind of funny even."

"Dana? Really?" It's difficult to imagine her being funny. Or nice.

"She's coming to the fundraiser. I talked to her yesterday," Sonya says.

"You still talk to her?" I ask.

"Yeah." Sonya nods and stands up. "Can I borrow the truck? I need to go see the caterer."

Everything going on is outside of me. Every time I think I get what's happening, another layer reveals itself.

"I should probably go with you, Sonya."

After all, if Vangie Ann doesn't get her junkie ass home soon, this place will be my responsibility. That is, of course, if we can keep it afloat.

* * *

Dear Tabitha,

I'm sorry it's taken me so long to write to you. I don't know what to say, I guess. I'm out here and you're still in there. Doesn't seem right. I didn't know how much I relied on you until I didn't have you anymore. You always knew what to say to calm me down, to make me feel loved and content. Even when I was locked up.

My sister has taken off. I'm trying to run the Blankenship House, but really the other girls are running it just as much as I am. There's a girl here with a brand new baby. I've never been around a newborn before. Samantha, that's the baby's name, doesn't cry much. She just sleeps and poops. I never knew how perfect tiny babies were. I hope that doesn't make you sad. Have your kids been to visit lately?

Do you remember when that big Russian bitch tried to make me her wife and you pummeled her? I think about that sometimes when I'm blue. The look on her face when she realized you had the better of her. That was priceless. You came out of that without a scratch, and that big woman looked like she'd been in a car wreck. It's strange how the view of romance changes when you're locked up.

I hope things are going okay with Maria. Getting a new cellmate must be quite an adjustment. But maybe it's a nice change after a decade of living with me.

I miss you, Tabitha. Things would be easier if you were with me to help me deal with life. I knew I couldn't depend on you forever, but it would be nice if I could. I'll come visit soon.

Love always,
Cass

By the time I finish writing the letter, my face is wet and snotty. I didn't know how much being without her would hurt. It's like being sucker punched in the gut every time her face coasts through my mind.

It's not something the girls here would understand. None of them have been locked up for more than a few months at a time. I'm permanently separated from my best friend.

Chapter 38

It's August fifteenth, and I'm a grown woman dressed up as a pirate. No matter how much I wanted this day not to get here, it big fat got here anyway.

"Cass, the band's here." Sonya's broad smile makes her look almost pretty in her slutty nurse outfit. I don't have the heart to tell her that it's so tight you can tell one of her boobs is bigger than the other.

"Tell them to set up out back, okay?"

She nods and leaves my room, Vangie Ann's room. I stroke the "One Day at a Time" necklace. It's cold and solid. I slip the chain around my neck and hide the necklace behind my fluffy shirt.

It's not too hot today, a rare occurrence in Arkansas for an August day. Fate has smiled on us displaced women for once. I step out into the backyard and admire the work of the caterers. Tables and chairs under a big white tent. A buffet table at the front. The guests should start arriving in the next hour, and everything looks perfect so far.

"Hello, Cass," says a husky female voice behind me.

I turn to see Dana, her robust figure stuffed into a French maid outfit. A laugh erupts in my stomach, but I choke it down before it escapes my mouth.

"Dana," I say with a nod. "Good to see you."

"Sonya asked me to come help. Do you know where she is?" Dana's eyes search the small yard, cluttered with chairs and tents.

"She's probably in the kitchen with the caterers." The band crosses the yard, guitar cases and microphone stand in tow. "She's been handling pretty much everything."

"Well, this place means a lot to her."

"Yeah. Thanks for coming, Dana."

She's staring at me with her arms at her sides.

"I worked with Judith at the bank for eight years. That's why I can't be friendly with you. Even if you didn't kill her."

I nod and watch as she ascends the steps into the House. She's wearing those big-soled shoes that nurses wear, even though they don't match her outfit.

There are about fifty people in our backyard. Tilly weaves in and out of the clustered crowds, wearing a slutty witch costume and heels. Her heels keep getting stuck in the ground but she refuses to change shoes.

"I never get to wear heels. I'm wearing them even if I have to stand in one place," she said earlier in the evening after pulling herself out of the ground twice.

I'm reviewing the silent auction table when Mack shows up. There are certificates for beauty treatments, baskets of fancy foods, a vacation to Gulf Shores condensed in a glossy folder. The blue grass music makes me wish we could have music in the backyard all the time.

"Nice eye patch." He's wearing his regular khakis and short-sleeved button-down.

"Thanks." I flip the eye patch up on my forehead so I can see. "Nice costume. Are you supposed to be an accountant?"

"Ha ha," he says. "Good turnout."

"Yeah. Not bad. It will help." Everything depends on the auction at this point. Maybe we'll stay afloat, maybe we'll sink.

Maggie appears by his side with Samantha against her chest. Maggie's wearing a caftan that I found at the back of Vangie Ann's closet.

"Oh," Mack says as he looks down at the baby.

"Want to hold her?" Maggie asks.

"No, thank you," he says. But Maggie hands him the baby anyway.

Mack's eyes are huge as he takes Samantha into his big hands. He pulls her close and the panicked look is replaced with a slow, content grin.

"You're a natural," I say. My cheeks turn red like the first time I told a boy he was cute.

I don't have to feel stupid for long. Maggie turns to me with wide eyes and asks, "Did you hear people talking in the attic when you lived upstairs?"

"What?" I ask.

Before she can answer, Vangie Ann stumbles out of the backdoor, and I forget all about my boy troubles and the teenaged mama. I make a beeline for Vangie Ann. She's finally here, alive. But she's also messed-up.

The pastor from the Baptist church sees her and starts moving in her direction. But I get to her first.

"Turn around and go back inside." I grab her arm and shuffle her toward the door. Her skin is sticky and hot.

"This is my place, Cass. You can't tell me what to do." She jerks her arm away and looks around. "This looks fucking great."

The pastor is two steps away.

"Please, V. Let's go inside."

"No. I'm hungry." She crosses her arms and sticks out her chin. She marches away from me, bumping into the pastor on the way to buffet table.

I take off after Vangie Ann and grab her arm. "Like hell you are." I pull her toward the door. She jerks her arm from my grasp.

"I'm just here for the party. I'm not staying."

"Sister Blankenship. Your party is lovely." It's Pastor Denton, leaning in to hug V around the shoulders.

I'm surprised to hear him call her "Sister." I hadn't realized she was an active part of his flock.

"Well, thank you. It's good to see you, Brother Denton." She smiles with fake sweetness. "You see, my sister here just got out of jail and she has completely taken over." Vangie Ann and glares at me. "Great job, sis."

"Are you okay, Sister Blankenship?" He puts his hand on her shoulder and stoops down to face her.

Vangie Ann's bottom lip starts to tremble. She tightens her lips and snaps away from the pastor.

"I'm not okay." She looks around the yard. Her hands drop to her sides and she draws them into fists. "I'M NOT OKAY!"

Her screaming proclamation stops the motion in the yard. Every person, all there to help her and the rest of us displaced women, turns to her and stares. The guitar player sends one last note into the air. The rest of the band has already stopped playing.

"What are y'all staring at? Huh? Think you're fucking better than me?" She's turning on her heels and surveying the faces in the small crowd.

"Vangie Ann, please," I say.

"I made this place what it is. ME!" She jabs her thumb into her chest. Her shoulders drop.

I grab her arm again and pull her toward the door. She doesn't have much fight left, and I'm able to pull her all the way to the bedroom.

"What the fuck? You've just made yourself at home, haven't you?" she asks.

My clothes are on the hastily made bed, and my makeup is on the dresser. There's no denying that I've moved in.

"It's just until you come home. It's so Maggie and the baby can have the whole room to themselves."

"Who?" She squints at me, and I can see deeper lines in her face than a couple of weeks before.

"Maggie. She's new here and she just had a baby." TJ's baby. A detail I don't bother to mention.

Vangie Ann grinds her teeth and stares at me. "Well, it seems like you have everything under control."

"If you're not here to stay, I think you should leave." I have to push the words out. I'm afraid of losing sight of her. "You're high, and you've already made enough of a mess."

"I'm not here to stay." She crosses her arms and leans back a little. She sways slightly, unsteady on her feet. "I'm just here for the fundraiser."

"You're not helping." I can't help TJ with Maggie. This situation tells me that. Maggie can't end up like Vangie Ann.

"Fuck you." She loses her balance and falls back a few inches against the wall.

"The bank is going to take the House." I don't know how to make her understand how much we need her.

"What do you want me to do about it?" She shrugs, a pathetic motion that takes more effort than it should.

"Get out." I can't stand to watch her anymore.

"This House is mine!" She puts her hands her hips and stomps her feet.

"And I want you back here. But not like this. Mack's here. He can take you to rehab right now." I'm not sure he can, but if Vangie Ann agrees to it, I'll find a way.

"I don't need rehab. I'm fine." She rakes her hair away from her face with her nicotine-stained fingers, and the track marks in her arm are clearly showcased.

"Please, V." I grab her hands in mine and squeeze, hoping she'll feel some sort of connection to me. Her hands feel like bones covered in damp, dull sandpaper.

"This day was supposed to keep us going for six months." She looks down at her hands and starts working a loose cuticle. Two of her yellow nails pinch the tiny piece of hanging skin. "There ain't enough people out there for that."

"We'll figure it out. You need to come home. But you have to sober up."

She yanks the cuticle. Blood encases the edge of her fingernail, and she wipes it on her cut-off shorts. The maroon streak mark on her shorts leg escapes her attention.

"Who the fuck do you think you are? You can't tell me what to do. I can have you kicked out of here."

"Really? Do you think the cops will listen to a junkie? Look at yourself, V." I grab her shoulders and turn her toward the mirror that sits on top of the dresser.

Vangie Ann searches her appearance like she's looking at a stranger. She reaches up and touches her hair, wild around her head and face. She puts her hands on her hips and thrusts her face forward. She balls her fist and brings it to the mirror in a loud crash. Glass collapses in shards all over the dresser and floor. I jump back to avoid it.

"What the hell are you doing?" My voice emerges as a screech. "GET OUT!"

Vangie Ann stands in front of me, blood pouring from her hand. She stares at it in awe, like she's watching a butterfly emerge from a cocoon.

She grabs a t-shirt from the bed and wraps it around her hand. She walks out of the door, and I'm stuck in place with my jaw dropped.

"That's my favorite t-shirt" I whisper, and shuffle in the pile of mirrored glass.

I don't know how many minutes I stand in that pile. My feet don't seem to want to move through it. It's almost beautiful, the way the ceiling fan fixture jumps the light around on the shards. A silver glint here, a rainbow against the wall.

"What the hell?" Lucinda walks in. The familiar smell of her makes the moment even more peaceful. "What happened here?"

"Vangie Ann stopped by." My toes kick a large shard over to its side, where the light can play better tricks with it.

"Holy shit." She picks her feet up high, one by one, and steps closer. But I'm surrounded, and she can't get within three feet of me. "Where is she?"

"I made her leave." And the tears start. I tell them to stop. *I'm done with you. Said so when we buried Aunt Rita.* But the tears don't listen. They just pour down my face like they're coming from a water hose with no nozzle.

"You made her leave?" Lucinda asks quietly as she holds her hand out to me.

"I'm sorry."

I shuffle out of the pile, pushing glass out of the way with my stupid pirate boots. My hand finds Lucinda's. She pulls me close and lets me cry on her shoulder until her blouse is wet and sticks to her skin.

Chapter 39

The phone ringing from the kitchen jolts me out of my sleep. It's still dark outside, that blackish-purple right before the sun wakes up. The clock reads 4:32 a.m.

My heart races, forcing me to my feet. The phone never rings in the early morning hours for a good reason. Even I know that, and this is the first phone I've had full access to in ten years.

"Hello. Blankenship House." The words ride out of my throat on a gasp of air.

"Cass? It's Danielle." It sounds like she's laughing.

"What's up?"

"TJ and Vangie Ann…" She's not laughing. She's crying, sobbing, choking on her breath and tears.

"What happened? What's going on, Danielle?" The clock on the stove flashes 4:33. It flashes the number then goes dark at one second intervals. *Why have I not fixed that? It can't be difficult.*

"They were in a car wreck. They're both in the hospital." Her voice is even, but she keeps sniffing. I want to tell her to go get a tissue, but I don't.

"Are you there now?"

"I just got here. I haven't seen either of them yet."

"I'm on my way." I put the phone back on the receiver, and I'm lonely. There should be someone waiting in my room, eager to hear about the phone call. Open arms to envelop me and soothe my fears.

I turn on the overhead light in Vangie Ann's bedroom. The harsh, bright light makes my eyes feel like they've been punched. I turn it off, and switch on the small pink-shaded lamp on the bedside table. My jeans and t-shirt are still on the floor from when I changed to my nightshirt. I pull my t-shirt over my head, and something scratches my left shoulder. A small circle of blood forms on the shirt, and I remember the glass from the mirror. Vangie Ann. I kicked her out and now she's in the hospital.

Bandage. There has to be one here somewhere. I go across the hall to the bathroom and pull open the drawers and open the cabinet under the sink. I pull off my t-shirt and see a glimmer of silver from the middle of the bloody hole in my shoulder. I try to grasp the piece of glass, but it's tiny. The trying-to-grasp becomes desperate-digging-with-my-fingernails. Blood pools in the wound. There's a first aid kit under the sink. I pull tweezers from the drawer, and antibiotic cream and a bandage from the kit. I pinch the glass with the tweezers and pull it from my shoulder. It's small. Nearly insignificant. It's strange how something so small could cause so much trouble.

* * *

When we were little girls, our mom told us stories about fairies. They were stories she made up herself. The fairies all had silly little names like Tulip Ice Cream or Tallulah Pickle-Pants. Vangie Ann's eyes would glaze over when Mom started telling the stories. She would hang on each word intently. I was more interested in Vangie Ann's reaction than in the stories themselves.

"I wish I lived in the fairy world," she'd say when Mom finished the story. "I would have wings and sprinkle fairy dust everywhere."

"You live here, Evangeline." Mom would hug us both and say something like, "You are my little fairy babies and you live on earth with me."

After Mom died, we decided she was probably in the fairy world. We both knew this wasn't true, but it felt good to pretend. The fairy tales died with Mom, and the fairies hadn't crossed my mind in a very long time.

Looking down at my sister, swollen and full of tubes, I wonder if she's in the fairy world now. Maybe she's sprinkling fairy dust and not in any pain. The pink streaks in her hair are not blood, but a natural consequence of slipping into the fairy world.

There's a machine breathing for her, another one pumping her full of drugs, another one doing something else. I'm not sure, really. I asked but forgot to listen to the answer. All I could do was stare at her, at the puffy flesh sealing her eyes shut.

Danielle said they hit a tree. TJ took a corner too fast and ran right off the road. The tall pine was broken in half.

A nurse walks in and looks at the machine. She writes something down.

"How is she?" I ask, hoping that the numbers on the machine indicate an improvement.

"About the same as before." In other words, really fucking bad.

The nurse leaves and a man walks in. It takes me a couple of seconds to realize it's Wayne, and he's here because he's TJ's dad.

"How is she?" he asks. His face looks haggard.

"Not good. How's TJ?"

"He's going to be okay." Wayne sits down on the chair near the window. "He has a concussion and a few broken bones."

It's not fair that TJ is going to be okay. He was driving the car. He did this to my sister.

"I kicked her out yesterday. She came back and we were having the fundraiser and she was high." I put my head in my hands and lean forward in my chair. "I kicked her out."

He stands and walks over to me. I feel his hand on my back. It's warm and soothing.

"This ain't your fault." His voice is just above a whisper. "You called Lucinda yet?"

"No. I'm waiting another couple of hours. No reason to wake her up."

"Vangie Ann was thrown from the car. She wasn't wearing a seatbelt."

My stomach flips and flops, threatening to empty itself on the floor. "That's not like her. She always wears a seatbelt."

"She's been doing a lot of things lately that aren't like her." He rubs my back for another second then moves back to his chair. "I thought Judith dying was the worst thing that could happen to this family. The bad shit doesn't seem to ever stop. Not for long, anyway."

"Do you know where they were headed?" I know it doesn't matter, but I need details for this to make sense.

"They were headed south on 31." He shrugs. "Don't know why they were on the highway at 2:00 a.m. Nothing TJ does makes much sense these days, though."

"Is Melody here?" I look up as he winces.

"Yeah. She's with TJ. She knows I'm in here."

I repeat the only thing important that I remember the doctor saying. "Vangie Ann might not survive."

"I'm so sorry, Cass." He chokes on my name and starts to shake. "My son. He's such a damn mess."

I walk over to him and sit on the small window ledge, and drape my arm over his shoulders. He leans into me and cries like I've never seen him, or any other man, cry before. His tears make it unnecessary for me to cry. It's like he's doing it for both of us.

I look up and see Melody staring at us through the glass pane in the door. She moves her finger in the "come here" motion. At first I think it's for Wayne, then I realize it's me. I get up, leaving Wayne to grieve on his own.

When I open the door to the hallway, Melody is standing with her hands on her hips and her jaw set.

"Hey," I say.

"How is she?" she tilts her head toward Vangie Ann's door.

"She's in real bad shape."

"She was in fine shape before you got out. And TJ wasn't doing as bad, either." Her eyes are full of rage.

"Fuck you," I say, because nothing more appropriate comes to mind.

"You know I'm right." Her arms drop to her sides and she walks away.

My instinct is to follow her, make her face me, and punch her in the nose. I can't though. Not here, not today.

Chapter 40

"Do you know what they was doing out there?" Lucinda lights a cigarette and inhales likes she's sucking down a soda.

"No." The breeze brushes against my face, but offers no relief against the heat. "TJ ain't telling anybody."

She wipes a tear, and her ring sends a flash of light. Her makeup is streaked, her tears have cut tracks all the way down her face.

"She looks terrible. All swollen and bruised. Doesn't look like Evangeline at all. Your dad would be heartbroken."

The thought of my dad seeing Vangie Ann in the hospital sends a sharp pain through my gut. I can't imagine he would be very proud of either one of us right now.

"I know." I'm rocking slowly in the chair. "All I can think about is what if I hadn't kicked her out? What if she had stayed here instead of going back to TJ?"

"You did what you had to do, I guess. If you had kept her here, or even called the cops, she could have been locked up instead." Lucinda takes another drag and lets her words hang around my neck. She's not looking at me. "The fundraiser was good, right? You girls made some money?"

You girls. Makes it sound like we are a sorority house instead of a home for ex-cons and victims of domestic abuse.

"No. It was a disaster. We made enough to buy groceries for a week or two." When I kicked her out, I thought I was saving Blankenship House. "A lot of people left after she showed up."

Lucinda nods in response, staring into the street.

"If she doesn't come back…" It will be over, done. We'll all have to find a new place to live before the end of this month. That's what I want to say, but she doesn't let me.

"Don't, Cass." Lucinda finally turns to me. "Don't talk like that. She'll be okay."

"You heard the doctors. She might not."

"Doctors can't account for miracles, and miracles happen all the time." She stubs her cigarette out in the ashtray. "I read a story just the other day where this girl was on her deathbed with cancer. The doctors told her parents to start planning a funeral. Can you imagine a doctor saying something like that? Maybe it wasn't that exactly, but something like 'start making arrangements.'" She looks down at her hands, straightens her rings and takes a deep breath. "Anyway, she was nearly dead and then suddenly she was fine. The cancer started shrinking and now it's completely gone. There's no explanation. All we can do is pray."

Sunday school taught me a lot about prayer. Every Sunday in my pretty dress, I prayed to Jesus and meant every word of it.

When my mom was run over and lying unconscious in a hospital bed, looking a lot like V does right now, I prayed for two whole days that she would live. She never even opened her eyes.

I didn't pray again until I got arrested. Then I spent hours praying that I wouldn't get sent to prison. My first two years in, I prayed every day that I would get out. That Wayne or someone else would come to their senses and get me released. Hours that brought me nothing but sore knees and disappointment.

My words to God: *bring her home.* Then Vangie Ann came home wasted and violent, and I sent her back to TJ. The power of prayer.

Saying this to Lucinda would do nothing but hurt her feelings and start a fight. So I take my turn staring into the street, seeing nothing new, and finding no answers.

Tilly walks outside, breaking my painful train of thought, letting the screen door slam behind her. "That damn baby won't stop crying." She sticks a cigarette between her lips and lights it.

"Samantha barely cries." I stand and walk over to the porch rail. "What are you talking about?"

"Any crying is too much. Makes me want to stick my head in the oven." She looks down at Lucinda. "Oh sorry. That was insensitive."

"Why? Evangeline didn't try to kill herself." Lucinda lights another cigarette and props an elbow on the chair arm. She leans to the side and looks up at Tilly. "Babies are supposed to cry. That's how they communicate."

"Yeah, I guess. I just wish she could do it somewhere else." Tilly blows a puff of smoke out. I don't know how she said so many words while holding in that much smoke.

"You be nice to Maggie and Samantha. They need us." I look into the street again.

"It's nice to be needed, isn't it?" Lucinda asks without looking at me. There's no reason for me to respond.

***

"I want to move back in, me and my boy." Dana stands before me with a suitcase. Troy peeps from behind her and grins.

"What happened?" It's rude to ask, but it's my business now. I'm not just a resident here anymore.

I stand aside and let them walk in, and I close the door behind Troy.

"Elijah's drinking again. He threatened to beat me up last night. This time for no reason. It's not safe." She puts her arm around Troy and pulls him close. He looks down at the floor.

"This place doesn't have a revolving door," I say.

"It kind of does," Sonya interjects. "This is my third time to live here."

I cut my eyes at Sonya, then look back to Dana. "Are you going to stay this time? Vangie Ann's still gone. She's in the hospital." I do my best to deliver the words stoically, to hold myself together.

"Yeah. I heard. How's she doin'?" There is pain in her gaze. Even though her life is falling apart, she feels sorry for me and my sister. I feel bad for noticing that her hair is still dirty.

"Not good."

Dana looks at me with her eyebrows raised, waiting for details that are stuck in my throat, the words going through my brain on a continuous loop. *She might die. She might die.*

"Well, we're here. We need a place to stay." She stands up straight. "Are you going to help us not?"

I recognize her prideful stance. The stance of a woman who's been beaten down but refuses to accept pity or adopt shame.

"You can have your old room."

"Thank you." She looks down at Troy. "Troy's goin' be starting back to school next week."

"Are you excited, Troy?" I bend down a little so I can talk to him face-to-face. He has freckles, a lot of them that I couldn't see until I was close.

He shrugs and says, "I reckon."

"Will you be in second grade?"

"Yeah."

"Do you know that I used to teach second grade?" I cross my arms over my chest and smile.

"When you was in jail?" He cocks his head to the side and scrunches his eyebrows together.

Dana doesn't tell him not to ask questions like that, nor does she laugh at his sweet ignorance. I guess a question like that is no big deal around a place like this.

"No. Before I went to jail." I put my hand on his shoulder. "I had a regular life before jail."

"Are you going to the hospital today?" Dana asks.

My knees crack as I stand up. "Yeah. In a couple of hours."

"If Sonya will watch Troy, I'd like to come with you. Vangie Ann's been real good to us." She maintains her prideful stance, and it works on me.

"I'll watch him," Sonya says before slipping past me to get to the kitchen.

"You can come with me."

"All right." She nods and turns to Troy. "Let's go upstairs and get settled in."

Troy follows her up, turning to look at me every few steps. He's trying to make peace with the idea of me being a school teacher and the woman he thinks killed his mom's friend. So I stick my tongue out and cross my eyes.

Chapter 41

The phone wakes me from my early morning slumber once again. I'm so afraid of what awaits on the other end, I almost don't answer. If I don't hear the words, it won't have happened. Vangie Ann won't be in the hospital. Or dead.

My shaky legs take me to the phone.

"Hello." No formalities.

"Cass?" A female voice, choking on sobs.

"Danielle? Is that you?" My knees bend and carry my butt to the floor.

"TJ's...he's in jail."

I release a sigh that I'd been holding in my gut. It's not V. She's still alive.

"I don't care." It's the truth, and my internal filter isn't awake yet.

"That's so mean." Her words are muffled by tears.

"Are you okay?" Or course she is. Her sibling isn't on his deathbed.

"Yeah." She chokes out a sob that turns almost to laughter. "He's safe now, right?"

"Where are you?"

"Hospital. I came here to visit him and the cops were here taking him away." She's sniffling now. That seems better than the sobs.

My afternoon yesterday was spent at the hospital. Me and Dana, holding vigil at Vangie Ann's side. The swelling had gone down, and I got to see her eyelids flutter a few times. Flutters like butterfly kisses on an angel's cheek. Those little flutters proved to me that she's alive in there. I don't want to go back now, not when I had finally found some relief in sleep.

I really don't understand why she's so upset about TJ. He's in jail, not dead. He probably hasn't even been charged with anything yet.

"I'll be there in fifteen minutes." I'm careful to keep my feelings out of my words.

The entire way to the hospital I'm tempted to turn around and go back to bed. I don't know why I'm doing this. I don't even want to see Danielle.

She's waiting for me in the hospital lobby. Her face is puffy and red, and her eyes are swollen. I pull her into my arms, and her sobs return. So much for cutting her out of my life for not telling me the truth.

"Where's Wayne?" I whisper to the top of her head.

"He's with the doctor or somebody. Something about TJ's release paperwork. I'm not sure. There have been so many people around." She pulls away and wipes her tears with a crumpled tissue. "Do you want to go see your sister? I'll go with you."

"Yeah. Let's go." She grabs my hand. Her tiny hand makes it feel like I'm holding hands with a child.

Vangie Ann is still unconscious. The doctors told me yesterday that her body is healing. That it's not a bad thing for her to be out this long. So many tubes are hanging out of her face and arms that she looks like something from a science fiction movie. Someone has washed the blood out of her hair and her face looks better than it did yesterday. There's a cast on her left arm and left leg, which is held in the air on a sling.

"How's she doing?" Danielle asks. She stands over Vangie Ann with her arms crossed.

"Not great. Broken arm, broken leg, broken ribs, broken pelvis, severe concussion. There was some internal bleeding but they think that's under control now. She might make it. But she might not." I sit on the chair beside the bed and touch my sister's unbroken arm.

"I think I know where they were going." Danielle is still standing over my sister, her eyes focused on Vangie Ann's swollen and bruised face.

"Where?"

"I think they were going to Mom's grave. It's the only thing that makes sense." Danielle reaches out and touches a lock of Vangie Ann's hair, tracing the curl with her fingertips. "Do you still want to know what happened?"

I sit up straight and give Danielle my full attention. "To your mom? You know I do."

"I can tell you." She crosses her arms again and turns to me. "But you're going to hate us all."

"I'm willing to take that chance."

"I don't know if I am. You mean too much to me." She sits down in the window seat and collapses into tears. "I don't want to lose you again."

"You'll lose me if you don't tell me." Maybe my words are hateful. Her brother was just arrested, but I can't help it. "I mean it."

The door opens and a nurse comes in. "Oh. I didn't know anyone was in here. Visiting hours haven't started yet today."

"I know. But I'm her sister."

The nurse nods and busies herself at Vangie Ann's bedside. She's checking machines and writing things down.

Danielle stands up and walks toward the door, and I follow. I want to beg the information out of her. To cry and plead until she tells me the truth. At least something I need would come out of this nightmare. But I don't. She looks small, scared, and exhausted.

Wayne meets us in the hallway after a few paces. He looks ten years older than he did two days ago. He walks faster when he sees me. When we reach each other, he wraps his arms around me and squeezes.

"Cass. Oh, Cass. I'm so glad to see you."

"Thanks, Wayne." I return his hug, hoping Melody doesn't appear. That would be the last thing either one of us needed, an angry Melody.

"At least I won't have to worry about him being on the streets for now. I don't know how long he's going to be gone, but he'll be off the streets." He says the words quietly so Danielle can't hear. I can smell the coffee from his breath. "He'll be charged with vehicular homicide if Vangie Ann doesn't make it."

He releases me and grabs his daughter's hand. "Come on, baby. Melody's looking for you."

"Okay," Danielle says with a sigh. She turns to me and says, "You should have been our mom."

"Stop it. Don't do this right now." Wayne doesn't look at me when he says this. His gaze is focused on Danielle.

I don't respond to her words. I don't know how. Part of me is still sad that I missed out on the life I had planned. The other part of me is glad I didn't have a hand in raising Wayne's messed-up kids.

Chapter 42

I have a date. Okay, it's not a date. But Mack's driving me to see Tabitha. We'll be in the car together all day. And I'll see Tabitha. Tabitha's face should bring clarity and peace, perspective.

Staring into Vangie Ann's closet, I quickly realize I can't borrow her clothes. It would be too weird since she's in the hospital, and because her clothes are so slutty. Mack probably thinks the worst of me since I slept with Wayne. No need to solidify his opinion with a stripper dress.

Samantha cries from upstairs. The sound is sweet and gentle. Apparently the cries don't get shrill and loud until later. Tabitha told me that once when she was telling me stories about her babies. There were three babies, now three teenagers who live with her mother. Her mom brings them to visit when she can afford to make the drive, which has been increasingly infrequent over the years.

The crying stops quickly, and I know Maggie has the baby in her arms.

I put on one of my three sundresses and brush my hair. I already applied my makeup as carefully as if I was about to go to prom.

There's a knock at the front door. I suck in a deep breath, walk the short hallway, and pull the door open. Melody stands on the other side.

"Why are you wearing a dress?" Her makeup's been cried off.

"I have a meeting." The truth is too much to explain. *Sorry that I don't have much time to console you over your incarcerated stepson and/or recently dead mother. My attractive parole officer is taking me to see my former cellmate/lover. Does this dress make me look pretty without looking slutty?*

"Can I come in?"

"Oh yeah. Sorry." I stand aside and she walks in. "Do you want something to drink? A Coke or something?" A hug seems normal under the circumstances. But Melody doesn't get close to me. She has the look in her eyes that she had when she came over to confront me about her husband.

"No." She walks into the sitting room and sits on the couch. "Thank you," she adds.

"I'm sorry about TJ." I sit down, too.

"Yeah. First my mom dies and now my son is in jail."

The word "stepson" comes to mind and wants to jump out of my mouth. Correcting her would be a mistake.

"I know what you're thinking, Cass. You're so easy to read."

"What do you mean?"

"You're thinking he deserves it."

"That's not what I'm thinking, but I won't deny it." I sigh and purse my lips. "I was thinking that he's your stepson. Not your son."

Melody glares at me and juts her chin out. "He was a teenager when I married Wayne. I was there for some of the hardest shit. I never gave birth. TJ and Danielle are my kids."

"What is it with us Blankenship women not bearing children?" I've never really thought about until now.

"I don't know. You were in prison during the bulk of your childbearing years, Vangie Ann was on drugs for some of hers. Tiffany ain't having no kids. And I married Wayne and he didn't want more kids." She shrugs.

"Well, I guess you cleared up that mystery." I wanted more time to figure it out. Just like Melody to take that from me. "I could still have kids, you know. I'm not too old."

Melody grunts in response before changing the subject.

"Vangie Ann might not make it, huh?" Melody's staring at me like she's waiting for me to cry.

"But she might. There's been some improvement."

"There's been too much grief lately. Too much hardship. It's like God has forgotten about me." She takes her gaze off of me and looks to the floor.

"We all go through hard times." My hand goes to her shoulder and she flinches. I leave my hand anyway. She brushes it away.

"Why don't you leave? Isn't there somewhere else you can go?" She's looking at me again. This time with tears in her eyes and her jaw set.

"I had a transfer application filed when TJ turned me in for seeing Wayne." I sit back in my chair, pushing myself as far from her as possible without getting up. "I'm supposed to go to California. I want to leave just as bad as you want me to."

"It would make my life easier if you would leave. Danielle adores you. Do you know that?"

"I kind of figured."

"She talks you up to Wayne. I've caught her." Melody stands up and looks out the window. "I gave her her first box of maxi pads. I'm the one who helped her get ready for her first date. But she wanted you for a mother, and she'd still take you now."

"I don't know what to say, Melody. I was the first woman in her life after her mom left. Maybe she's attached to me for that reason."

"And Wayne? Well, he'd rather have you, too," she says as a single tear rolls down her cheek.

"That's not true, Mel. He loves you."

"Just please, please leave."

I get up and stand beside her at the window.

"I'm staying away from your family as best I can. I'll continue to do so. I promise. But I'm not allowed to leave right now." I don't know why she doesn't understand that those kids keep coming to me.

I should already be in Camarillo helping rich ladies pick out dresses for parties, matching purses to shoes. Spending evenings reading books in the lowering sunshine with no one expecting more from me.

"Maybe we can leave then. Wayne could open a shop somewhere else." She turns to me and says, "Danielle could stay here with you."

"This isn't the place for Danielle. She's never been in trouble."

"What makes you think that? Just because you've been away, time stopped?" She shakes her head and turns back to the window. She parts a larger spot in the open blinds with two fingers. "That girl has been in trouble. She's better now that she's on the right medication."

"I had no idea."

"Why would you, Cass? She's not your family."

"Look, Melody. I'm sorry for sleeping with your husband. I'm sorry for the effect I've had on your family. I meant you no harm, but it was beyond shitty. I'm trying to be better than that." By setting my sights on my shacked-up parole officer instead. I'm such a hypocrite.

"I hope you are trying to be better. I really hope you are. I can't take any more heartbreak." She turns toward me again.

"I won't hurt you again." And I mean it. If there was any doubt in my mind about ever revisiting Wayne's Wrangler snake, it's gone now.

"I believe you." She glances out the door, then steps toward me. "Your parole officer just pulled up. I'll be leaving now."

His work sedan sits on the street. I'm relieved that we will have air conditioning for the long trip.

"Okay. If you ever decide you want to be my friend again, I'm willing to try." I walk her to the door.

"We'll see, okay?" She puts her arms loosely around me, and I return the half-assed hug.

"Bye, Melody."

Watching her retreat, my mind replays a scene from our teen years. She came over to bitch at me about a boy she liked who liked me instead. A boy who meant nothing to me, and meant everything to her for about one month. He was insignificant, but she was mad at me and I got mad at her in return.

I know things are different now. This is real life. The consequences and the players matter. Wayne isn't just some boy who drives a Firebird and passes me notes in sociology.

Mack approaches, taking me out of my teen years and bringing me back to the front door of the Blankenship Home for Displaced Women and Children.

He's wearing his standard khakis, but with a deep blue polo shirt instead of a button-down. The small change makes him look younger, more relaxed.

"Everything okay?" he asks, nodding his head toward Melody.

"Yeah. Just family stuff."

"I bet she's pretty wrecked, huh?" He's standing in front of me now, his broad shoulders blocking my view of Melody as she gets in her car.

"Yeah. It's a rough time."

"You ready?"

"I just need to grab my purse."

When I return, Tilly and Sonya are surrounding Mack like he's a movie star.

"Did you play football in high school? I bet you did." Sonya's rubbing his shoulder.

Mack's face goes bright red. "Yeah."

"I bet you could bench press me," Tilly says and squeezes his bicep. "I'd really like you to try."

"Ladies, back off," I say.

Sonya and Tilly smile at me and remove themselves from Mack.

"I won't be back until this evening. Can you guys cook dinner? Dana will probably help if you ask her. She's helping Troy with his homework right now."

"You look pretty," Sonya says. "Where are you two headed?"

"Mack's taking me to see Tabitha." I smile without trying.

"Isn't that a conflict of interest? I mean your new beau taking you to see your girlfriend?" Tilly asks with her head cocked. She's really thinking this over.

"Mind your own business." I turn to Mack. His entire head is blushing. "Let's go, Mack."

As we walk down the sidewalk to his sedan, I turn back to the House to see Tilly and Sonya watching us through the window. I smile, flip them off, and loop my arm through Mack's, simply because I can't resist.

When we get in the car he says, "I didn't know your cellmate was your, um, girlfriend."

"Of course she was. I was in there a long time." I pull the mirror down and check my lipstick.

Mack starts the car, and doesn't ask any questions. Even though I would like for him to ask instead of forming his own judgments.

Chapter 43

I sit at a tiny table in a room full of tiny tables waiting for Tabitha to emerge. It's the same place where my dad saw me last. He could hardly take visiting me here. His heartbreak was written all over his face.

I see Tabitha when she comes out of the door. Her hair is no longer cornrowed, but instead it's in a soft afro. I stand and when she reaches the table, I pull her into my arms. Unlike my dad, she's still alive. I can keep from breaking her heart.

"No touching!" A guard shouts from the corner.

We pull apart and sit down in the plastic chairs.

"You look beautiful. I love your hair." My eyes search all of her that I can see. Her skin is so soft it's almost velvety. It's not fair that we can't touch.

"You look beautiful, too. Makeup *and* hair dye. A dress. Girl, you are a sight for sore eyes." She's smiling. It's the best thing I've seen in ages, second only to Samantha's perfect face.

"I miss you, Tabitha. So much. I wish you were with me." My bottom lip trembles but I don't let the tears fall.

"I miss you, too." She leans close toward me, as close as she's allowed. Her eyes dart side to side and she begins to whisper. "We don't have much time, so you have to listen."

"Sure, okay." I nod, keeping my hands flat on the table, centimeters from hers.

"Before I ended up here, I was saving money so I could take the kids and leave Cassius. I buried it in a coffee can in my mom's yard." She bites her bottom lip and looks down. "It's only two thousand dollars, but my oldest wants to go to college and can't afford it."

"What do you want me to do?"

"Here." She slides a piece of paper toward me. There's an address written on it. "It's buried at the bottom of a weeping willow tree. Dig it up and take it home."

"Take it home? Don't you want me to give it to your son?"

"Yeah. But I want you to put it in your own checking account, then write checks directly to Ray's college. Don't let him waste it." Tabitha looks up with moist eyes. "I don't know if he's any good with money. He might be, but I really don't know. I'll mail you the school information."

"Sure. Anything you want."

"Who's that?" She tilts her head toward Mack. He's standing against the wall with his arms crossed.

"My parole officer."

Her eyes search him up and down. "The girls around here would love that."

She always calls men "that" instead of "him." Abused women do what they can to empower themselves.

"How's the new roommate? You two carrying on yet?"

Tabitha's mouth turns up a little. "Not yet. She'll come around, though."

"Of course she will." We lock eyes. "I love you." The words come out choked.

"I love you, too. Thanks for coming to see me."

"Sorry it took so long." The words aren't enough.

"Write me when it's done, okay? Let me know." She's nodding at me.

"I promise."

A tall muscular female guard places her hand on Tabitha's shoulder.

"I have to go." Tabitha says the words slowly, holding on as long as possible.

"Okay. Keep writing, okay?"

"You, too." Tabitha stands and puckers her lips at me, kissing the air.

I pucker my lips in return as Tabitha stands and walks away with the Amazon woman guard. She should be leaving with me, helping me navigate life like she helped me navigate prison.

* * *

"You okay?" We're halfway home when Mack asks. The first hour and a half was full of silence, except for the sound of the sedan slicing through the wind.

"Yeah. Thanks." I look out the window. It looks like the trees are passing us instead of the other way around.

"You probably don't want to hear this."

"Then don't say it."

"I have to." Mack looks straight ahead. "If you keep your attachments to prison, you're more likely to go back."

"Are you calling Tabitha an 'attachment'?"

"Yeah. Just think about it, okay?"

I nod in response, even though I don't intend to give it any thought at all. I'm not abandoning Tabitha or going back to prison. There's nothing to consider.

"You see the best in people, but you overdo it." His hands fidget on the steering wheel like he's not quite sure where to put them.

"What the fuck does that mean?" I sigh, wishing we could go back to silence.

"Wayne and his kids were the beneficiary of Judith's life insurance, yet you believe his innocence." Mack glances at me quickly, not removing his eyes from the road for long.

"Yeah." I turn my body toward him.

"His cousin was the prosecuting attorney. And when it was all said and done, Wayne and his kids inherited seven hundred and fifty thousand dollars." He glances at me again, this time with his eyebrows raised. He looks like he's about to say, "duh."

"What are you getting at? Just spit it out."

"You know what I'm getting at. Wayne did it. He killed her for the money and set you up. Stop being so blind."

"He couldn't have set me up. Wayne had no idea I'd show up at her apartment."

"Why were you at her apartment anyway?" he asks.

"She called me out of the blue. Said she wanted to clear things up. He couldn't have known, could he have?"

"I don't know. Maybe he was just going to take his chances with not getting caught, then you made it easy for him." He reaches his right hand to my arm and leaves it there for a beat. "Just think about it, okay?"

"It doesn't make sense." Does it?

"Maybe that's not quite it. But there's something here you're not seeing. That woman dying worked out really great for Wayne. He and the kids got a windfall, and he didn't have to worry about her coming back for the kids."

"Or the kids watching their mom wasting away to addiction anymore." I see her face, pretty and fresh like Danielle's, then gaunt and pockmarked from the drugs. I don't know why anyone would do drugs that made them lose their looks.

"Here's what I think: you thought it was Wayne the entire time you were in prison. You get out, you see him, you sleep with him. And then believe him because you want to."

"I believe him because I believe him."

"You believe him because it hurts to think that someone you still care about after all these years could have fucked you over in such a huge way." Mack's cheeks turn rouge, from anger or embarrassment. Or maybe a combination. "If you think I'm wrong, tell me what you think happened."

I sigh deeply and say, "I'm not sure. Maybe it was Matt Morgan. Tilly said he came home with a pistol that night."

"If you're right, you'll never clear your name. Matt Morgan is dead and gone." Both of his hands are on the steering wheel and he's staring straight ahead. "I think you'd rather never clear your name than admit that it was Wayne."

"You're wrong." My voice comes out louder than I intend. "I thought it was him the entire time I was away. I hated him for it, and I was used to hating him."

"But you stopped hating him and started caring about him again."

I don't know if he's right or if he's wrong. But his words hurt. Helpful to hurtful, not what I need right now.

"Just get me home, please." I look out at the passing trees and try not to think.

Chapter 44

Danielle's waiting on the front porch when we get back. She's sitting in a rocking chair watching traffic.

"Somebody wants you back, even if it ain't Wayne," Mack says. He nods toward Danielle and looks back to the street.

"Thanks for the lift." I get out without waiting for him to say goodbye. I feel like an asshole. It was really sweet of him to take me to see Tabitha, but the lecture reduced my gratitude.

Danielle stands up when she sees me walking up the driveway. "Hi, Cass."

"Hey, Danielle. Why are you here?"

"Just wanted to see what you were up to." Her mouth turns up for a second, then goes right back down. As usual, Danielle's face can't decide if it's happy or sad.

"You here to finish our conversation? Are you ready to talk?" I'm trying to be tough, but I'm tired from the trip to the prison.

"Melody told me she asked you to leave town. You're not going to, are you?"

"Not yet." I unlock the three locks and push the door open. Danielle follows me in.

Blankenship House is quiet when we walk in. No baby crying, no Troy stomping, no Sonya laughing. It's not late enough for everyone to be asleep. Something's off, but I don't know what.

I walk up the stairs and Danielle follows. If I have to keep running the place, I'm changing out the lavender stair runner. I hate it.

They're all in Maggie's room. Every last one of them. Maggie is shoving clothes in a backpack. There's a sadness weighing in the air that reminds me of the hospital when Aunt Rita was dying. The sadness that comes from knowing someone is leaving you, and you'll never see them again.

"You can't do this," Sonya says. "We'll miss you guys."

"It's what's best. My aunt will take care of us." Maggie shoves a onesie in her bag and looks over at her sleeping baby. She's still young enough that voices don't wake her.

"We'll all take care of you." Dana is sitting on the extra bed. Troy is planted in her lap with his head resting on her breasts like they're pillows.

"What's going on?" I step into the room and make my presence known. Danielle follows silently behind.

Maggie stops packing and looks at me. "My aunt sent me money for us to come join her. I'm getting on the train tomorrow."

"You can't leave, can you? Isn't this part of your probation?" I should already know the answer to these questions.

"I talked to my probation officer. My PO's submitted my transfer and he's having it expedited so I can get going. I'll have a new probation officer in Mississippi."

"Is this what you want?" I already know the answer. She wouldn't be packing if she didn't want to go.

Maggie nods and looks down at Samantha. "It's the right thing to do."

"But we'll miss you," Tilly says.

"I'll miss you guys, too." Maggie starts packing again, shoving those big t-shirts as far down as she can. She's running out of space in the backpack.

"Is your aunt good to you?" Dana strokes Troy's hair and his eyes start to close.

"She's the best," Maggie says.

"No, Maggie," Danielle says. "Your baby will need both parents."

"What do you know?" Sonya crosses her arms and looks at Danielle.

"Sorry. I just, well, I don't think she should take the baby away." Danielle's cheeks flush pink and she looks to the floor.

Maggie stops and folds her arms across her chest. "Danielle, you know as well as I do that your brother isn't ready to be a father. At least in Mississippi I'll have help."

Silence falls across the room. Dana opens her mouth to speak, but closes it instead.

The thought of Maggie taking the baby away from us makes my heart hurt. She's only been with us a little while, but it feels like she belongs to us, to the House. But it's nobody's decision but Maggie's. And it's probably best if she gets away from TJ.

"Are you sure, Maggie?" I put my hand on her shoulder so she'll look at me. There are tears in her eyes.

"Yes." She turns back to her task.

"My aunt has a big enough house for us, and there's a college a couple of miles from her house. She thinks I can go there. There's financial aid and assistance for people like me."

"What will I tell TJ?" Danielle asks.

"I don't know!" Maggie shouts. Samantha wakes with a shrill cry. Maggie picks her up and squeezes the baby to her chest. "It's my choice."

"Leave her alone, Danielle," Tilly says.

"I have to handle this. I have to figure it out. I'm a mother now." She rocks side to side, and Samantha's cries die down. Maggie sits on the bed, still her holding her baby.

I sit next to her. "Just promise that you'll come back if things don't work out."

Danielle glares at us from the doorway.

"I promise." She looks at me with her brownish-orange eyes. I think she's telling the truth.

"Will you send pictures of Samantha?" Tilly asks.

"Now Tilly, when did you start caring about the baby?" I'm smiling, even though it's fake, to try to lighten the mood.

"I don't know. It was the weirdest thing. Samantha's the only baby I have ever liked. She seems smarter than the others." Tilly's smiling, too. But she looks like she's on the verge of tears.

Dana stands up, pushing Troy to his feet. "I'm taking this one to bed." She wraps her arms around Maggie.

Troy shuffles across the hall behind his mama. He mumbles, "Goodnight."

"How are you getting to the train station?" The nearest train station is over an hour away, and I don't want to take her.

"My cousin is coming to pick me up." She looks down at Samantha, whose tears are gearing up again. "I need to get some rest, ladies. My baby's hungry, and I have a big day tomorrow."

"Okay. I'll be downstairs."

Danielle walks downstairs with me and sits at the table. "I don't want her to take the baby away."

"You haven't had anything to do with Samantha." I hold a glass under the tap and take a sip of water.

"Well, no. But I think having a baby would make TJ clean up his act." Danielle looks at her hands, flat on the tabletop. Her fingertips are painted pale blue.

"Do you really?" I ask.

Danielle looks up at me and smiles softly but doesn't speak.

A wash of cold rushes my blood. If I know one thing, it's that the baby needs to be as far away from TJ and Danielle as possible. "I need to change. Please leave."

I walk down to Vangie Ann's room, my room, and peel off the heels and dress. My jeans and t-shirt are still on the floor from when I took them off earlier. I want Danielle to leave, and I want the goodbye with Maggie to be over with. Sentimentality has no place here. We're all in transition.

* * *

"Evangeline is awake." The doctor on the phone speaks with a cadence that indicates hope. Maybe not much hope, but a little is better than none.

"Really?" I gasp, as if it might be a cruel joke and really she's dead.

"Yes. She's asking for you." I can tell she's smiling.

"I'm on my way."

The morning started with Maggie and Samantha getting ready to leave Blankenship House. I haven't known either of them long, but they became a part of our little family so fast. And it felt like they needed us: me, Sonya, and Tilly. None of us were used to that feeling, but adapted quickly and happily.

With them leaving, I'm reminded that no one really needs me. I was gone for a decade, and life kept going for everyone else. I became insignificant.

The other girls feel it, too. Sonya isn't out of her room yet, and I could hear her crying when I pressed my ear against her door earlier. Tilly is already outside smoking on the porch and staring into the street. She isn't in the mood to talk, a point she made clear as soon as I tried to engage her.

I walk past Tilly on the way to my truck. "Vangie Ann's awake." I take the porch steps in one leap. When I get to the truck, I turn to see Tilly smiling.

The hospital feels like my second home since I've been out of jail. I'm starting to lose track of how many times I've been here, and there's no time to count it up right now.

When I walk through the door, Vangie Ann is sitting up. There are still tubes in her arms, but her face has no machines attached. She looks mostly like herself. I dash to her side, uncertain of what to do. Is she still angry? But she holds her arms out as far as the tethers will allow, and I wrap her in my arms.

"I've missed you so much." I cry into her hair, those embarrassing tears I swore I was done with.

"I'm sorry," she whispers.

We hold each other like that long enough for my lower back to start hurting from bending over. I sit in the chair next to her and hold her hand. Her nails are broken and the paint is chipped.

"Want me to bring stuff to do your nails later?" I ask.

"Yeah. That'd be great." She smiles at me and her lips look they're about to crack.

"I'll bring Chap Stick, too."

"Can you tell me what happened? The doctor told me there was a car wreck, but that's all she would say."

"I'm not sure, really." I study her fingernails for a second and wonder what shade of pink polish to bring back. I decide to bring a few bottles so she can choose. "You were in the car with TJ. It was early in the morning, like two o'clock."

"Is TJ okay?" She squints her eyes and her crow's-feet are more prominent than they were a month ago.

"Yeah. He's in jail, though."

Vangie Ann leans her head on the pillow. "Why is he in jail?"

"DUI. They were also waiting to see if it was going to be vehicular homicide." I squeeze her hand to make sure she's real. "We almost lost you."

She sighs. "I'm sorry. I don't know what came over me. I've been clean so long. I've heard about relapses, but I didn't think I'd have one. I'd come too far."

"It's okay." That's a lie, but it's the right thing to say.

"I'm forgetting something about TJ. It's so weird. There's this nagging feeling. You know?" She squeezes my hand back. The squeeze brings a strange relief.

I shake my head because I don't know.

"Maybe I'll remember later." She shrugs and releases my hand so she can smooth her hair.

"I met Gabe." The thought pops in my head and comes out of my mouth before I have time to decide if it's a good idea or not.

"Really?" Her lips turn up slightly and she says, "Handsome devil, ain't he?" Her cheeks turn pink, and I know she's thinking about the parts of him I haven't seen.

The kiss he laid on me flashes in my mind, and my cheeks turn pink, too. I'm glad Vangie Ann can't read my mind. "Yeah, he is. You don't see men like that every day."

"Thank the good Lord for that. Men with those looks will lead you down the path to evil." Vangie Ann's grinning now.

"What about TJ, though?" I don't want to embarrass her right now, but it's bugging me. I've never seen Vangie Ann with a man who wasn't good-looking.

"Well, he had plenty of meth. And he's not so bad when you're around him for a little while. He's kind of like an injured puppy."

"An injured puppy who looks like the banjo kid from *Deliverance*."

"He does not." She tilts her head toward me. "He's not handsome, but he's not ugly."

"I think we'll have to agree to disagree." I sit back in my chair and stretch my legs out.

"We weren't having sex if that's what you think."

"Thank God," I say. The relief is only second to finding out she was awake this morning.

"We were way too high to have sex. Needles are crazy."

"Thank God." I never thought I would be relieved that my sister used needles. "Did he say anything to you about his mom?"

"He talked about her a little. He's still really angry." She rubs one of her fingernails against the sheet. "TJ really needs therapy."

"No. Well yeah, he does. But what I meant was did he mention anything about the night she died?"

Vangie Ann looks at me and then looks to the wall, her eyes are squinted. "It seems like he did. But I don't remember."

That figures. "If you remember something will you let me know?"

"Of course."

"Let's make a list of stuff you need from home." I stand up to find a piece of paper while my sister, frail and tiny, remains in the white-sheeted bed.

Chapter 45

It's late in the evening when Elijah shows up. I can see him through the peephole. This time there are veins bulging in his forehead and neck. It's enough to make a woman asexual.

He's banging on the door, but I have the good sense not to open it this time.

"Go away, Elijah. You're not welcome here." The door is closed, and I'm shouting directly at it.

Bang, bang, bang. "I need to see my wife." He's turning purple.

"Not going to happen."

Tilly joins me. She's grinning like this is the most fun she's had in years. "Get off the porch, bacon grease."

"Bacon grease?" I ask her.

She shrugs.

Dana has emerged from her room and she's standing at the top of the stairs. "Elijah?"

"How'd you guess?" Tilly asks with a smirk.

Bang, bang, bang. "I'm not leaving before I talk to my wife."

"I'll call the cops if you don't leave right now." I glance at Dana and she's hasn't moved from her perch.

"Call the damn cops. I don't give a shit!" he shouts at the door.

Tilly darts toward the phone, a sudden sense of urgency taking her over.

There's a crash in the sitting room, and I jump backward a few paces. I turn to see a chair from the front porch placed in front of the sofa like it belongs there. Glass covers the carpet, and Elijah is facing me with his red eyes and purple jowls. I expect him to say, "Heeerrreee's Johnny."

"Tell that bitch I want to talk right now!" He's coming in through the window, one leg in and one leg out. "She ain't leaving me!"

Tilly emerges from the kitchen with a broom. She's holding the straw end and swinging the handle at his head. She hits him across the face twice with a solid *whack*,

whack and he falls backward. One tennis-shoed foot is hanging through the broken window. The shoes are white leather, stained with dirt and something oily. A shard of glass rests in his ankle, and blood is pouring out in a thick line down the wall.

Dana bounds down the stairs. She gasps when she sees her husband's bloody foot hanging in the living room. It's a strange sight: a part of someone's leg busting through a window like he had kicked it instead of throwing a chair.

"Mommy?" Troy is at the top of the stairs and slowly making his way down. He's in his pajamas and has a small velour blanket tucked under his arm. He looks like a toddler, and I want to hold him.

"Go back to our room and close the door," Dana says, but Troy stands frozen. "Now!"

Troy's eyes jump to discs and he sprints to the bedroom.

Dana opens the door and I follow. We stand looking at her husband, immobile and messy. My instinct is to kick him to see if he's alive, but that seems rude.

Dana kneels down to his side. "Elijah? Elijah?" She slaps his face, bloody from the broom handle striking his nose.

"That ain't helping." Tilly's standing behind me.

Dana puts two fingers to his neck. "Do either of you know CPR?" She turns around and looks at us. There's an animalistic panic covering her face.

Tilly and I both shake our heads. I'm pretty sure I wouldn't put my mouth on Elijah's even if I could save his life.

"He's still breathing," Dana says. She stands up. Her face is as white as paper. She falls to his side with a thud.

"Well, shit. What do we do now?" Tilly lights a cigarette.

"Call an ambulance, I guess." I bend down to Dana and make sure she has a pulse. Neither of them are dead yet.

* * *

"Death comes in threes." Vangie Ann says when I tell her about Elijah's massive heart attack that played out half in our sitting room.

"Elijah hasn't died yet. And that's an old wives' tale." I'm brushing her hair. Her curls are going from tangled to puffy. "And anyway, Aunt Rita and Elijah didn't even know each other."

"I just feel like Aunt Rita dying was just the beginning. Bad stuff is coming."

The police questioned Tilly about her hitting him across the nose with the broom handle. It didn't take long to figure out that the broom handle blow didn't really hurt him. And that he deserved that whack across the nose. They still put the fear of God in her. I was scared, too. Having the police in the House asking questions and snooping around isn't comfortable for anybody, but especially for ex-cons.

"Bad stuff has already happened." My first two months out of prison have been two of the worst months of my life, second only to my first two in prison.

"How's Dana holding up?" Vangie Ann leans back against the pillow, even though I'm not finished brushing her hair.

"She's okay. Elijah's in intensive care. He's weak." I place the hairbrush on the tray beside the bed. "Dana probably feels empowered for the first time in a long time."

"I wonder if they'll go home." Vangie Ann is looking at her nails.

"Ready for your manicure?" I grab her hand and look at her nails. They're chipped, and a few have broken bits of fake nails still glued on. Even in prison, mine never got quite so bad.

"Yeah. Did you bring everything?" She looks at me and almost smiles, but not quite.

"Three different pinks."

"Thank you."

"How much longer are you here?" It's a question I've been reluctant to ask. She's been granted a future, and I'm afraid talking about it can make it disappear.

"Hopefully only another three or four days." A flash of something, fear or dread or both, appears in her eyes. "Take my cell phone with you. It's on the table there."

I pick up the phone, crusted with blood and dirt. "I'll clean this up for you. How did it survive the wreck?"

"It was in my shorts pocket. Still works and everything."

I slip the phone into my purse. "I'll get your room ready." I grab my purse and start pulling out fingernail tools.

"What do you mean?" She looks at me with her eyes squinted. Then the memory hits her. "Oh. Right."

"You can have it back." I say the words quietly like a secret.

"Look, something's been nagging at me. Right before the wreck, me and TJ were fighting about something. I can't remember what exactly, but it seems like it has something to do with you."

"Maybe you'll remember later. Don't push yourself too hard, okay?"

She gasps. "My recovery journal."

"Where is it?"

"Either the trailer or the cabin. Find that and maybe you'll get your answers." Vangie Ann shrugs and looks down at her hands, bending her fingers to get a better look at her jacked-up nails.

Chapter 46

"We're going home, Miss Cass." Troy is dragging his suitcase down the stairs when I walk in.

"Are you excited?" I'm not sure that's the right question, but it's all I've got.

Troy stops his progress down the stairs and looks at me. "Well, my toys are there."

Dana appears behind him with her suitcase. "How's Vangie Ann?"

"She's good. Better." I walk up the stairs halfway and grab Troy's suitcase.

Tilly emerges from the kitchen. "You leaving?"

"Yep. It's safe to go home for now," Dana says. She drags her suitcase to the bottom of the stairs. "Elijah will be in the hospital a while. I'm filing for divorce while he's there. Getting a restraining order. Getting rid of all his stuff. It's a fresh start."

"Good luck." Tilly looks at me and says, "I'm taking her room."

"Like I give a shit," I say. "I mean, I'm not really in charge anymore as soon as V gets back."

I squat down so I'm eye level with Troy. "Sorry about my potty-mouth, big guy."

"That's okay." Troy wraps his arms around my neck. "Mama told me not to repeat anything I hear in this House."

"That's good advice." I squeeze him in my arms. He's so thin I could wrap my arms around him twice.

"We'll stay in touch," Dana says. "Troy really seems to care for you."

"Thanks for letting me know." I start to hug Dana, but decide against it. Instead, I just say, "He's a good kid."

She nods and leads Troy to the door. "Thanks for everything, Cass. And good luck."

The state of my life must be pretty crap for someone like Dana to wish me luck. Or maybe that's just her way of being nice.

Tilly's brewing coffee in the kitchen. I sit at the table.

"Here you go." She sits down at the table with a cup of coffee for each of us.

"Thanks." I take a sip. It's too bitter, but I know I'll drink it anyway. It's better than prison coffee.

"Is TJ still locked up?" Tilly sits back in her seat, looping one elbow over the back of the chair.

"Yeah."

"And you need to find Vangie Ann's recovery journal?"

"Yeah."

"Then what are you doing here? Go look for clues." She smiles and slaps the table. "But first you better make sure the son-of-a-bitch isn't out of jail."

"I'll call Danielle." I stand up and head to the phone.

Danielle confirms that TJ is still locked up. Mack isn't answering his phone, so I get in the pickup and head to his house. The address from the phone book takes me down a dirt road outside of town. Now I know why his truck is always so dirty.

The driveway is rocky and leads to a house with green siding and a screened-in front porch. I imagine him sitting on the porch in the evening with his lady at his side. The thought makes me feel queasy and doubt my decision to just show up. I almost turn around twice while I'm waiting for him to answer the door.

The woman who answers the door takes my breath away. She's wearing a purple track suit, and her hands are covered in clunky rings. She has several dainty chains around her neck, and her hair is arranged in a perfect gray circle.

"Yeah," she says and puts her hand on her hip. She's hasn't bothered to open the screen door.

"Hi. I'm looking for Mack. Do I have the right house?" I back up a couple of paces in case I need to take off.

"Yeah, honey. Come on in." The woman pushes the screen door open and I see her in her full aged glory.

"Thank you. My name is Cass."

"Nice to meet you. I'm Edith." Edith turns and yells, "Mack! You have company!" She turns to me and asks, "Can I get you a glass of tea?"

"No, thank you." I stand in one spot, unsure of what to do with myself.

Mack appears wearing jeans and a t-shirt. I've never seen him look so young and handsome. He looks from me to Edith and back to me again. His face goes crimson.

"Cass? What are you doing here?"

"I'm sorry. You weren't answering your phone. I need your help."

He steers me by the elbow to the front porch. "What's going on?"

"Wait, first what's going on with you? You can't tell me that Edith is your girlfriend." I point to the front door as if he doesn't know who I'm talking about. "She's the woman you live with?"

The red of his face somehow goes even deeper, almost to a purple. "She's my mother."

"But, wait. You said you live with a woman."

"I know, I know. And I do. I live with my mother. I couldn't very well tell you that, could I?"

A laugh emerges from my stomach and pops out of my throat. It's an obnoxious guffaw, and it feels super.

"Thanks a lot." Mack crosses his arms over his chest.

I take a few deep breaths and my laughter subsides. "I'm sorry, Mack. You could have told me. Who am I to judge? I live with my sister in a halfway house."

"Why are you here, Cass?" His hands drop from his sides and he stares at me.

"We need to go to TJ's right now. He's still locked up. Vangie Ann said she remembers that they were fighting about something, and she thinks it was something to do with me. Let's go see if we can find her recovery journal." The words pour out quickly.

"We can't just break into his house."

"You're right. We might have to break into his cabin, too."

Mack sighs and says, "Let me get my shoes."

My laughter picks up again in the truck. It starts with a snicker that bursts forward while I'm holding my breath to keep it back. This happens again and again, until the dam breaks and my laughter fills the car.

"You're a parole officer," I wipe a tear and catch my breath, "and you live with your mother. Some tough guy you turned out to be."

He smiles from the corner of his mouth. "I know how it looks. But if I tell you the complete truth at this point, you're going to feel like an asshole."

"Oh, really? Try me, mama's boy." It had to be some sort of financial hardship on his part that landed him there, and it was a temporary situation that has become semi-permanent.

"She's sick. That's why I need this money. It'll get worse."

"You're shitting me," I say, and I hope he is. "She looks fine. Didn't seem to have any trouble moving around or anything."

"It's dementia, Cass." He looks straight ahead at the road. "Told you you'd feel like an asshole."

"She didn't seem, well, like she's losing it or anything."

"It comes and goes. Some days she's sharp as a whip. Other days, she can't find the right outfit and shoes to wear to work." He glances at me for a beat and turns back to the road. "Mom's been retired for over a decade."

"Wow. You really do know how to make a girl feel like an asshole." I look down to my fingers twisted up in my lap.

"I didn't want to do that. And the reason I didn't tell you I lived with her wasn't because I'm embarrassed." Mack sighs and taps his knuckles lightly against the window. "I didn't want you to know what kind of baggage I got."

"Holy shit, that's so stupid. Look at my baggage. You could have at least told me to make me feel better about my life."

He grins and says, "I guess you're right." Mack stares straight ahead again. "It's just that sometimes I think of you in ways I shouldn't. You know, like the wanting to kiss you and stuff. It's all driving me crazy."

A broad smile over takes my face, and I do my best to squish it down to a normal smile that doesn't make me look insane or overmedicated.

"You're going to make a break for it as soon as you're able. I don't want to get attached," he says.

"Just because I'm leaving doesn't mean we can't enjoy our time together."

Mack pulls into the trailer park. Our conversation had distracted me from the death stink. He puts the truck in park, turns to look at me, and says, "Maybe you're right." My stomach responds with a tiny flip.

Chapter 47

"How close were you to TJ?" Mack's standing in the kitchen, digging through drawers. The countertops are piled high with dirty dishes and food wrappers.

"We were close, I think. I mean, I was with his dad for almost two years. Those kids didn't have a real mom at that point. Danielle took to me more than TJ did, but I think he liked having me around." I'm in the living room, only a few feet away from Mack. I lift a couch cushion and a cockroach lands on my shoe and scurries across the threadbare carpet. "This place is disgusting."

"TJ has been in a lot of trouble the past few years." He's flipping through a stack of papers.

"Yeah. I feel bad for him, but he's such an asshole." I pick up another cushion, uncovering ashes and potato chip crumbs.

"I'm sure he's not what you had in mind when you thought you'd be raising him."

I let the cushion drop and turn to him. "No. I guess not."

He doesn't look up. "What exactly are we looking for?"

"A notebook. V's recovery journal."

"Something like this?" Mack holds up a notebook with a cover that was once red but has faded to orange. The column of spiral metal has been flattened.

"No. It's brown leather."

I walk over and take the notebook from his hands. The cover resists opening, so I fold it against the metal to see pages and pages of drawings. Each one more macabre than the one before. Women, naked and arranged in various states of dismemberment. Men in helmets or hoods that look like animal heads with antlers wielding sharp, bloody weapons.

"Oh my God," I whisper, unable to speak at a normal volume because the wind has left my lungs.

Mack slides behind me and looks over my shoulder. "What a sick fuck."

"This is no help." I close the cover and push the notebook away from me. "I'll hit the bedroom. You keep searching in here."

"That was the last drawer. I'll go with you."

The short, dark hallway opens into a small bedroom. The mattress is bare except for various stains. The air is tainted with nicotine and chemical sweat, mixed with the ever-present stench of the chicken plant.

"I wish we'd brought rubber gloves," Mack says. He lifts the mattress, and I look beneath. Nothing but dirt.

Mack picks up a pile of sheets from the floor, releasing a stale sex smell, and tosses the pile on the bed. A pair of pink silky panties drops from the pile, panties I've seen at home in the laundry.

I turn to a dresser and start digging. The first drawer is nothing but underwear and socks. The second is t-shirts. There's a towel in the third, and just under the towel are two notebooks. I take them out and toss one to Mack. Illegible phrases and more drawings.

The remainder of our search yields nothing.

"All right. Want to head to the cabin?" Mack is washing his hands at the sink. He grabs a paper towel from a roll on the countertop.

"Yeah. We have to get this done." I'm not prepared to keep digging in TJ's filth, but it's the only option. "I'll call the girls on the way."

* * *

I'm on the phone with Tilly when the call-waiting beeps. Tilly's telling me that she made loaded baked potatoes for dinner, and she saved one for me.

"Hold on," I say and hold the phone in front of my face. I'm not sure how to switch Vangie Ann's phone over, so I just hang up. It rings immediately.

"Hello?"

"Cass?" It's Vangie Ann. I haven't heard her voice on the phone since I was in prison.

"Hey, V. What's up?"

She takes a breath so deep it sounds like a gust of wind against the phone. "TJ took off my seatbelt."

"What?"

"I think he did. It's all cloudy. But we were fighting. You know, in the car. He reached over and I thought he was about to hit me but he unfastened my seatbelt."

"Why would he do that?" I ask.

"I don't know."

On its own, this information does nothing. But I can't push her to remember more. It won't work.

"Well, thanks for letting me know." I'm not sure if there's something else I should say.

"I'll call you if I remember more."

"Okay, thanks." I hang up.

"What's up?" Mack asks. His eyes dart over to me and back to the road.

"Vangie Ann said that she thinks TJ unfastened her seatbelt before the wreck." I press the small plastic phone against my palm.

"He was trying to kill her." Mack doesn't look at me. He keeps his eyes straight ahead.

"You think?" TJ, the child I used to tuck into bed on the nights I stayed at Wayne's house. He's grown into a mess of a man, but I can't imagine him trying to kill my sister.

"Yeah. She said she thought they were fighting. He took off her seatbelt and slammed the car into a tree." He says the words as if it's a reasonable conclusion.

"Why would he want to kill her over a fight?"

"Maybe he wanted to silence her." This time he does look at me for a beat. I want to hold his gaze longer so I wouldn't have to think about my sister, bloodied and bloated. Asleep and silent in her hospital bed with tubes and machines everywhere. My sister, brutalized like one of the women in TJ's drawings.

Mack's phone rings and I jump from the sudden noise.

"Hey, Mom." He stares straight ahead and then pulls over to the side of the road. "No. Don't do that. I'll be right there. Just wait."

He puts the phone down on the console. "My mom wants to go out looking for my dad. She thinks he's missing."

Dead for over a decade, but her unreliable memory still believes he is alive. I don't think my generation knows that kind of love.

"Okay. We can try to do this tomorrow." I pat him on the arm and put my hands in my lap.

The sun melts as Mack does a U-turn on the highway.

Chapter 48

Mack rushed into his house after making me promise I would go straight home. But I'm a liar. I have to go now. TJ could get out of jail at any time, and I have to find Vangie Ann's recovery journal. It's finally making sense: why the weapon was there for Matt Morgan to find. A murderer wouldn't have left the weapon. I just need to find proof. Or at least the beginning of proof.

No lights shine from the cabin. The trailer door had opened easily with the aid of Mack's credit card. I'm not so lucky out here in the woods. Fortunately I have a flashlight.

Vangie Ann's phone rings from my pocket as I search for a key along the porch rail. It's Tilly again. I don't want to hear about the damn baked potato, so I put the phone back in my pocket.

I pick up a terra-cotta flower pot near the doorstep. There's a little soil and a dead flower in it. I turn it upside down and the contents dump out. There's no key on the bottom. I keep on turning stones and lawn art, and feeling around the edge of the porch rail.

The phone rings again. "What, Tilly?"

"I've been calling you for ages."

"Sorry. What's up?" If she says "potato" I'm going to scream.

"Maggie was here a little while ago. She's looking for you. She left Samantha and got in the car with Danielle."

"Why is she in Arkansas?"

"She said changed her mind and took the first train back."

"But she got out of here." It's not right. Maggie has slammed the door that was open to her future. "I'll be home soon. Take care of Samantha. We'll figure this out."

"Okay." Tilly hangs up, and it takes a second for me to remember what I'm doing.

Key. One of those rocks that hides a key. There has to be one. I shine my flashlight under a bush, and yellow eyes stare back at me.

I'm getting ready to break a window when I hear a car rolling up the long gravel driveway. Danielle's Jeep. I feel like I should run, but there's no point. My truck is parked in plain view. She knows I'm here. So I take a seat on the porch steps and wait.

Maggie and Danielle appear two minutes later. They're both giggling like one of them just told a joke.

"Hi, Cass," Danielle says. She balls her hands into fists and rests them on her hips. "What are you doing?"

"I need to find Vangie Ann's recovery journal. She left it here and she needs it." I stand up so I can be taller than Danielle. "Maggie, why are you here?"

"It didn't work out." Maggie shrugs and grins. "It's fine, though."

Danielle pulls the keys out her front jeans pocket. "Let's go in and find this journal." She's excited, like we're going on a treasure hunt.

Maggie and I file behind her and go in the cabin. Danielle turns on the lights. It's a completely different place than the last time I was here. No ashtrays, no garbage, no drugs. It's spotless.

"Who cleans this place?" I ask.

"Melody keeps it clean. She hates it when it's dirty." Danielle smiles at me sideways like she's telling me a secret. "She hates it when anything is dirty."

"We can help you look," Maggie says.

"Okay, thanks. It's a journal with a leather cover."

I go to the kitchen. The drawers hold nothing of interest. Not even creepy notebooks. I don't know why I chose this room to start. They weren't spending any time in the kitchen.

The girls are in the bedrooms, and I look under the couch. No crumbs, nothing. The same under the cushions. Melody can clean better than anyone I know.

"Is this it?" Danielle asks. She's coming from the hallway, holding Vangie Ann's journal open and reading as she walks.

"Yeah."

Danielle smiles her creepy doll smile and reads aloud: "The suicide note came in the mail two days later. TJ hid it from his dad, but his dad found it a few months later. They all knew Judith killed herself and they let Cass go down for it for an upfront cash payment and trust funds for TJ and Danielle. Cass's freedom cost $750,000."

I start to sway and sit back on the couch. I gasp for air.

Maggie appears behind Danielle. "Why did you do that, Danielle?"

"She needs to know the truth so we can move on. Plus she told me if I didn't tell her the truth she wouldn't be my friend anymore. I can't have that."

Maggie raises her hand and I see that it holds a dainty revolver. It looks girly, like a toy. But it's definitely real, and it's meant for me.

Chapter 49

"Time for me yet?" TJ asks as he walks in the front door.

"Oh, Cass! I bailed TJ out today. He's been waiting outside." Danielle is still smiling. I wish it were comforting, but it's unnerving. She turns to Maggie and looks at her like she's a child. "We don't need the gun. Everything's going to be fine."

"Danielle told her the truth," Maggie says to TJ.

"Why did you do that?" TJ asks. His jaw is set, but not grinding. His face looks normal. Weathered, but normal.

"So we can move on. I'm tired of keeping the secret. Now we can be a family like we're supposed to be." Danielle puts her hands up like she's saying the most obvious thing in the world.

"We don't need the gun," TJ says. He reaches into his pocket and pulls out a pill bottle. "I brought Percocet."

"WAIT!" I realize I haven't said anything in a while so I shout over the others in the room. "Your dad knew that Judith committed suicide and he still let me rot in jail?" A Percocet buzz would really help me deal with this. But I don't think a warm, relaxing high is what TJ has in mind for me.

Danielle walks over and sits beside me on the couch. She puts her hands on my thigh. "Yes. And he's very sorry about that. He couldn't tell everyone that his son told such a big lie."

"And there wouldn't have been any money," I say.

"And there won't be any money for my baby if you talk," Maggie says. She's still holding the revolver, a detail I hadn't quite forgotten but had chosen to ignore.

"We're not going to shoot her, Maggie. We can't hide that," TJ says. "She has a history with opiates." He shakes the bottle of pills.

"I'm not taking that," I say.

"Come on, Cass. Either you get shot in the head, or you get to get really high before you die." TJ crosses the room and sits beside me on the couch.

"We're not hurting Mom," Danielle says on the other side of me.

"Danielle, we don't have a choice. She'll tell." Maggie comes closer, still gripping the gun.

Vangie Ann's journal sits in front of me on the coffee table. I pick it up and hold it to my chest. I close my eyes and try to remember how I said the right words to the parole board. I have to do it again.

"I won't tell. I want to be your mom." I put the journal on the table and lean toward Danielle. "All I've ever wanted was to be your mom."

Tears pool in Danielle's eyes and she says, "Really?"

I nod. "Yes, really."

"She's lying," TJ says. "We'll make it easy on you. Take a pill or two every few minutes until the bottle is gone. You'll have a great buzz, throw up a few times, and then go to sleep." His voice is oddly soothing.

"Maggie, is that what you want?" I'm not surprised that TJ wants me to die, but Maggie?

"It's for the best. I'm sorry." Maggie sticks her bottom lip out and frowns. "Things will be so much better for Samantha than they've been for me."

"You can't raise her from jail." I grab Danielle's hand and squeeze it. Without her as an ally, I'm doomed.

"That's why you're going to overdose." TJ hands me two white round pills. "Or we can shoot you and bury you in the woods."

"I need water." I hold the pill in my palm.

TJ goes to the kitchen and returns with a glass of tap water. No ice.

"Can I talk to Wayne one last time before I die?" I ask Danielle.

"Take the pills," Maggie says and points the revolver at me. "Hurry up before the CIA gets here."

"CIA?" What the actual fuck is going on?

Danielle whispers, "She's off her meds because of the whole pregnancy and breastfeeding thing. Don't worry. She usually holds it together, and we'll get her back on them soon."

I swallow the Percocet. Under any other circumstances, I would sit back and wait for the warm euphoria to envelop me. Instead I'm just trying to figure out how I can keep from dying tonight. I can't just give up and take it like I did when it came to my prison sentence.

"Good girl," TJ says. "One more." He's holding a pill between his fingertips.

I nod and take the pill from him.

"Why won't you let me have a mom? It's not fair." Danielle jumps up and crosses her arms over her chest.

"It's going to be okay, Danielle." Maggie sits on the floor on the side of the coffee table. She still has her revolver, but it's resting in her lap now. "We'll all be together. You can help me with Samantha. You don't need a mom. Anyway, you still have Melody."

"I got rid of Melody." Danielle looks down to her feet.

"What do you mean?" TJ asks. He's smiling, not at all alarmed by the possibilities.

"I didn't kill her if that's what you think!" Danielle laughs like it's an anecdote. "I just told her that Cass was coming back to Dad. She got all mad and left."

TJ laughs so hard he starts to shake. The couch cushions jiggle up and down. "I bet she was so pissed."

My stomach rolls. The Percocet is kicking in. "I haven't eaten in a while. I don't feel so good." I stand up, and Maggie grips the revolver. She lifts the gun, but doesn't point it at me. "I need to throw up."

"Let her go throw up," Danielle says.

"Wait. You can't take your phone to the bathroom." TJ stands up and blocks my path. My stomach is inching up my throat.

"She doesn't have a cell phone. She doesn't know how to work them." Danielle is still laughing, and TJ steps aside.

I dash down the hall and into the bathroom. I lock the door and sit on the floor. I pull Vangie Ann's phone from my pocket and scroll through the phone numbers. I know I should call 911, but I don't know the address of the cabin. I just know that I'm off of the highway. I need to call Wayne or Mack. But before I can decide which one, my stomach empties into the toilet. I don't see any pills floating in the vomit. They're still in my system, but I can handle three Percocet. Things are not dire yet.

"You okay in there?" TJ shouts through the door.

"Be out in a sec," I say.

Melody's number is in Vangie Ann's contact list. I select her name, but nothing happens. I have to push something else. I find the button that reads "call," and put the phone to my ear. After four rings, it rolls over to voicemail.

"Melody," I whisper into the phone, "the kids have me at the cabin. They're going to kill me. Call Wayne or Mack or the police or something."

I push "end" on the phone, and realize my skin is itching everywhere. I scratch and scratch, and then I realize that everything is going to be fine. Even if I die, at least it will be easy and I don't have to do this shit anymore. Tears form in my eyes and pour down my face. Fucking opiates.

I struggle to remember Wayne's phone number. It's been a long time since I called it, but I had it memorized for a long time. I run my finger over the numbers, hoping for muscle memory to kick in.

TJ bangs on the door. "What are you doing, Cass?"

"Throwing up. Leave me alone." My voice is weak. I want it to be stronger.

The door knob starts to jiggle. He's trying to unlock it. It would only take a screwdriver.

He says in a jovial sing-song way, "You better not throw them all up. I'll boil the rest down and shoot them in your veins."

Wayne's number pops into my head, a miracle from memory. He picks up after three rings.

"Hello?"

"Wayne. I'm at the cabin. TJ is trying to kill me. Maggie has a gun." I throw up, but don't bother moving the phone away from my face.

"Cass? Cass?"

"You have to get here and talk some sense into your evil children. You owe me, motherfucker." I lean over to throw up again. The phone drops from my hand into the toilet. It's floating in the water and stomach acid.

"Who were you talking to, Cass?" The door is open and TJ is looking right at me.

He marches over and grabs me by my hair and drags me across the floor. Pain spreads across my scalp in protest, but the pills soften the hurt.

"No, TJ!" Danielle rushes to his side. "That's our mama!"

"You're talking crazy, Danielle!" TJ shouts.

"You always talk crazy, Methy McMethface!" She swings her arm back and slaps TJ across the face. He lets go of my hair and grabs Danielle with both hands. He slams her against the wall.

"Fucking stop it!" Maggie shouts from the end of the hall. She charges forward with the gun in one hand and the pill bottle in the other. "You are not going to ruin this for me, Danielle."

Maggie points the revolver at Danielle and tosses the pills to TJ. He lets go of his sister and catches the bottle.

"Put those down her throat." Maggie points at me with her free hand.

I try to jump up, but my balance doesn't seem to exist. I topple back onto the floor before I get my feet flat.

TJ pries open my bottom jaw and pours the bottle into my mouth. I'm kicking and clawing at him, and I'm not sure how many pills go in. Maybe ten, maybe twenty. I try to spit them out but he puts his hand over my mouth to keep it closed. The pills start to dissolve and a few make it down my throat. I stop struggling for a second, and TJ relaxes his grip on my face. I push him away with my remaining strength, and find my way to my feet.

I can see the front door, but it feels very far away. I dig in my mouth and pull out Percocet as I take steps forward. Everything itches. I want to strip down and scratch everything, but there's no time for that.

My hand wraps around the doorknob, and Maggie's hand wraps around my arm. "No, you don't," she says.

The revolver is pointed at my chest. It's so small and cute, I just want to pet it. I grab the barrel and point it toward the ceiling. Maggie grabs my wrist and tries to point the gun at my face. My prison instincts kick in, but they're foggy and confusing. I lean forward and sink my teeth into Maggie's cheek. She screams and drops the gun. My stomach turns and creeps up my throat as I bend down to pick it up.

I spit out a mouthful of her blood and throw up on the floor. A few pills come up this time, but I still don't know how many I've ingested.

Maggie is screaming. Screaming so loud and it echoes in my head. I point the gun at her. "Be quiet," I say, "or I'll shoot your fucking face off."

TJ and Danielle are staring at me. I bend over and vomit. I raise up and point the gun at TJ.

"This is your fault." The gun shakes in my hand.

"Don't do it," Danielle says. "You'll go back to jail." Tears stream down her face. "My plan is ruined."

The door opens and Wayne walks in. His eyes dart around the room. "What the hell?"

"You knew." I point the revolver at Wayne. There are so many people I want to shoot.

"She knows everything, Daddy. We can be a family now." Danielle's smile has reappeared through her tears.

"Give me the gun," Wayne says and holds out his hand.

My feet feel unsteady. I sway back and forth and my stomach lurches. I stumble backward, the gun slips and I try to grasp it. The gun discharges as I crumple to the floor.

My eyes start to close as Danielle screams at the top of her lungs, "MAGGIE!" I don't understand why everyone is being so loud.

Chapter 50

My sister is home. Vangie Ann's on crutches, moving slow, and going to narcotics anonymous meetings every single day, but she is home. We're sitting together having coffee at the kitchen table when TJ Talbot shows up on our doorstep.

"Call the police," I say before opening the door.

"Don't let him in," Vangie Ann says when she spots TJ.

"It's okay, V. Just call the police."

TJ looks better than normal. He's not grinding his teeth, he doesn't look sweaty or greasy. He's not a frightening sight today.

"Hi." I'm staring at him as I open the door. He looks almost handsome. He looks like the man he should look like. "Did they let you out on bail?"

He nods and says, "Apparently I'm not a flight risk."

"Why are you here?"

Tears rest in his eyes, but they haven't made their way to his face. "Can you come sit with me on the porch?"

"Okay." I walk out onto the wooden porch. The humidity shortens my breath for a moment.

TJ sits down, and I sit across from him, far enough away that he can't touch me.

"You look nice," I say.

"Thanks." He smiles, revealing the yellowed teeth. "I had an appointment with my lawyer today."

"Oh."

"Melody verified everything with the cops." He pulls a cigarette from his pocket and lights it. "It seems that my whole family is pretty much fucked."

"She knew, too?" I'm not sure my capacity for forgiveness is big enough for this.

"Yeah."

"I'm sorry for how your life turned out." And I mean it. Even though I hate TJ right now, things should have been better for him.

"The secret got bigger than me or Dad or Danielle." He looks at me out the corner of his eyes and takes a drag of his smoke. "We knew we'd have to pay back money that we'd already spent, and we'd be in trouble for hiding evidence. Dad didn't know how to handle it."

"I know." I look down at my hands on my lap.

"I told Vangie Ann the truth. I thought she would be on my side. Like we were best friends or something. But she wanted to tell you." His statement ends in a cough.

"Is that why you unbuckled her seatbelt?"

TJ looks at me and nods.

"What's going to happen to Danielle?" I don't know why I care. There's something like pity left in me, I guess.

Even though Maggie is dead, and it was my bullet that killed her, and it never would have happened if not for TJ and Danielle. Even though Samantha will live with Maggie's aunt in Mississippi, and we'll never get to see her grow. I'll always feel guilt over Maggie, but it will be manageable.

"Not sure. Either prison or the looney bin."

The soft swoosh of a passing car catches my attention. Then I hear the unmistakable click and look up, expecting to see a gun in my face.

"TJ, no." The words emerge softly when I see him with the gun pointed to his head. The cops should be here in a second. I have to stall.

"It's the only way to finish this." A tear rolls down his cheek, but he doesn't wipe it away. "My mom wanted you find her, you know. It was in the suicide note. That's why she called you."

I jump up but don't have anywhere to go. I don't want his brains on my face. So I stand in front of him. The sirens sound from a few blocks away.

"Samantha will be an orphan."

His eyes scan my face, and I stand perfectly still. "She's better off without me." Peace washes over his eyes. Maybe I've gotten through to him.

TJ pulls the trigger, and the left side of his face detaches from his head. The gunshot rings in my ears. My feet are stuck. There's so much blood. It doesn't seem possible for that much blood to fit into one person. His body is slumped over the side of the chair.

Vangie Ann is standing next to me. I don't know how long she's been there.

"Cass! Cass!" She pulls me into the House.

I want to tell her that she was right about death coming in threes. But the words can't find their way out.

"What was that?" Sonya and Tilly bound down the stairs. I'm not sure which one spoke. Then I realize what they are about to see.

"Don't go out there," I say, but it's too late.

Tilly releases a scream that must have formed all the way down in her toes. It reminds me of the time Vangie Ann found a garden snake under her bed when we were kids. I manage to stop myself from saying it.

The cops pull up as Vangie Ann pushes past me and hobbles back to the porch. I just stand in the middle of the floor like a wax figure. I should go to the porch instead of standing here being useless, but I can't figure out why. No amount of people on the porch can put TJ's head back together.

Chapter 51

"How much are you willing to invest?" Vangie Ann is limping around the kitchen, making a pot of coffee.

"Don't know. Depends on how much you need." Dad's death paperwork is spread out in front of me on the kitchen table. "I'm going to California when I can, so I need some money for that. But you can have most of it."

Vangie Ann pulls a chair away from the table and sits down. "I want you to be my partner. You'll buy into the place."

When she says that, it feels like she's attaching a tether to me. It's not like I haven't thought about staying. But I know myself. I'll end up in a relationship with Mack, working with Vangie Ann, and never pushing myself to do anything different. It would become another prison, this one with an herb garden and a box-store membership. I have to go while I still have a chance at a new life. And I want to get away from the Talbots. I see TJ's face everywhere I go. I feel Maggie in the House. My heart is officially broken.

"You can just have it, V. No strings attached."

"Okay." She smiles.

"I'm giving some money to Mack, and I want to put some back for Tabitha's kids." I gather the paperwork into one pile and tap it on the table. "I'll spend this money before I have it."

I put my hand over hers and we sit like that for a minute.

"Do you think Dad would be proud of me for showing everybody I'm innocent?" I ask.

"Well, I wouldn't say 'innocent.'" A slow smile spreads over her face, a face with a couple of new scars that shrink a little every day. "He's smiling down on us from Heaven, Cass."

Then Sonya and Tilly charge down the stairs and interrupt.

"What's going on in here? You're not lezzing out, are you? I saw that once on Jerry Springer. These two sisters were lovers. It was nasty." Tilly rambles as she grabs a coffee mug from the cabinet.

"No, weirdo. Sisters are allowed to hold hands," I say, but I still take my hand away.

"Hey Evangeline, the toilet's acting up again. I'm going to call Paul." Sonya's hair color is fading, but it still looks nice. I'll have to do a touch-up soon.

There's a knock at the door and my heart flutters like a tiny bird. I know it's him. Tilly opens the door. "Hello, handsome."

Mack walks in. "Hi, Tilly." He sees me at the table. "You ready, Cass?"

"Yeah." I stand up. "I'll be back late tonight, ladies."

I walk out with Mack and he puts his arm around me, his big paw rests on my shoulder. "How far is the drive?"

"Four hours each way."

His arm slips down my back and he grabs my hand. We hold hands all the way to his truck. Mack opens the door for me, and I feel like a lady.

We take off down the road toward Tabitha's weeping willow tree.

The End

Acknowledgements

This book started from a seed of an idea several years ago. Fortunately, the idea grew until I filled up a lot of pages. It's been a long journey for me from aspiring to published author. I can honestly say that though writing is a solitary task, I would not have finished writing this novel without the help and support of some wonderful people in my life. Without the love and unwavering support of my husband Richard, I would never make the time to write a word. And my children Samuel and Molly have been my continuous cheerleaders, even if they're too young to read my stories.

Thank you Mom and Dad for raising me in the south, a place where inspiration flows freely. I was in a wonderful, supportive critique group for several years. Every member helped me get the words out. Thank you Jeanne Adwani, Pete Magsig, Annette Weathers, Adrienne Losh, Kate Kansteiner, Lynne Nickle, Cate Stidwell, and Bobbi Busard. So many friends have read my work over the last ten years and helped me keep going. My early work was so terrible I'm lucky they still like me. Thank you Austin Bailey, Chris Harris, Jesse Suphan, Deedee Ulintz, Whitney Lawrence Morehead, Kim Bridge, Kim Degroff, Kim Pisano, Kim Hebbes, Karin Killian, Sharon Carty, Abby Holt, Jenna Brand, Laura Kemp, Natasha Sinel Cohen, Sara Kraemer, Karen Slagell, Melissa Jackson, and Susan Jones. And to my little cousin Joshua Morehead for letting me pester him with questions. Thank you to Katherine Pfieffer for taking a million shots to get a few great author photographs. Your patience didn't go unnoticed! To Linda Epstein for all of the advice and encouragement- thank you for not letting me give up! To Ashlee McCaskill, my dear friend who put together a collection of my crazy ramblings decades ago to prove to me that my writing could form a book. And to her parents Linda and Don who have always celebrated my craziness as if I was one of their own.

Thank you to Zara and Allan Kramer and the rest of the Pandamoon Publishing family for believing in me. To my editors Rachel Schoenbauer, Heather Stewart, and Kathy Davidson for making it better. To my fellow gamma class Jessica, Dana, Sarah, Brian, Francis, and Meg- this is one helluva ride! To Elgon Williams and Christine Gabriel for elevating us all! And thank you Don Kramer for my amazing cover!

Please forgive me if you helped and I didn't mention you by name. Let me know and I'll get you next time. Because there will be a next time!

About the Author

Penni Jones is a writer, mom, and blogger extraordinaire of Scapegoats and Sacred Cows (http://scapegoatsandsacredcows.com/). Her work has appeared in *Six Sentences*, *Bird and Moon*, *The Northville Review*, *Women on Writing*, and *Newport Review*.

Penni is a native Arkansan who currently lives in freezing cold Michigan. Penni has worked as a bartender, restaurant manager, bank teller, payroll specialist, event planner, and office manager. But she has always been a writer. She specializes in novels set in the Dirty Deep South.

On the Bricks is her debut novel. Her second, *Kricket*, is scheduled to be released by Pandamoon Publishing in Spring 2017.

Thank you for purchasing this copy of **On the Bricks** by Penni Jones. If you enjoyed this book by Penni, please let her know by posting a review.

Growing good ideas into great reads…one book at a time.

Visit www.pandamoonpublishing.com to learn more about other works by our talented authors.

Mystery/Thriller/Suspense
- *122 Series Book 1: 122 Rules* by Deek Rhew
- *A Flash of Red* by Sarah K. Stephens
- *A Tree Born Crooked* by Steph Post
- *Fate's Past* by Jason Huebinger
- *Juggling Kittens* by Matt Coleman
- *Knights of the Shield* by Jeff Messick
- *Looking into the Sun* by Todd Tavolazzi
- *The Moses Winter Mysteries Book 1: Made Safe* by Francis Sparks
- *On the Bricks Series Book 1: On the Bricks* by Penni Jones
- *Southbound* by Jason Beem
- *The Juliet* by Laura Ellen Scott
- *Rogue Alliance* by Michelle Bellon
- *The Last Detective* by Brian Cohn
- *The New Royal Mysteries Book 1: The Mean Bone in Her Body* by Laura Ellen Scott

Science Fiction/Fantasy
- *Everly Series Book 1: Everly* by Meg Bonney
- *.exe Series Book 1: Hello World* by Alexandra Tauber and Tiffany Rose
- *Fried Windows in a Light White Sauce* by Elgon Williams

- *The Crimson Chronicles Book 1: Crimson Forest* by Christine Gabriel
- *The Crimson Chronicles Book 2: Crimson Moon* by Christine Gabriel
- *The Phaethon Series Book 1: Phaethon* by Rachel Sharp
- *The Sitnalta Series Book 1: Sitnalta* by Alisse Lee Goldenberg
- *The Sitnalta Series Book 2: The Kingdom Thief* by Alisse Lee Goldenberg
- *The Sitnalta Series Book 3: The City of Arches* by Alisse Lee Goldenberg

Women's Fiction
- *Beautiful Secret* by Dana Faletti
- *The Long Way Home* by Regina West
- *The Mason Siblings Series Book 1: Love's Misadventure* by Cheri Champagne
- *The Mason Siblings Series Book 2: The Trouble with Love* by Cheri Champagne
- *The Shape of the Atmosphere* by Jessica Dainty

Made in the USA
Middletown, DE
21 April 2017